CHASING AFTER LOVE

CHASING AFTER LOVE
An Eros & Co. Novel

KERRI KEBERLY

CHAPTER ONE

The hustle and bustle of the Sacred Forest's winged community normally didn't bother Apollo. In fact, he usually didn't notice. *This* morning, however, the forest at the foot of Mount Olympus was frantic with avian activity. The sharp trilling and loud screeching were impossible to miss, and as he bent down to brush the dirt from the tips of his dress shoes, feathers drifted down from the tree tops.

A nearby robin flapped to another branch at the loud scoffing he directed toward the narrow, winding path before him. The prolonged sound ruffled even more feathers as it ricocheted off tree trunks with alarming velocity. Straightening, he reached inside the breast pocket of his suit coat, and, phone in hand, resumed his journey, willfully ignoring the *No Cell Phones* sign as he pulled up his contacts and pressed speed dial.

A soft voice, one he'd heard many times over the centuries, floated into his ear. "Morning, boss."

"Good morning, Calliope. Could you see if Hephaestus can pave the path that leads to . . . my spot? Gods know I've walked it enough. I'm tired of getting my shoes dirty."

"Sure, but Heff's more in to metal working. You know, forging weapons and stuff for you guys."

A faint *click* came from the other end of the line. She was biting her nails again. He could hear it even through the chorus of anxious chirps and persistent squawking.

Speaking of, what in Hades' Realm was up with these birds?

Along with the nail biting, Apollo ignored the warning bells going off inside his head and took a sip of his coffee. "He's also a stone mason, Calliope."

"Sorry. You're right," she replied. "I'll put a call into him ASAP and see what his schedule looks like." After another tiny biting sound, she continued, "Do you think it could wait a few days, though? I'm still working on compiling the numbers you wanted for the next staff meeting. You know, showing how many advances in modern medicine were made last year?"

Apollo stopped walking, his lips stretching into a thin line. He wasn't going to be able to ignore the biting, the bird chatter, or the questions much longer. "Are you having trouble keeping up, Calliope?"

She was a great assistant, the most revered of the muses, which was half the reason why he'd chosen her, but he was the one who gave the orders. *He* asked the questions, not the other way around. No questions meant no chance of giving the wrong answer. He preferred to keep the house of cards he'd built, the one where he appeared to know everything, intact.

"Are the demands of working for me too much? Because if you can't handle it, I'm sure one of your sisters would jump at the chance. And stop biting your nails. It's unbecoming." Apollo took another sip of coffee, narrowing his eyes at a large raven peering down at him. It cawed loudly as he passed by, no doubt reprimanding him for being so callous.

"Of course. And, no, I can handle it," said Calliope.

Apollo softened, pushing the bird's judgment and the nagging feeling something was wrong aside. "I'm glad to hear it. You do good work."

He liked Calliope, and despite her unseemly habit of gnawing on her fingernails, she was perfect for the job—efficient, reliable, and perhaps most important of all, organized. Way more than he was, that was for sure.

She asked a lot of questions, however, which, due to obvious reasons, was always a bit problematic. He didn't want to look weak in front of anyone, ever, but especially not her. Which was why the raven was probably right, he shouldn't be so hard on her. If she ever decided to leave . . . Well, he was positive he'd never find another assistant as faithful as Calliope.

He cleared his throat, issuing his next request in a gentler tone. "Let me know how soon he thinks the work will be done. In the meantime, can you see if there's a less filthy route I can take? I prefer not to magic myself there. It wrinkles my suit. You know how I feel about wrinkled Versace."

"Sure thing," she said, laughing even though what he'd said wasn't meant to be funny. He always strived to look his best. Looking impeccable gave off the same impression. "I'll get right on that." She paused for a beat before starting again. "Hey, do you—"

Apollo lifted his eyes toward the sky, inhaling a breath and exhaling his sigh slowly. He didn't like being short with her, but she should know all his virtues by now. Patience wasn't one of them, and what little he had was currently evaporating like water on a hot day. "Look, I appreciate your dedication, Calliope, I really do, but I've got to go, okay?"

"Oh, okay. Yeah, of course. See you later, then."

Sorry for rushing her off the phone, but grateful she didn't ask another question, he nodded and said, "See you later this afternoon," before ending the conversation with a press of his thumb. After tucking his phone into his pocket, he stepped around a jutting stone and tried to ignore the renewed swirling in the pit of his stomach.

A cloud slid in front of the sun, throwing the forest in shadow before quickly passing. It wasn't long before another took its place, and the sky dimmed for several seconds until the sun muscled its way out again. Back and forth, light and shadow fought for dominance, mimicking the current struggle for control going on inside him. Proving the god of sun and light shined brighter than the rest of the divinities on Mount Olympus was a constant battle.

He forced himself to inhale deeply, so the scent of pine mingling with the fresh mountain air would urge the clouds to dissipate. A satisfied smile curled his lips when the giant orb in the sky began to shine brightly again.

Apollo continued down the path, careful not to stir up any more dust. He hadn't minded running around in the Sacred Forest in the old days, and his morning walk was usually pleasant, but gods, the *dirt*. It was bothersome now that he'd grown accustomed to the glittering luxury of the mountain.

These days, he preferred to spend most of his time there, especially since Zeus, reigning king of the gods—deadbeat father extraordinaire—had started Life Industries, the other-worldly managing company created to help secure their existence. Sure, they all had to work a 9-5 to ensure the nectar and ambrosia stores stayed full, but they did it. They had to keep themselves from fading into oblivion somehow. It was hard work, with long hours, but none of them liked the alternative.

Mandatory day jobs aside, he'd take the sparkling atrium, lush, well tended gardens and a huge corner office over wild, overgrown woods any day. Honestly, the only reason he stepped foot in this gods-forsaken forest anymore was to see her, the love of his—

Apollo skidded to a stop. The paper cup he'd been holding slipped from his grasp at the same time his mouth dropped open. Another round of hysterics came from the birds, but he still heard the plastic cover pop off the rim when it hit the ground.

His eyes remained glued to a spot in the forest he knew well, and, more specifically, what wasn't there. Not knowing what to do, and certainly not believing what he was seeing possible, his gaze dropped to the hot, black liquid mixing with the dirt around his feet. It wasn't until the muddy, caffeinated mess fully engulfed the soles of his expensive shoes that he tore his eyes away and directed them back toward the gaping hole in the forest floor.

Keeping his person free of filth no longer mattered. In fact, a snarling chimera could have dumped a whole pot of coffee on his head and he wouldn't have cared. She was gone.

That's what the damned birds were going on about.

In an instant, Apollo closed the distance between himself and the place where an ancient laurel tree had been firmly rooted just yesterday morning. When he reappeared at the edge of the depression, he blinked a few times before closing his eyes. He prayed that when he opened them again, he'd discover they'd only been playing tricks on him. They weren't, of course, and when he found the hole was still there, he sank to the ground, grasping for something to steady him. Ironically, all he found was dirt.

"This can't be happening," he murmured, ignoring the mess he was making of his designer suit.

The memories of why he'd walked an uncountable number of times to visit this place, this tree, every morning before heading to work came barging in, right on cue, and the fight he'd picked with the god of love, Eros, centuries ago began replaying in his mind.

First the way he'd laughed at the younger god's gilded bow and arrows, saying they were nothing more than a child's play things, with no *real* power. Not like his silver bow. Then the way Eros had risen to the challenge, shooting a leaden arrow, filled with revilement and hatred, into the heart of the nearest soul, a water nymph by the name of Daphne. That was, of course, right after Eros had shot Apollo with a golden arrow, to which his heart had promptly filled with an overwhelming need to chase after her.

Apollo tried shaking the unwelcome thoughts away, but it was no use. Another memory, an earlier one, shouldered its way to the forefront. His traitorous brain pressed rewind, beginning the events of that fateful afternoon in an earlier spot. Now he saw himself stumbling upon the god of love in the Sacred Forest. It hadn't been long after Apollo had finished destroying Python, the serpent sent by Hera to harass his beloved mother. He'd been headed to Mount Olympus to toss the beast's carcass at Zeus's feet, as evidence that abandoning Apollo and his sister Artemis had been a mistake.

The only thing he'd proven, however, was that, in his rush to judgment regarding how much ridicule Eros could withstand, Apollo was rather adept at making terrible decisions. He'd been so hopped up on adrenaline after destroying Python, he simply hadn't been able to resist cajoling the god of love. What he should have done was continue dragging the giant snake through the forest and kept walking. Instead, he'd decided to prolong the thrill of victory, and Eros had been an easy target—or so he'd thought. Eros had snapped, soundly and swiftly, and cursed him with one of the worst cases of unrequited love in the universe.

He remembered the moment well, and how he'd promptly

forgotten all about schlepping Python up the mountain because he'd had a new mission—chasing after Daphne. And he chased her, all right. Like it was his job. He'd gone on running after her until she'd finally gotten fed up and asked her father, Peneus, to save her. The old bastard had turned her into a tree.

"Daphne?" He pushed himself up, wiping his hands on the thighs of his dress pants as he peered into the surrounding forest. His eyes darted around in search of nymphs. He knew they were there. The forest was riddled with them, and he broke out into a sweat wondering what they were thinking. "Daphne, are you here? Come out. I just want to talk, I promise."

Silence.

Apollo's skin tingled, and when he looked at his hands, they were trembling. The urge to chase Daphne had diminished significantly after she'd been turned into a tree, and it had been a huge relief, but it seemed as though the old engine was firing up again. He inhaled a shaky breath. His ego had received blow after excruciating blow from her constant rejection. It had been demoralizing to say the least, and he didn't want to go back to that horrible old song and dance.

Apollo stood, unsure of what to do next as he fought to remain calm despite the thoughts rioting inside his head. He was too old for this. Too important. Cushy job, more than his fair share of adoration . . . he liked things the way they were. Well, other than his father not giving a damn.

Not long after Daphne had been turned into an evergreen, Apollo had broken down and accepted his father's offer to work at the fledgling Life Industries. He'd agreed because he was desperate to see if he could regain some semblance of normalcy. It turned out throwing himself into the job of being the god of every damn thing had been exactly what he'd needed.

However well becoming a workaholic had worked, he hadn't been able to forget about Daphne completely. He couldn't. The curse wouldn't let him. So he'd come to visit her here, in this very spot, since the day she'd been transformed. Religiously, as he felt there might be a chance she'd finally give in, however slight. Or was it more out of habit? Either way, she was gone, uprooted and torn out of the ground, with no trace of the long, slender trunk and graceful limbs that had towered above the rest. The only sign she'd ever been here was crumbling dirt.

There had to be a way to break this ungodly curse. It just needed to be something other than crawling back to Eros. That he refused to do. There was no way he was going to risk embarrassing himself again.

If that was the case, and it was, the first thing that needed to happen was figuring out where Daphne was. Several seconds passed, and it became clear that if any of the inhabitants of the Sacred Forest knew what had transpired, none of them were talking. In fact, the whole place had gone quiet. Even the chatty cardinals and screaming blue jays had halted their bickering. They all wanted to see what he would do next.

The sun disappeared behind a much bigger, thicker bank of clouds. "For Fates' sake, Daphne, just come out, will you?"

More silence.

Gods dammit. He should have never messed with Eros. If he hadn't, he wouldn't be standing in the middle of the Sacred Forest begging like a fool.

Apollo's frustration mounted at the lack of response, and when he finally opened his mouth to speak again, his voice sliced through the stillness like a razor blade. "Look, I know you're unsatisfied with the way things have been. Perhaps we can come to a compromise. But in order to do that, I need to have your full cooperation."

He was the epitome of a Greek god—tall, strong, beautiful, and good at everything he tried. How in Hades' Realm could she not see that?

Probably because she'd figured out it was all a farce.

"By my fellow gods, come out this instant!" The words burst out, the last of his patience disappearing. Surely she would answer him, he just had to be a bit stern is all. Then again, the last time he'd made such a demand of her, things hadn't exactly gone as planned.

Even more silence.

Apollo went rigid, mashing his lips together to keep the howl of rage from escaping. It still managed to break free in the form of a frustrated growl that vibrated in his throat. He inhaled calming breaths for several minutes, forcing his shoulders back down. When he finally collected himself, he tugged the cuffs of his dress shirt into place. One never knew what kind of mythical creatures were lurking about in the Sacred Forest. If his momentary lapse in strength and character should find its way to Leto, Life Industries receptionist, gossip queen—and his mother—it would be all over Mount Olympus in a heartbeat.

He gulped down the anxiety trying to claw its way up his throat, and then drew in a lungful of air to keep it there. Daphne obviously still wanted nothing to do with him, and he wasn't going to get help locating her from any of the other nymphs. That left one person he could rely on.

After speed-dialing his assistant's number again, he brushed at the dirt and debris that clung to his pants while waiting for her to answer. She picked up on the second ring.

"Hey, boss."

"Hi. Meet me in my office in twenty minutes, will you?" he asked in a rush as he made his way over to a stone bench so he could sit down. His compulsion to chase Daphne had been manageable while she was a tree. Now that she'd transformed back into a nymph, he could feel it ramping up again. The thought of chasing her once more, of enduring more rejection, made his gut churn. On top of that, keeping the fact that she'd obviously ran the minute she got her legs back out of the gossip mill was going to be exhausting.

"What's wrong, you sound—"

"Must you ask so many questions?" he snapped, raking a hand through his hair. He immediately regretted the harshness of his tone, but he'd been unable to stop himself. Another reminder that, underneath all the confident smiles and chiseled, muscular physique, he was nothing but weak. "Please, just wrap up whatever you're doing and head to my office."

"Sure thing. I'll see you there in a bit."

"Thank you, Calliope." Apollo ended the call before gripping the edge of the bench, steeling himself against any more memories of his foolish days of youth. He willed his lungs to take in oxygen, but they protested, lamenting over the impossibility of the task being asked of them, which was to help him stay calm and clear-headed enough to find Daphne as soon as possible.

ASAP? He needed to find her like yesterday.

With numb fingers, he dialed another number. One he knew by heart.

"Life Industries. This is Leto speaking, how may I direct your call?"

"Good morning, Mother."

"Oh hello, darling."

"I need a meeting with Zeus right away." As soon as he said it, his jaw tightened. He absolutely hated to admit it, but going to his father for help might be the fastest way to bring this situation to an end.

"Why didn't you just stop by my desk?" asked Leto. "Are you not at work yet? What's wrong, darling? You sound—"

"Can you clear his schedule, please? I'm not at the office yet, but I'm on my way in and I need to speak with him as soon as I get there." He knew full well that wasn't going to cut it even before the words left his mouth.

"Oh? What's going on?"

His mother would burst if he didn't give her some kind of explanation.

"Not much. It's just that several health crises down on Earth have reached epidemic level, and I need to go over next steps regarding whether or not we expedite their discovery of cures."

It was the truth. Humans were a mess.

"Oh, yes. They're about due, poor things." Faint tapping and clicking came from the other side of the phone. "Okay, I've rearranged his schedule. You have a meeting for 9:30 a.m., darling."

"Thanks, Mom. Be there shortly." He hung up before she could ask him whether or not he was available for movie night, a longstanding Friday night tradition with him, his twin sister Artemis, and their mother.

The stone bench had gone cold without the sun to warm it, and he stiffened in an attempt to subdue the full-blown shudder already trembling his core. To stave off another bout of regretful memories, he waved his hand and a lyre appeared. Just holding it made him feel better, calmer. There were exactly two things that were ever successful at soothing him during times like these. One of them was his lyre. The other was on her way to his office.

He plucked at the strings, aimlessly in the beginning, but soon the first movement of Beethoven's Moonlight Sonata poured out of him. With each brush and sweep of his fingers, his racing thoughts slowed and the knot in his stomach untangled. What was done was done. He couldn't go back, so he might as well forge ahead.

He continued to play, hoping somehow, wherever she was, Daphne would feel his melancholy. If only she'd hear his sadness in the melody, maybe she'd be moved to tears and come rushing back, ready and willing to listen. To discuss the curse like adults and find ways to work around it.

If she did come, there was more than a good chance he would forget all about finding a way to break the curse and start relentlessly pursuing her again. Gods knew, their situation was screwed up, but, at this point, it was a risk he was willing to take.

After finishing the second and third movement, his tight muscles were blessedly looser. He waved away the lyre and sat quietly, listening to the wind rustle the leaves. He dragged a breath in through his nose and tried to relax further, but the unmistakable scent of a storm yet to come left his stomach churning again.

"No one has anything to say, then?" he called out. "If you do, say it now. This is your last chance."

Apollo tilted his head, listening to the Sacred Forest one last time before he got up to leave. When he stood, ready to snap his fingers and disappear, Pegasus stepped out from behind an enormous ancient oak.

Apollo stared into the iridescent creature's lavender eyes for a moment before it spread its wings and gracefully leaped into the air. Apollo watched him fly away, wondering what the purpose of the encounter had been if not to impart information leading to the whereabouts of a certain missing nymph. He was about to go when Pegasus doubled back. Rearing in mid-air, his immense wings stirred up fallen feathers and dirt as he said, *"Look for the love you seek in the last place you'd expect it to be."*

Apollo pinched the bridge of his nose and shook his head

as the winged horse turned and galloped off into the clouds. Good old Pegasus, ever the helpful creature. Too bad the wisdom he'd just imparted was basically useless. There was no time to decipher vague assertions. What he needed was concrete answers. Better yet, an exact location. That would be nice.

Besides, he wasn't looking for Daphne so he could profess his love to her. He'd already been there and done that. Now the goal was finding her so he could break the curse and end his misery. He didn't need a mystical winged horse to tell him that.

CHAPTER TWO

Apollo flashed his work badge at the Spartan warriors on either side of the entrance to the Hall of Olympians. The lips of one of the sentries curled into a faint smirk, and Apollo knew he was still gloating about that damned wooden horse. Gift his ass. Odysseus may have out maneuvered his champions to finally breech Troy, but, in the end, Apollo had seen to it that persistent mortal bastard never came out on top again. Ten years to get home? He should have made it twenty.

A slight nod of approval from the other guard made Apollo's teeth grind, but he kept a passive look on his face. He didn't need permission, didn't even need the badge. He was Apollo, undefeated victor, and if he'd had more time he would have had no problem proving it.

Gods, he was sounding more like his father every day.

His nostrils flared with disgust at the thought as he strode under the carved marble frieze and into the prestigious wing of Life Industries where the partners' offices were located. Right now he needed to get to Calliope, not waste time noting all the flaws he'd inherited from Zeus. That would come later.

In about fifteen minutes or so.

He purposely kept his gait steady and unhurried as he made his way down the covered promenade, even though every muscle in his body was either tight or twitching. Most of them were doing both.

Dionysus slouched out of his office, a mess of crumpled papers and empty alcohol containers practically tumbling out after him. Apollo stopped himself from rolling his eyes as the god of wine and overindulgence pulled his door shut.

Apollo gave Dionysus a curt nod as they passed one another, trying to remain unreadable, but the stench of stale cigarette smoke threatened to ruin his stoic facade. That and the fact that, while Zeus had no problem abandoning him and his twin sister, he'd actually sewed an unborn Dionysus into his *fucking leg* to save the godling from imminent death. The part that really stung was Apollo had gone on to accomplish countless great and wondrous things, while Dion had done nothing but grown from a little disaster into a big one.

Nope. Zeus hadn't lifted a finger to stop Hera from trying to prevent Apollo from being born, and he'd been trying to wrap his head around that for centuries. He was so much stronger than Dion, so much brighter. How did Zeus not see that? Everything that Apollo had ever done, all the victories he'd ever won, was to try and gain the love, even just a single ounce, and respect of his father. Yet, Zeus saw nothing, acknowledged even less, and it made Apollo constantly feel as though he'd done something wrong.

Apparently, that something was having been born.

When Apollo finally got to his own office door, he unlocked it with a wave of his hand and slipped inside to wait for Calliope. The lamps sensed his presence and automatically clicked on as he walked over to the cabinet that held a crystal decanter filled with nectar.

Apollo set down the coffee he'd gotten for Calliope and poured himself a glass, his eyes grazing over the sleekness of his enormous corner office as he sipped. Everything was made of glass and brushed metal, and all the furniture sported clean, modern lines. The gleaming illusion of an imposing high-rise cityscape outside his window and numerous trophies lining the shelves on his walls usually reassured him of his greatness. They did nothing of the sort at the moment. But the nectar did. As always, it infused his being with strength and power. *More* strength and power, which, right now, and especially during his meeting with Zeus in a few minutes, he'd need.

He walked over to the wardrobe that held a change of clothes, unzipped his pants, now with grayish brown spots of drying dirt on the knees, and let them fall to the carpeted floor. The knock on the door a moment later was soft.

"Hey, boss, you wanted to see me?" said Calliope as she entered. Her sleeveless blouse just skimmed the waistband of her modern-fit chinos, and her Executive Assistant badge, clipped to an unused belt loop, dangled at her hip. When she looked up from closing the door, she stiffened, freezing in place when she noticed his state of undress. She swung the door back open in a hurry.

"Sorry."

"You're fine."

It's not like she hadn't seen him half naked before, or fully naked, for that matter. They had only been together once or twice, but who knows what would have been if Daphne hadn't entered the picture.

If he hadn't picked a fight with Eros.

She re-entered, her eyes flicking to his snug fitting boxer briefs as he pulled on a clean pair of perfectly tailored pants.

When she bit her lip, the feeling of vitality flowing through his veins intensified.

"I got you a mocha from Siren Coffee," he said, nodding toward the cup sitting next to his glass of nectar. After tucking in his dress shirt, he zipped up and strode over to his desk. He pulled out his chair, took a seat and gestured to an elegant leather sofa occupying space near a window, inviting Calliope to do the same.

Her cheeks pinked. "Thanks."

Apollo's thoughts raced around his head at break-neck speed as she grabbed her coffee before taking a seat. Panic at having to catch one so he could explain the situation with any amount of calmness swelled, but Apollo swallowed it down, wrestling his urge to spill his guts like a bumbling idiot into submission. He knew exactly how to handle situations like this. He would simply . . . He would just . . .

Oh, gods, what in Hades' Realm was he going to do?

His eyes glanced over the smooth ivory skin of Calliope's shoulders before moving to the band made of delicate laurel branches encircling her head full of long, russet curls secured at the nape of her neck.

Instead of focusing on the problem at hand, his mind began to wander. It wasn't just once or twice, it had been four times, all before his scuffle with Eros. But even after he'd been cursed, he hadn't forgotten those nights—and one afternoon—with Calliope. In fact, he often recalled the way her neck curved when she arched her back, offering herself up to him so he could . . .

He cleared his throat. "I have a problem, and I need your opinion on how to fix it, but I also need your complete confidence, as I do *not* want what I'm about to tell you to get back to my mother." He lifted his glass and took a sip of the rose-colored liquid.

"Yes, of course. Mum's the word." Calliope set her coffee

down to open her ratty, leather-bound notebook. She plucked a pencil from behind her ear and proceeded to give him every ounce of her attention.

Apollo clasped his hands together in front of him, squeezing them tight as he wrangled the right words in line before allowing them to leave his mouth. "Daphne is gone."

He swallowed, waiting for Calliope's reaction. Honestly, how could three simple words be so hard to say? Never mind. He knew the answer to that. Even though he was speaking the truth, as he always did, just saying the words aloud bruised his ego.

Even worse, it made him look bad.

Calliope squinted her eyes at him as though she couldn't quite comprehend what she'd just heard. "I'm sorry? What do you mean she's gone?"

Apollo's lips thinned even more as a short burst of air rocketed from his nose. Questions. Always with the questions. "I mean she's no longer a tree, Calliope. I went to the Sacred Forest to see her, as I do every morning, and the tree is gone." He rubbed his temples, wishing there was no need for the words he was about to say next. "Daphne is gone and I need your help finding her."

"Me?" Calliope's brows lifted when she pointed at her chest.

"Yes, you." Apollo abandoned his aching head to take another sip of nectar. Sure enough, it filled him with a shot of vitality, and the throbbing subsided. "Who else can I count on?"

The flush of color spreading across Calliope's cheeks flooded his mind with something he shouldn't have been feeling. Not then, anyway. He'd seen plenty of women, both goddess and mortal, blush in his presence. Evidence of sexual attraction should not be affecting him like this. Yet, the delicate pinkness splashed across her face made it hard to concentrate.

Determined to stay focused, he shook away the memories of their lovemaking, and by the time he fixed his eyes out the window, his focus on Daphne had returned.

"I'm sorry," she continued. "I just thought maybe you'd ask someone more powerful for help."

Apollo nodded, pleased he'd had that bit of foresight, at least. "I'm on my way to Zeus's office in a few minutes. Hopefully I can get him to call her back to Olympus. If he refuses, then we'll have to locate her the old-fashioned way, by actually looking. I'm relying on you to come up with a plan B . . ." He sighed, already knowing he was going to need one. "You know how unreliable Zeus can be."

Biggest understatement ever. Other than quarterly staff meetings, he rarely saw—or spoke to—Zeus. Despite being the most accomplished of the king of the god's sons, their bond could be most accurately described as a raging trash fire. The meeting was going to be interesting, to say the least.

"Of course," said Calliope. "There's got to be someone else who can tell us where she's gone. I'll make a list."

"Right. She's not in the Sacred Forest, that much I know. And since nymphs aren't allowed on Olympus unless summoned, she's obviously not here. I doubt she'd hide in the Underworld, but maybe. Elysium and Earth are possibilities as well. It will take a considerable amount of time searching both without an exact location."

"I bet her father, Peneus, would know where she is," replied Calliope. "Aside from Zeus, he's the only one who could have granted her respite."

As soon as the words left her mouth, Calliope's gaze shot down to the floor. She peeked up at him a moment later, with an apology on her lips, no doubt, but it was too late. His jaw had already set at her choice of the word *respite*.

"Do you think I wanted any of this to happen?" He knew she hadn't meant it the way he'd taken it, yet he was powerless to stop himself from feeling upset. Or was it hurt? "The curse will go on forever so long as she runs. I'm unable to stop, Calliope, which is why I have to find her. Do you understand?"

His gaze fell to the glass in his hand when Calliope's blue eyes, round and luminescent as a newborn godling's, dropped in deference. He swallowed hard when she began to scratch small circles onto one of the pages of her journal with her pencil. As far as she knew, he was perfectly content to chase Daphne, and he found himself wanting to confide in her that he wasn't. Not by a long shot.

"So you think she called out to her father again?" he went on, deciding his personal information was on a need-to-know basis only. "It does make sense he'd be the one most likely to know where she's disappeared to, doesn't it?"

Callie perked up again, clearly relieved he wasn't angry. "Usually the god or goddess who casts the magic is the only one who can undo it, so, yes, that would make perfect sense. You know, you could always go see Orea, too, she might know something."

"Orea?" Apollo arched one of his eyebrows. Who in Hades' Realm was she?

"Daphne's cousin," answered Calliope, as if she'd heard what he was thinking. "The woodland nymph who was—"

Apollo shook his head and shrugged, his lips turning downward, forcing his bottom lip to cover its mate in a pronounced pout. "Never heard of her." This influx of new information was overwhelming, and it was becoming a struggle to keep it straight. Thank the Fates for Calliope.

"Don't you remember that whole thing with Eros and Orea?" She stuck her pencil behind her ear so she could fold her arms. "She was recruited by Hera to try and get him fired a few years back. Orea agreed, you know, on account of the fact she was still pretty pissed that he shot Daphne instead of her during your—ahem—*argument*. There were actually two nymphs nearby, but Eros only shot one, which was Daphne. You do know that, right?"

"Hmm." Apollo didn't remember the other nymph being there when Eros had let his arrows fly, but he did remember Hera trying to get the god of love fired from Life Industries recently. Cupid had won that battle as well, which made being cursed by him even more infuriating.

Apollo drained the last of his nectar and set the empty glass on his desk before swiveling his chair to face the window. He crossed an ankle over one knee and steepled his fingers, bringing them to his lips. It was a poor attempt at keeping his mind clear. He only had a few minutes left, and he needed to figure out how to convince his father to give a damn.

He pushed out of his seat and stood, sliding his hands into his pockets as he made his way over to the wide expanse of glass. He looked past the city streets and beyond the skyscrapers to zero in on the horizon. His gaze searched, moving back and forth, as if he could pinpoint the exact location at which Daphne had disappeared into its misty, blurred line, where Heaven and Earth met.

She'd bolted like a bat out of Hades' Realm, and the funny thing was, he didn't know if he blamed her—if he could run away from this mess, he would. Instead, he had to carry the weight of his centuries-old mistake on his shoulders, pretending they were strong enough.

"Dammit, Daphne," he muttered, praying the meeting with his father would bring about a quick resolution. "Where in the world are you?"

aphne squeezed her eyelids shut in an effort to stop her head from spinning. It only succeeded in making the dizziness worse. Long, flowing tresses were a huge part of a nymph's identity. But that was exactly why she had to do this. Besides, it was only hair, and she was determined not to let it define her. Not anymore.

She also didn't want the relentless bastard to recognize her.

"Cut it," she said, heart pounding in her ears.

"All of it?" replied the woman, her bottle-blonde hair teased and sprayed within an inch of 1985. "That's pretty drastic, sugar. I mean, what is it, almost down to your knees? It's so long and silky. Some of us would kill for hair like this, you know." The woman took the liberty of raking her fingers through the ends of Daphne's hair.

"Cut it," repeated Daphne.

"Okay, okay, but can we at least start at the bottom of the shoulder blades and work up? So it's not such a shock? I'd hate to have you leaving here in tears."

She met the mortal woman's gaze in the mirror, which

was friendly but surrounded by more makeup than necessary for such lovely brown eyes. Daphne looked down at her dirty bare feet resting on the chrome and wiggled her toes, which were so much smaller now that they weren't roots, and pondered how much of her old life to cut away.

It didn't take long. She'd been waiting for this moment for ages.

"Yes, I'm sure. Just cut it."

She'd gone into the hair salon because the sign in the window read: *Free haircut with Locks of Love donation.* The word *free* had caught her attention. After that, it hadn't been difficult to decide someone was going to get a whole lot of blonde locks. Cutting her hair would be sad, but all she wanted, more than anything right now, was the free part.

"Okay, then." The woman snapped her gum. "You definitely got enough for three donations. You want to do a pixie cut and try for four?"

Daphne tapped her collarbones, deciding that length seemed like a good place to start fresh. "How about up to here?"

The woman peered at her in the mirror, sliding the tie she'd slipped around Daphne's hair down to the middle of her shoulder blades. "I think that's a good length for you. Say, we don't get many new people around here. You're not a criminal on the run up from Texas, are you? Or one of those Salt Lake City sister wives?" Her southern accent was as heavy as her suspicions.

Daphne shook her head. She hadn't broken any laws, and she hadn't left a commune, although she had been a prisoner of a different kind. Her father had made good on his promise to save her should she ask to escape the unwanted advances of a certain someone. That certain someone had been Apollo, and he'd chased after her until she'd hadn't been able to stand it one moment longer. A shiver ran through her just thinking about it.

"You cold, sugar?" The woman began snipping at the hair below the hair tie.

"No, just . . . Yes, I'm a little chilly." Daphne looked at the women in the mirror again, prepared to enchant her. She hoped all humans didn't ask this many questions.

"So you won't mind telling me your name and what brings you to Oklahoma, then, right? Because, no offense, you don't look or sound like a Sooner." The woman planted her hands on her hips, scissors in one and a chunk of liberated hair in the other.

Daphne drew in a sharp breath, pleased at both how the hair skimmed her clavicles and how effortlessly the weight of her old life had been cut away. "My name's Daphne," she said absently, awed by her new look. It seemed to change the shape of her face, make her eyes a bit greener. She felt lighter, and hope filled her chest. Maybe running had worked this time.

"You like it? It'll look even better once I even it up." The woman placed what remained of Daphne's old life in a bin full of other rubber-banded chunks of hair. "You got a last name, Daphne?"

"Brooks," answered Daphne, the sun sparkling off the pristine waters of a Sacred Forest stream flashing in her mind.

"Well, it's nice to meet you, Daphne Brooks. My name's Sadie Carson. Now where was it you said you were from?"

"Um . . . the . . ." The words "sacred" and "forest" caught in Daphne's throat.

Sadie nodded, backing off and focusing instead on shaping the ends of Daphne's hair. After a few moments of silence and several rounds of gum snapping, she said, "Sometimes a girl just needs her privacy, and I can respect that. What do you say we throw in some low-lights to go with your new cut? Maybe go a couple of shades darker?"

Before Daphne could answer, the bell over the door jingled, announcing the arrival of a tall, dark-haired man in a tan cowboy hat and a Caddo County sheriff's deputy badge pinned above the pocket of his navy short-sleeved uniform shirt. A huge German Shepherd stood at his side.

Daphne gasped, a little at the dog's size, but more at the man's imposing stature. His height was impressive, but it was the set of his jaw, with its strong lines that were hard and soft at the same time. The contradiction sent her heart galloping.

It also could have been the size of the weapon holstered and strapped to his belt.

"Hey, Ladies," he said. "How y'all doing this afternoon?"

In spite of her strong disinterest in mortals in general, his deep voice, and the sweet, slow drawl of his words, caused a sensation to spread through her, like water warmed by the sun.

"What's up, Sammy?" chirped Sadie.

Sweat dampened Daphne's underarms. It was an odd, uncomfortable sensation, and all she could do was nod at the man with smooth, bronze skin and look away before her pits could get any damper.

Get ahold of yourself, Daphne.

In her experience, gods only wanted one thing: Control. She wasn't clear on mortals yet, but if she had to guess, she'd say that men, mortal or otherwise, were all the same. It made her muscles stiffen until they trembled, and the urge to take off nearly made her bolt out of her seat.

She clenched her jaw instead.

Despite what kind of effect this particular male mortal was having on her, it was inconsequential. She was to be the master of her own fate. If she couldn't do it in the Sacred

Forest, she'd do it here, even if she had to pretend to be mortal for the rest of her days. All she needed to do was blend in and stay hidden. She was determined to never be trapped again, not by a god and certainly not by a man.

At least, that was the plan.

The dog barked and Daphne jumped, startled out of her thoughts. Her gaze went directly to the canine; ears alert, stance serious, attention trained on her from lack of response to its partner.

"It's all right, Zeus." The man signaled for the dog to sit. "His bark is worse than his bite." One eyebrow slid up. "Unless someone decides to break the law. Ain't that right, boy?" Zeus barked again, and Daphne offered them both a weak smile. When the animal's name finally hit her, she nearly giggled.

Controlling or not, at least some of them had a sense of humor.

The man turned toward Sadie. "And you know when the badge is on you're supposed to call me Deputy Carson."

"Oh, you ain't never gonna be nothin' but my little cousin, okay?" she snorted. "You need to respect your elders."

"Fair enough, Sades." Deputy Carson nodded with a resigned smile. "So, old man Owens said there was a woman wandering around over in Nowhere, possibly high on something? You haven't seen anyone suspicious around Fort Cobb, have you?"

Daphne swallowed. Why was he looking directly at her?

She caught Sadie's eyes widening at her in the mirror, and Daphne tugged at the hem of the 2XL *Welcome to Nowhere, OK* T-shirt that hung to her knees underneath the nylon smock. They were in Fort Cobb, which wasn't far from Nowhere, and she knew full well Sadie had put two and two together.

Daphne's cheeks warmed, and she pressed her lips

together at the memory of the old man's face. He'd been behind the counter working on a crossword puzzle when she'd stepped out from behind a rack of T-shirts with only her hair covering her gods-given curves. The poor man had been as red-faced as a cardinal, sputtering out directions for her to put on one of the shirts. Right quick, as he'd put it. Mortals and their modesty. When he'd told her she owed $12.99 plus tax, she'd run out the door.

She'd asked her father to send her to the middle of nowhere, and he'd obliged. Literally. Nowhere, as it turned out, was a bait shop in Oklahoma, on the corner of County Street and a dusty old road that didn't even have a name.

Her father always did have a wicked sense of humor.

"It was me." The words slipped out of Daphne's mouth before she could stop them. Why she thought it was a good idea to blow her cover, she couldn't say.

Yes she could. This man was a mortal. Nothing more, nothing less. Certainly nothing to fear. There was no reason to cower. She'd give him an excuse—and enchant him if she had to—and be on her way.

Deputy Carson squared his broad shoulders and folded his arms. "Mind telling me what you were doing in the bait shop naked then?"

His voiced wasn't raised, but despite her best effort to remain poised, his suddenly serious and authoritative tone made her rethink the probability that her hasty plan would work. She never had been good at thinking ahead, and her impulse control was much weaker down here on Earth, obviously. She'd opened her mouth without a good explanation at the ready, and now she would pay for it.

"Well shoot, Sammy, isn't it obvious?" Sadie placed her hands on Daphne shoulders and squeezed before catching her eyes in the mirror. "She ain't from around here, are you, sugar? Well, you're not the only person to go skinny-dipping over in the reservoir. If you're sticking around, the first thing you need to know about the locals is how much they love their practical jokes. You gotta hide your clothes so they don't steal 'em and make you walk home in your birthday suit. Not that it ever happened to me in my day, I'm just saying."

Daphne exhaled, grateful for the life-line.

She *had* felt the pull of the lake, but had gone in search of a disguise instead. That was the deal as long as she was down on Earth. She had to do what mortals did, which meant eat, sleep and, most important for her, blend in. Also, at some point she supposed, get a job and work herself half to death.

Diving to the bottom of a lake sounded nice right about now, and it made her want to groan in frustration she wasn't doing just that. Water always soothed her soul. Why her father had decided to turn her into a tree when she'd cried out for help, she never understood.

But beggars can't be choosers. Apollo had been relentless, and her father could have turned her into a fig for all she cared. Just as long as she could stop running. And here she was, on the verge of possibly having to flee again. Maybe leaving the Sacred Forest had been a mistake.

"This is Daphne Brooks, by the way," said Sadie. "She needs a ride to the real estate office."

Daphne opened her mouth to protest—she'd walked from Nowhere to Fort Cobb just fine, she could manage a few more miles—but Sadie slammed her foot down on the chair's back pedal. Daphne's stomach looped, first from the sudden drop, then from the chair whirling around so fast the room spun.

Sadie pulled Daphne to her feet, clamping the back of the smock closed as she pushed her toward a back room. "We're just gonna get her things and you can take her to Jimmy's, if you don't mind."

"Sure, happy to help," replied Deputy Carson, seeming to forget all about locating the mysterious streaker running around Caddo County.

Maybe he already knew he'd found her and felt sorry for her.

Or was planning to lock her up.

The velcro strip made an awful tearing noise when Daphne ripped off the smock. Panic clawed at her insides. "I'm not helpless, I can figure things out on my own."

Sadie rummaged through a large tote bag before pulling out a pair of cut-off jean shorts and a tank top. "Oh sure, with what money?"

"How do you know I don't have any . . . ah . . . money?" said Daphne, catching the clothes that Sadie threw over to her.

"Well, you're not wearing pants, and you sure as shit ain't carrying a purse, so unless you've got it stuffed where the sun don't shine, I reckon you don't have any. Now gimme that t-shirt." Sadie held out her hand so Daphne could get rid of the evidence that the naked woman who'd nearly put old man Owens into cardiac arrest was her. "Listen, folks around here might not have much, but we do what we can to help each other out. I don't know who you're running from or what he's done to you, but I know a woman gunning for her freedom when I see one. Here, take these, too." Sadie pulled a pair of sandals from the bag and tossed them at Daphne's feet. "Sammy—Deputy Carson—is a good guy. Go with him, he'll help you find a place to hide—stay."

Sadie dug into the front pocket of her jean skirt before pulling something out and pressing it into Daphne's hand. "It's not much, but it'll let you eat until you can find yourself a job. Welcome to Oklahoma, Daphne Brooks."

Daphne stared at the crumpled green paper rectangles in her hand. Mortal currency. Daphne knew Sadie must have worked hard cutting hair to earn it, and the woman's kindness overwhelmed her into silence.

"You come back as soon as you can," Sadie continued, grabbing Daphne's shoulders and turning her toward the door. "We'll give that new cut of yours a different color so that sorry SOB you're hiding from won't even recognize you. Free of charge."

CHAPTER FOUR

$\mathcal{A}$pollo appeared outside Zeus's office in a flash of light. He blew out a breath as he straightened his tie. The king of the gods peered at him through the floor-to-ceiling glass door, and he fought the urge to shrink under that indifferent gaze. Had Zeus *ever* looked at him with pride? Not that Apollo could recall.

He squared his shoulders and, pushing the massive door open as if it weighed nothing, strode into his father's office.

"Good morning. Thank you for meeting with me on such short notice," said Apollo as he walked toward a set of chairs stationed in front of the desk. He took a seat, reminding himself to keep his chest and his head held high.

It hardly mattered because, like the self-important ass he was, Zeus had already gone back to signing paperwork. Yet, Apollo remained silent, sitting and waiting patiently until Life Industries' CEO looked up and nodded curtly.

Apollo held in a growl of frustration. That's it? That's all the greeting he was worth? What else had he expected? Fanfare? A ticker tape parade? Yeah, right.

Considering his track record of making huge mistakes, it

wasn't outside the realm of possibility that this meeting fell directly under the category of *Wrong Move, Hotshot*. Especially if he couldn't keep the look of disappointment off his face long enough to convince Zeus he wasn't bothered by the slight. Apollo needed to stay focused. Be strong, not just appear strong. He couldn't afford to get sidetracked with his daddy issues.

"I trust you scheduled this meeting for a reason other than to stare at me?" asked Zeus, sliding off his glasses and dropping them onto a mound of papers before lacing his fingers together.

Apollo willed the placid look on his face to remain intact. He really shouldn't be surprised Zeus was treating him as though he were nothing more than an employee. What he wouldn't give to make it not sting every time.

When Apollo finally responded, he said the words slowly so he wouldn't shout them. "Your most accomplished son sits before you, and you ask if he's scheduled a meeting?"

Zeus stared at him, unmoved. More than unmoved. Impatient.

Screw it. Two could play the *Who's the Bigger Dickhead?* game. Apollo unleashed a derisive snort. "I'm the patron of organization and formalities, of course I scheduled a meeting."

Zeus pulled in a slow breath, massaging his temples with the finger and thumb of one giant hand. "Okay, you've got my attention. What do you want, Apollo? A raise? Is that it?"

His patronizing tone raked its claws down Apollo's calm demeanor, which was already irritating enough, but saying Apollo had his attention added even more insult to injury.

Apollo wanted to burst out laughing at the irony, but he managed to keep it together enough to at least appear unfazed. If he wanted Zeus's help, he had to forget the bastard had left his mother high, dry, and very much pregnant so he could marry another woman. "No. No raise. It has nothing to do with Life Industries, actually. I need your help with a personal matter."

Zeus lifted a brow, folding his arms as he sat straighter in his seat. Apollo stared back at him as a cavalcade of thoughts paraded through his mind, the forerunner being how his father had gotten this far through immortal life being such an unscrupulous bastard. One who abandoned his own children.

Not entirely true. Zeus had relationships with plenty of his offspring. Just not Apollo.

Zeus broke the silence first. "Well, what is it? What do you need help with?"

Apollo didn't *need* help with anything. What he *wanted* was a show of respect for once. Barring that, how about a simple: I'm proud of you, son. I'm sorry I handed your mother, you, and your sister the shit end of the stick when I left to be with Hera.

"Daphne's gone," Apollo said through clenched teeth.

Zeus let out a heavy sigh, which gave way to a grunt. "You're still going on about that nymph? She is going to be the downfall of you yet, Apollo. You're obsessed. If you ask me, you should be happy she's gone. Maybe now you can finally get on with your life."

Being cursed. One more thing he'd done wrong. Add it to the list.

Apollo's frustration poured through the cracks beginning to appear in his calm exterior, allowing a scathing sneer to creep onto his face "You think I should be *happy* she's missing? And I'm not obsessed, I'm cursed. Believe me, if I could stop I would, but I can't." Zeus opened his mouth, presumably to say something, but Apollo pressed on. "And really? You're going to speak to me about being obsessed? You and your uncontrollable lust. My mother was *pregnant* when you declared Hera your seventh wife. Do you even know what that has done to Artemis? She reviles marriage."

He wanted to point out what it'd done to him, too, but his pride wouldn't let him.

Zeus leaned forward and gripped the sides of his desk, the thick glass making a crunching noise under the pressure. "Hera was a better match, and your sister has chosen to live a life of celibacy on her own. She's a strong, independent goddess. The fact that she refuses marriage has nothing to do with what happened between your mother and I. We weren't meant to be."

Apollo's aura grew brighter. Hotter. He was close to dropping all pretense now. "Oh, of course, how convenient. You just weren't meant to be. And you don't think Daphne and I are meant to be together, either? Is that what you're saying?"

"What I'm saying is I don't have time for this nonsense. I have all of mankind to run. You know what happens if they stop believing? It's bad enough they no longer worship."

The conversation was going south, and Apollo knew he should stop, but he'd finally had the courage to call his father out on not giving two shits about him and Artemis, and the son-of-a-bitch was worried about worship?

"No time? Ha! That's rich coming from you. You've never had the time for much of anything besides battling Titans and seducing women. So again, don't speak to me of things you know nothing about."

"Trust me, I know things. I wouldn't be king if I didn't. Sometimes you have to follow your heart, no matter how much destruction it causes. Speaking of, perhaps you should see Eros if this is a matter of the heart."

"Eros?" snorted Apollo, the mere suggestion ratcheting his anger up a notch. Zeus knew their history, that he and Eros were not on speaking terms, and he didn't appreciate the insult added to injury. "What would that chubby man-child be able to do?"

Zeus folded his massive arms. "You know full well what he can do."

He did, and Apollo didn't want to admit it, so he made a conscious effort to redirect the attention back to the reason he'd scheduled the meeting in the first place. Even if he was able to work something out with Eros, Zeus was the quicker route to finding Daphne. "I'm asking *you* to help me."

"You know I can't, Apollo. If I show you favor, all the others will be in here asking for something, especially the Titans." Zeus snickered. "What's left of them."

Apollo finally snapped, his aura glowing white-hot and his skin blazing like the sun. He slammed a palm down on the top of the desk, leaving a red, glowing handprint in its wake. "You're the king of the fucking gods! Just call her back to Olympus for a mandatory meeting and I'll do the rest."

Thunder rolled in the distance, the force vibrating the office furniture, and the air crackled with electricity.

Zeus glared at him, deadly serious. "I said no."

Apollo's chest heaved, but other than that he remained still, not moving a muscle until the darkness blooming at the edge of his vision receded. As usual, he would get nothing from Zeus. "Fine. I'll do it myself. Just like I do everything else."

Zeus returned his glasses to the bridge of his nose before refocusing his attention on his paperwork. "You know, sometimes I don't know who you take after more," he murmured.

"What's that supposed to mean?" asked Apollo.

"Clearly, you got your ego from me," answered Zeus, his gaze lifting again.

Not exactly a compliment, but Apollo would take what he could get, especially since Zeus never talked about this part of his past, the part that acknowledged Apollo as his son.

"And from my mother?"

"Drama," said Zeus. "You can't stand it when there's no drama, can you?"

Apollo jumped up, the chair flying backward, unable to withstand the force of his indignation. That was it. Thinking he was unworthy was one thing, but insulting his mother was the last gods-damned straw. His father knew nothing about him. Certainly not that he avoided drama at all costs, and definitely not that all he'd ever done, practically from the moment he was born, was try to impress the one god who apparently was impossible to impress.

Apollo didn't bother to button his suit coat before storming off toward the door. He knew he should leave without saying another word, too, but that would be like stopping a Kraken once it's been disturbed from its watery slumber. Impossible. "Thanks for nothing," he spat the words over his shoulder. "I'll be sure to give my melodramatic mother your regards."

"Apollo," Zeus called after him, his tone commanding and icy.

"What?" Apollo responded just as coldly, halting but refusing to turn around.

"Did you try asking your mother if she's heard where Daphne is?"

Apollo dropped his chin to his chest, his shoulders falling along with it. No wonder Zeus thought him unworthy. He hadn't thought about checking the latest gossip to see if he could find out where Daphne had gone. His embarrassment was so immense he considered lying for the first time in his immortal life and saying that he had. Sighing, he muttered, "No," before exiting the office with as much dignity as he could muster.

Apollo ruled over so much, and had accomplished such

great things, but Zeus had managed to make him feel small and insignificant. Again.

Instead of magicking himself back to his office, where he could lick his wounds in peace, he hurried down the corridor that led out into the lobby and straight to his mother's desk. Despite her penchant for harvesting the latest intrigues on Mount Olympus, Apollo loved her dearly. She'd always been there for him and Artemis growing up. As much as he was loathe to admit it, talking to her was a good idea. One he wished he'd thought of himself because, while his forthright nature didn't approve of such a deplorable exchange of information such as gossip, perhaps he could use her love of whispers to his advantage. Just this once.

Apollo strolled arm-in-arm through the Atrium with his mother, making small talk as he guided her toward a bench in one of its many courtyards. He politely waited for her to finish some story about Dionysus foolishly dabbling with mortals down on Earth as a rock musician.

"Dion's a lost cause, Mom. He's a drunken brat who's never going to grow up . . ." He stopped before the floodgates burst open. He had his opinions about the god of wine. What he didn't have was enough time to express them all. Nor did he have the inclination to unravel a string of profanities in front of his mother. "So, not to change the subject or anything, but you haven't heard any rumors floating around about Daphne, have you?"

Leto's lips pressed together before the top one ended up caught between her teeth. It popped out as she pursed her lips. "No, why do you ask?"

He rolled his shoulders, hoping the small movement was enough to keep his composure. This might be his best chance at finally getting a lockdown on Daphne's whereabouts, but he didn't want to appear too eager and, Fates forbid, like he didn't have a handle on the situation. "You probably didn't know this, but it seems that Daphne has decided to take a break from the Sacred Forest." He didn't like what he was about to say next, because it wasn't exactly the truth. But it technically wasn't lying either. It was semantics. "A vacation."

His mother arched her eyebrows at him. "Oh, and where did she decide to take this *vacation*?"

"I don't know, but I miss her terribly, and I'd like to join her. You don't have any idea where she's gone, then?"

Leto cleared her throat softly. "Well, I hate to be the one to have to tell you this, but . . ."

Apollo swallowed hard, hating that look of pity in her eyes. He should have known—he should have skipped the meeting with his father and come straight to his mother.

Her eyes dipped as she smoothed the lap of her printed dress and crossed her Jimmy Choo-clad feet demurely at the ankle. "This is between you, me, and the fence post, darling, but Daphne isn't on vacation. Well, I suppose it's a vacation of sorts . . ."

Apollo wanted to plague nations, flip tables, punch a cyclops in the eye. How come no one else could see this mess wasn't all on him? He literally couldn't stop. Did they all think he enjoyed keeping such close tabs on Daphne?

"Rumor has it she's left for good," said his mother. "Tired of being a tree, I suppose."

Panic bubbled and popped in his stomach. He knew she'd run away from him, yet again, and was now hiding. If what his mother was saying was true, everybody on Mount Olympus knew it, too.

But he couldn't turn back time—Chronus had expressly forbidden it without a formal request or else Apollo would have tried—and, even if he could, he and his ego would probably make the same stupid mistake.

His only choice now was to find Daphne.

"Do you know where she's gone?" he asked, careful not to sound too eager.

"I don't know where she is, darling, but maybe you could use the GPS—oh, shoot, that only works on mortals, doesn't it? What about Eros? He and Psyche just got that promotion, I bet he could help you—"

"It's okay. She'll turn up. Thanks anyway, Mom." Apollo got up from the bench. Even though this entire mess was technically his fault, crawling to Eros with his tail between his legs was not an option. "Well, I better get back to the office."

"Are you coming to movie night?" The hopeful look on her face clawed at him. "Arti said she'll be there. We're watching *You've Got Mail.*"

"I'll try." He kissed his mother on the cheek, laughing to himself because he knew how much his sister hated romantic comedies. Their mother was over the moon for them, so they suffered through every movie night to indulge her. "I can't promise anything, though, work's been crazy."

"Okay, darling. Love you, and . . . Well, just try not to work so hard, all right?"

Apollo almost let a snort escape. If she only knew how hard he *always* had to work, at everything. And dealing with the rat's nest of emotions Daphne's disappearance dredged to the surface had shot to the top of the list.

Make that second on the list. His reputation as a strong and powerful god, one who was secure enough in his godhood to achieve greatness without a father's love, was at stake. He didn't know whether to laugh or cry about it, but was leaning toward the latter because of all the times his mother didn't have the scoop, of course it had to be when he needed it most.

CHAPTER FIVE

The atrium at the top of Mount Olympus had it all —dry cleaner, coffee shop, hair salon, and a gym outfitted with enough free weights to be every Olympian's wet dream—all surrounded by beautiful fountains, lush gardens, and strolling paths. A real paradise.

What it didn't have was a place for Callie to hide from her sister's scrutiny.

Her sister and fellow muse, Clio, took a sip of her nectar smoothie as she eyed Callie's journal. "How's the writing going?"

Callie knew it was a loaded question, and she hated loaded questions so she pressed her lips shut. As always, Clio saw the boundaries Callie put up and proceeded to cross them. Dove over them cackling with glee was more like it.

Clio pressed forward. "I'm surprised you've had any time for yourself working for *you know who.*"

Callie kept writing, refusing to give in and break down at her sister's insistence to bring the subject of her and Apollo up as often as possible. Clio stared at her, slurping her smoothie louder than necessary.

Callie gripped her pencil—which had stopped scratching its way across the page at this point—so hard her knuckles turned white. "Whatever, Clio, he's not that bad."

"Oh, really?" Clio made a scoffing noise. "When's the last time you had a day off?"

A sound of exasperation burst from Callie's throat. "I take days off all the time. In fact, I just went to that *Modern Man and How to Inspire Them* workshop not too long ago." She tilted her head at her sister. "Funny, I didn't see you there, Clio."

"Good gods, Callie," laughed Clio. "That workshop was at the turn of the century . . . *Two* centuries ago. And, I'm sorry, but modern man is always in the process of making history. I don't need a workshop to teach me that."

"Ugh. Don't you have some history buffs to drive crazy somewhere?" snapped Callie, trying to turn the conversation back on Clio. It never worked, but it was worth a try because this conversation was getting old. In fact, it was bordering on ancient.

"Oh, come on, Callie." Clio expertly sidestepped Callie's bait and switch. "Apollo's a jerk, admit it. He doesn't treat you very well. You should really stop trying to impress him. I mean, you're a muse for Fates' sake. People are supposed to be obsessed with *you*, not the other way around. If I didn't know any better, I'd think you were still in love with him."

Callie huffed. Still in love with him? Gods, this was getting ridiculous. How many times was she going to have to explain that, no, she was *not* still in love with Apollo because it, that thing between them, had only happened once.

Okay fine, four times, while working late, but they'd both just needed to blow off some steam. That's all it had been. Stress relief. Mind blowing, toe-curling stress relief.

Callie geared up to say as much when her phone crooned the words to *You are the Sunshine of My Life*. The ringing provided a much needed diversion, and also sent a pair of peacocks casing the cafe tables for pita scraps darting the other way. Her choice of ringtone, however, didn't help her case in the *I'm Not in Love With Apollo* debate.

Clio raised an eyebrow. "Need I say more?"

Callie rolled her eyes. "What? Stevie Wonder is a treasure." She glared back at the muse of history before answering her phone. "Hey, boss—"

"Where are you?" Apollo's voice blasted from the other end of the line.

The phone practically slipped out of her sweaty hand as she frantically pushed the volume button down several notches. "Um, I'm in the atrium eating lunch." She frowned when her sister mouthed the word *asshole* from across the table. Callie turned away, hunching her shoulders and lowering her voice. "Why, do you need something?"

"Yes, I need you in my office again, immediately."

Callie straightened. He already had her attention, but the small crack in his voice made it go from one hundred percent to *I'm-dropping-everything-now-I'll-be-there-in-two* seconds percent.

Apollo could be demanding—she was used to that—but it was only because he had so much on his plate. It only made sense that a god who accomplished so many great things would have a ton of responsibilities and obligations, wouldn't it? Apollo handled it all with aplomb. Well, she was actually the one who ran his schedule, making sure he was up-to-date and in-the-know, but who was keeping track?

Oh, that's right. Clio. Clio was keeping track. And if Clio was keeping track, Callie would bet her journals so were the other seven muses.

But there was something in his voice right now, an undercurrent of urgency that only Callie, being his longtime personal assistant and totally trusted advisor, could pick up on. He needed her, and it made her chest expand, spreading warmth from the tip of her ears to the ends of her toes. It also made her muscles soften until they were about as useful as overcooked noodles.

Her relationship with Apollo was complicated, she would admit that much, but he'd chosen to keep her on as his assistant, even after *it* had happened, and she was determined not to let him down. Not because she loved him, but because it was her job.

Clio chewed on the straw poking out of her smoothie and stared at Callie with disapproving eyes. Callie returned her sister's narrowed gaze. No way was she budging on this. She was not in love with Apollo. She simply had a very strong work ethic. "No problem. I'll head up as soon as I finish—"

"You can eat your lunch up here," said Apollo, his voice low. "Just this once."

Again, no trace of his usual overconfidence, only desperation, and Callie wished Clio could hear it for once. He wasn't an asshole—well, not all the time, anyway—just misunderstood.

"I'll be right there." The poem she'd been working on would have to wait. And Clio's snark? Well, she could just shove it where the sun didn't shine. "You want anything from Pegasus Cafe?"

"No, thank you. Just please come to my office as soon as you can."

No, thank you? Please? He might be more desperate than she thought.

Eros had done a real number on Apollo with that leaden arrow to Daphne's heart, and while Callie wanted to hold a grudge against the god of love for cursing the god of sun and light with a raging case of unrequited love, she couldn't. Apollo had deserved it.

But that was then, this was now, and she'd work with what she had as far as Apollo was concerned. Truth be told, his holier-than-thou attitude wasn't so bad. Not after you got used to it. And not when you knew why he put up a good front. Having Zeus as a father couldn't be easy, especially since he treated Apollo like he was nothing more than an employee. Even worse than that. Like some filthy satyr wandering the Sacred Forest, begging for scraps of magic. Certainly not like a son he was proud to call his own.

Callie ended the call and slid her pencil behind her ear, refusing to look at her sister, who, of course, was still staring at her when she closed her journal. "My gods, would you stop looking at me like that, Clio? Technically, he's your boss, too. I'm just taking one for the team, okay?" Metal screeched across the gray flagstones as she pushed away from the table.

"Whatever you say, Callie. Better you than me, though." Clio continued to slurp on her smoothie as Callie gathered her things and threw them into her bag. "Me? I've got millions of mortals to motivate. When was the last time you inspired a poet, huh? Bukowski?"

"It was Maya Angelou, for your information." Callie hooked her bag over her shoulder then leaned over and swiped Clio's smoothie from her hand. "I mean, it's not like I give Apollo *all* my attention. I'm just a super dedicated and loyal employee. I'm a problem solver, Clio." She took a long sip of the smoothie.

"You might be a problem solver, but you're not a miracle worker, Callie, which is why—"

Callie cut her off. "I can do my job and still have plenty of time to inspire the great poets of the world, okay? Quit being such a broken record." She was so done with this conversation.

Clio shook her head. "Not the point and you know it.

He's never going to change . . . but you just keep holding out hope that he will."

"Our relationship is purely professional!" Thoroughly exasperated at her sister's tenacity, Callie slammed the empty cup down and darted away before Clio could issue a rebuttal.

Purely professional. The irony of those words clanged inside her head as Callie literally ran toward Apollo's beck and call.

She race-walked around the base of the enormous fountain in the center of the courtyard, and her eyes flicked up to the centerpiece. Three water nymphs smiled innocently as they poured water from their urns. Nymphs. They had no real power to speak of, not like muses did. So why was everyone always falling in love with them?

Once through the doors of Life Industries, she hurried up the wide stone staircase, across the polished marble floor and through the gleaming lobby, waving to the receptionist on her way to the Hall of Olympians.

"Nice wrap dress, Leto," she said. "Diane von Furstenburg?"

"Thank you, darling." Leto covered the receiver of her phone with a hand. "Eros suggested it."

"Mr. Matchmaker sure knows his stuff. I'm headed to Apollo's office. He knows I'm coming."

Leto answered with a wink, a corner of her mouth quirking up. Callie knew that grin held meaning, but she didn't dare let her thoughts get carried away. If she did they would waste no time skipping off into a sunset hand-in-hand, and that kind of thinking was nothing but a fairy tale, a happy ending that was just that: A fantasy that didn't exist.

Sure Leto approved of an official union between her and Apollo, but it would never happen, because Apollo was her boss and she was his assistant. He was revered among gods and mortals alike for a great many things. He was legendary, and she doubted if a single mortal could remember what she represented without having to do a Google search. If there was one thing Apollo deserved for being the best, it was having the best of everything. There was no way he would ever consider . . . Even though . . .

She shook away the ridiculous thoughts and picked up the pace.

Both sentries smiled fondly, nodding when Callie showed them her work badge. She took the time to send them each a warm smile before hurrying into the Hall of Olympians.

A congregation of songbirds was holding a concert in the courtyard, and she wished she had time to grab a front row seat, maybe get a few more passages of the epic poem she'd been working on while she listened. But Apollo needed her, and when he needed her, everything else could wait.

She passed Demeter, goddess of the grain harvest. "Hey, Demi. Looking golden, as always."

"Good afternoon, Callie," replied Demeter with a wave. "You're looking positively sunny yourself."

The compliment put an extra spring in Callie's step, succeeding in pushing Clio's ridiculous warnings even further into the back of her mind. Everything was under control. She was not in love with Apollo and she could handle whatever the universe threw her way. Her resolve to do her job and nothing more hardened, and she knocked on Apollo's office door twice, their special signal that indicated it was her.

"Enter."

She did as any good *assistant* would do and went inside. "Hey, boss. You sounded concerned. What's up?"

Apollo skipped the pleasantries, which was fine because pleasantries weren't really his thing anyway.

"Zeus was no help," he said, his brow dipping low. "Now what?"

There was usually never a hair out of place on his achingly

handsome head, but they were currently raked into a series of golden spikes at his crown, standing on end as though he'd been intent on pulling each one out. Plus his eyes, and the way his brow creased over them like that . . .

She went noodles again. "Don't worry, boss. I'll think of something."

CHAPTER SIX

*E*very one of Daphne's bones rattled, including her teeth. She'd heard of mortal contraptions like this—what had Deputy Carson called it? A pickup truck?—but had never seen one up close. It was such an odd chariot. Instead of burnished gold, it was white, with two doors, four wheels, and cushioned seats. At least she didn't have to stand.

They rode in silence, and although they weren't saying much, it was comfortable. Maybe a little too comfortable. Every time she caught herself inhaling more deeply than necessary, she bit the inside of her cheek. He smelled of cloudless skies, of wind and rain and earth—all the things she loved—and it stirred something in her. Even though she wished it wouldn't, her stomach fluttered like leaves caught in a cyclone, and when he parked his dusty chariot marked *Sheriff* in metallic gold letters in front of a squat brick building, her instinct to run kicked in.

"Thanks for the ride, Deputy Carson. I appreciate it." She groped for the door handle, her knee already pushing against its hard, molded plastic. "I've got it from here."

"Now, hold on a minute." He cut the engine and pulled

the keys from the ignition. "First, it's not my habit to leave a woman in a strange place by herself, and second, call me Sam. My shift just ended."

"I'm fine, really. I can take care of myself."

Zeus threw his nose in the air and barked.

"Oh, I don't doubt that," replied Sam "But it would make my partner, here, feel a whole lot better if you at least let me help get a roof over your head."

Both Zeus and Sam's eyes locked on her, waiting for an answer. A small smile played at the edges of her mouth. She didn't want the hindrance of a roof, necessarily, but it was amusing the way both their heads were tilted at exactly the same angle.

"Okay." The word seemed to just fall right out of her mouth. Wasn't that something? She'd escaped the endless attention of a self-righteous, overbearing god who refused to take no for an answer, only to be intrigued by a mortal man to whom *she* couldn't seem to say no. That definitely hadn't been in the plan.

Zeus's tail thumped against the cab's back seat, and she tried to hide the smile that broke free as she hopped down onto the pavement and headed toward the building.

Sam somehow beat her to the door and held it open.

"Thank you," she said as she passed through.

Zeus trotted in after her and then dutifully sat beside Sam when he reached the counter. He tapped a bell and a tall, reedy looking young fellow clicked off a television mounted on the wall in a small conference room.

The door swung open and the young man hurried over to engage in the same kind of shoulder-to-shoulder, quick-pat-on-the-back hug the men back in her world also did. "Well look who's come to interrupt my afternoon soaps. Finally decide to sell that old farmhouse, Sammy?"

"Daphne Brooks, this is my cousin, Jimmy Weber. And,

no, I'm not selling the farmhouse. It's been in the family for almost a century."

Daphne laughed, a bit at how paltry "almost a century" was to her, but mostly at the similarities in the number of family members she and Sam seemed to share. "Another cousin?"

"Yes, ma'am, we're all family around here, one way or another," answered Jimmy.

"I can relate. I come from a big family, too." She had a big family, all right, with lots of cousins. Land, water, woodland, sea, sky . . . She even had relatives in the Underworld.

Sam lifted an eyebrow. "Which originally hails from . . .?"

Was he simply doing his job or was he actually curious? Whatever the case, it didn't matter. She needed to concentrate on keeping her business under wraps, with no more incriminating outbursts. "Let's just say it's somewhere far, far away and leave it at that."

Sam's chuckle made her smile, the sound flowing over her smooth and easy. She tucked the hair that had fallen into her face behind her ear. Her cheeks warmed the moment she realized it was an unsuccessful attempt to dismiss how good his voice made her feel.

"So what are you in the market for, Miss Brooks?" asked Jimmy. "Do you have a budget?"

The warm feeling wasn't done with her yet, and it made her think about home. She pictured herself on the bank of one of the Sacred Forest's babbling brooks, with the tingling bubbles rushing over her ankles, toes curling around slippery rocks . . .

"Miss Brooks?"

Daphne blinked, pulled from her daydream. "I'm sorry, what did you say?"

The plan. She should really stick to it. The problem was,

she hadn't thought through how she was going to navigate the mortal world, only never enduring another minute of Apollo. In fact, she thought it would be a lot simpler than it was turning out to be. There were quite a few more things to consider now that she was here, and it was clear her plan needed amending.

Even after being on Earth for less than twenty-four mortal hours, it was evident she couldn't exactly hang out in the woods forever without raising suspicion. Plus, that's the first place Apollo would look, seeing as she'd been a tree for thousands of years and all.

"What's your budget?" repeated Jimmy. "Are you looking to buy or rent?"

"Um, I guess I've never had a budget before." Whatever "having a budget" meant.

Both of Sam's eyebrows went up this time, and she knew exactly what *that* meant. If she had to bet her immortal life on it, this budget thing had to do with both her class and her means. More specifically, the bigger her budget, the more comfortable her life. A kept woman, that's what he thought. It was written all over his face and it made her jaw clench. If he only knew the half of it.

The warm, fuzzy feeling evaporated, and a cold dread snaked through her. Assumptions aside, she didn't have one of these so-called budgets, which meant she had no way to pay for anything a human being needed. She was a nymph, so she could survive in the elements without food for longer than a human, but that wasn't the issue. It was they now knew she existed. If she took off, they'd undoubtedly go looking for her at this point. Although her wiles worked here, her magic only worked at home. She could ignite a human's lust, enrapture their minds to muddle their thoughts, but she couldn't morph into a pond or a stream and hide. She knew because she'd tried, earlier that morning. It hadn't worked, and so she'd kept walking. Now she was here, wishing she could turn into carpeting.

"I kind of left in a hurry, so I don't have anything to . . . No way to, ah . . ." Wonderful. Not even a full day of freedom and she was already failing at it. She should just cut her losses and have her father bring her back to the Sacred Forest. The last thing she wanted to do was spend all her time muddling minds. "I'm sorry, coming here was a mistake."

Sam must have heard the waver in her voice. His look was intense, and her pulse began to race as he ran his tongue along the corner of his mouth, his eyes squinting in thought before the lines in his brow smoothed. "I'll tell you what. I need some help out at the ranch. I've got a loft above the . . ."

Jimmy laughed. "You call that a ranch? It's a farm, with an old farmhouse and, excuse my French, a rickety-ass barn out back. I'm surprised it hasn't fallen down on Samson and Delilah yet. That loft you built is pretty nice, though, I will give you that. You're good with a hammer. Now, women on the other hand—"

Sam threw dagger eyes at his cousin. "If you're so worried about my horses, you're welcome to use my tools to secure their safety any time."

Daphne picked up on the tension sharpening the edge in Sam's tone. Was it the horses he was getting defensive about, or the comment about not being good with women?

And, ooh, horses. She loved horses. Especially the kind with wings.

"Nah, I'm allergic to manual labor." Jimmy shrugged off Sam's comment. "Besides, I've got—hashtag—goals. You know how much I can make selling commercial property down in Texas? That's where it's at. Speaking of, how heartless of you to rip a young man's dreams out from underneath him by being so kind-hearted? I mean, clearly, I am too fabulous for this podunk town. Let me shine, Samuel. Let. Me. Shine."

Sam laughed, Jimmy's over-the-top antics seeming to do the trick of coaxing him back into his normally easy manner. "Well I don't mean to dull your sparkle, *James*, but I don't think Daphne here is going to be your ticket to becoming a real estate tycoon."

Sam couldn't have known how deep the comment would borrow itself under her skin. But it did, and it fired up the familiar tune playing on repeat inside her head, which made her want to scream.

Poor, helpless nymph. Poor, helpless nymph. Poor, helpless . . .

Someone, somewhere, always thought they needed to protect nymphs. She knew why, thanks to thousands of years living under a self-righteous patriarchal society, but it ground her gears all the same.

Nymphs were considered the weakest of the divinities on Mount Olympus, with little to no power beyond transfiguration and feminine wiles. However wrong or right, they were forced to use whatever they had at their disposal to be treated with respect. Truth be told, even if she preferred not to, she might have to use some of that persuasion down here at some point in order to survive.

She wasn't above it, but since Jimmy didn't seem to be interested in feminine wiles, and she'd just decided not to use them on Sam, now was thankfully not the time to deploy them. Regardless, as much of a nice guy Sam was proving to be, it appeared as though she wouldn't be able to escape the same notion here on Earth that nymphs were weak, helpless creatures in need of saving.

It made her pride flare quick and hot. "I said I can take care of myself."

Both men stared at her in a way that made her feel as

though she were a nine-headed hydra. Jimmy puckered his lips and scrunched his nose before turning his attention on his cuticles.

Make that ten heads. Apparently, the patriarchy was rampant everywhere.

"I'm sorry," Sam said quickly, his voice smooth as pebbles caressed by water for a thousand years. "I didn't mean to imply you weren't capable."

He'd taken off his hat and was holding it over his heart as a show of respect. And sincerity, which immediately dissolved her anger. Had anyone ever apologized to her in her life? Sweet Persephone, these human emotions were harder to swim against than a riptide.

"It's okay. I can see why you'd assume that. I mean, I did come from out of nowhere, with no way to pay for food or shelter."

"No need to explain." Sam shook his head, dropping his gaze to the counter before looking her in the eyes. "I shouldn't have assumed."

Daphne's lips parted, "It's okay," on the verge of coming out of her mouth again before she closed it, surprised that he'd actually owned up to his mistake. That would never happen on Mount Olympus.

"Hey, you got a green thumb?" asked Jimmy, his gaze flicking over at Sam before landing on her again.

"Yes, why?" Daphne turned toward him, her heart picking up at the thought of unstrapping the cumbersome shoes from her feet and digging her toes into a pile of dirt. Did she have a green thumb? Up until this morning, her whole body had been green.

"Did I forget to mention Sammy, here, is an overachiever who has a vegetable stand over at the farmer's market?" Jimmy folded his arms and pursed his lips in an exaggerated fashion. "Hmm, maybe she could help you out around the farm? She could stay in the loft, take care of Sampson and Delilah while you're on duty. Seems like fair work in exchange for rent to me. I mean, those garden plots aren't going to weed themselves, Samuel."

Sam shook his head at his cousin, and Daphne couldn't help but smile right along with him at the very obvious fact, and deliberate, she was gathering, Jimmy had just claimed Sam's idea for his own.

Meanwhile, arguments for both sides—a thousand times yes and one hundred percent no—jockeyed for position inside Daphne's head. She should not, under any circumstance, put the lives of these innocent souls in danger. Apollo was a loose cannon, and there was no telling what lengths he'd go to if he found her living among them.

On the other hand, why had the Fates dropped the answer to her *Now that I'm here, where can I hide?* problem into her lap, and with such a neat, handsome bow wrapped around it? If meeting Sam Carson was fate, should she really pass up their generous offer?

Also, how was it possible for a man to be so imposing yet not intimidating in the least at the same time? What if he was setting a trap, like Apollo had tried to do a thousand times? Did he want to catch her, too? She didn't exactly have the best track record when it came to men and their need to control women.

What did it matter, anyway? She was determined to keep to herself and not to get involved with humans. Plus, she loved animals, and Sam had three. That she knew of. Maybe there would be more. She'd have to refrain from setting them all free if she stayed with him, since he probably wouldn't like that, but if, by some miracle of Asclepius, she could manage to stay hidden, a "rickety-ass" barn would be the last place Apollo would look for her.

"I accept," said Daphne, before she could change her

mind and refuse the gift that had been so conveniently dropped in her lap.

CHAPTER SEVEN

*S*ampson, a bay rippled with muscle and a few extra hands taller than most quarter horses, took to Daphne immediately. His companion, Delilah, however, needed some convincing.

The gelding regarded Daphne through his long forelock. It took mere seconds before he reached his muzzle toward her. Delilah snorted when Sampson curled his lips around the carrot Daphne held out to him. The paint mare nickered in disapproval at his eagerness, eyeing Daphne suspiciously before turning away from the fence and heading out into the pasture.

A twinge of sadness touched Daphne's heart as she watched the mare leave. There had been something in Delilah's eyes that looked an awful lot like distrust. Daphne didn't get the feeling it was toward Sam specifically, or her necessarily, but toward humans in general.

When Zeus whined, Daphne looked down at him standing by her side. Her fingers twitched, eager to bury themselves into the thick scruff behind his ears and scratch. But he was a K-9 officer, and she wouldn't go up to Sam and start scratching him on the back of his head, would she? She settled for planting her fists on her hips instead. "Why's she so upset, huh, Zeus?"

"It's okay, he's off duty," said Sam, and Daphne immediately dropped down to pet Zeus. "And she was my ex's." Sam swung a saddle up over the fence to be oiled. He'd already changed out of his uniform, and the silver buckle attached to the belt looped around his worn Wranglers flashed in the light of the setting sun. "Left her with me when she took off. Poor thing's been mad at the world ever since. Won't let anyone ride her."

"Well, you're still a beautiful soul, Delilah," Daphne called out to the mare, wondering if she'd ever get the chance to break through. Probably best she didn't, since she didn't know how long she'd be staying. "However mad you are."

The annoyed whinny from the yard didn't sound like they would be friends any time soon, and Daphne could respect that. In fact, she should follow Delilah's lead and trust no one, especially of the human variety. She wasn't here to make friends. It would be hard enough not getting attached to Zeus and the horses; she should definitely steer clear of the mortals.

Except, so far, every one she'd met had been so nice and helpful, which was making it rather difficult to dislike them. Plus, now she was curious why Sam's wife had left him. Something she most definitely should not be curious about.

She gulped down her interest in the matter. "So those are my roomies, huh?" Sampson left the barn to go check on his grumpy mate, and Daphne gave Zeus one last scratch under the chin before standing.

"Yep. They're quite the pair. Luckily, you don't have to sleep in a stall, though. Let me show you the loft."

Sam swept his hand toward a set of stairs near the entrance of the barn. Daphne's eyes flicked to the solid swell of his bicep, the butterflies in her stomach having a moment before she convinced her legs to move.

She reached out and touched the planks of wood as she ascended the stairs. Zeus climbed the steps beside her, Sam behind her. She bit her lip to keep them from pursing. Did they think she would fall?

Poor, helpless nymph . . .

She trailed a hand along the wall as she continued upward, pushing the thought to the back of her mind when sturdy oak, weathered and gray, vibrated beneath her fingertips. The structure was certainly old, but it was solid, and promised to stand strong for years to come. Oaks were among the proudest hardwoods. Rickety-ass might be a more accurate assessment of soft-hearted pines. No, the oaks that had been used to make this barn would keep their word.

Something told her Jimmy just had something against barns.

Daphne rounded the top of the stairs, and a soft gasp passed between her lips when she took in the sight of her new hideout. She'd been worried Sam would offer up the couch or a spare bedroom in his tiny farmhouse, and that she'd have to find a way to refuse. Not because she balked at the sleeping arrangements. Water nymphs were chaster than their tree-hugging cousins, woodland nymphs, but it wasn't ending up in his bed she was worried about. It was how she'd handle sleeping under a roof, in a cramped space, when she was used to sleeping beneath the stars.

But this place squashed that worry flat. The loft was open, uninhibited by walls to separate lounging from eating or sleeping. A large set of windows spanned the entire back wall, displaying the row of trees lining the far end of the pasture like a larger-than-life painting.

Her gaze followed the rays of sunset slanting down from two large skylights above a bed that was on a raised platform.

The bed posts were fashioned to look like tree trunks, one at each corner of the skylight. The realistic-looking leaves canopied the bed, but left an open space in the center for viewing the sky unhindered.

She smiled, delighted she'd be able to gaze up at her twinkling friends—it was rude not to look them in the eyes when one said goodnight, after all—and a powerful feeling raced through her, something she couldn't quite identify, but the more her eyes swept over the loft, the more the feeling grew. Awe? Joy? Gratitude? She decided it must be a combination of all three.

When an expanse of fireflies lit up the shadows among the leaves, her brows lifted. They furrowed when she noticed the tiny lights were white and unmoving, and not fireflies as she'd first thought. She looked at Sam, whose hand was still on the light switch he'd flipped over by the stairs.

"Cool, huh?" His smile was wider than she'd seen it so far. He was proud of this space, and it caused a little dip in her belly.

"Very cool," she said, the words coming out as a breathless mix of sadness and longing, happiness and delight. It seemed as though the space had been built with her in mind. A temple paying homage to her way of life.

The novelty of appliances, with their numerous handles and knobs, drew her toward the kitchen. She stopped, distracted by the dining table sitting stoically under a light fixture made of antlers.

Sam must have noticed the expression on her face because he said, "Dropped during shedding season and collected in the spring."

Daphne nodded, sighing as she placed a palm on top of the table, compelled to say hello to the wood that hummed beneath her fingers.

"Hi," she whispered.

The wood responded silently, and the longing to splash in the nearby river almost sent her racing down the stairs. There was one close, just beyond the trees. She could feel it. But the reclaimed oak assured her it was happy in its current form. Sam had done right by it.

Thank the gods—all except Apollo, because that might encourage him further—she was a water nymph. If she would have been a woodland nymph, she might have seen visions of the varnished planks as saplings before they were cut down. She didn't know if she would be able to withstand the sadness.

She meandered over to one of the far corners of the loft, opened the only door and peeked inside. An old claw foot tub, fitted with a stand-in shower, greeted her. She'd probably frolic in the stream whenever possible, but it was good to know this modern bathing contraption was here should she be so inclined to try something new.

"I finally just finished hooking up the water. The pressure isn't the greatest, but it works."

"It's perfect," she said with a smile. Sam's gaze dropped to his cowboy boots as he tucked his fingers into the front pockets of his jeans. It seemed the man had a hard time taking a compliment.

"It's more than perfect, actually," she continued, her cheeks warming. An easel tucked into the corner by the window, with unused tubes of paint stuffed into its tray, caught her attention. Who had this place been for? Him or her? "You must have spent a lot of time making it special."

Sam nodded, opening is mouth to say something, but a massive growl from her belly made his eyes go wide. It sounded like thunder echoing through an empty canyon. The fact that her mortal shell could produce a noise so loud and ominous scared her a little. But not as much as the strange rumbling sensation that accompanied it, as if a stack of stones were grinding against each other as they tumbled into the burning pit of her stomach.

"You must be starving," he said, his eyes flicking toward the kitchen that was undoubtedly bare. "I'm not doing anything fancy for dinner tonight, just cheese lasagna, but you're welcome to join me. We'll see about getting you some groceries tomorrow. I think Sadie's got the day off. I'll call her tonight and see if she'd mind taking you."

"Sure, okay. And cheese lasagna sounds great," replied Daphne, clenching her stomach muscles. She couldn't remember the last time she'd eaten, and the mere mention of food set off another round of ravenous snarling from her midsection. She spread a hand over her belly, which did nothing to quell the ferocity of its growling, in both volume and length of duration. "Oh wow, that was frightening. My apologies."

Sam chuckled as he shook his head. "No apologies necessary. Dinner should be ready in about twenty minutes. I stuck it in the oven when we got home."

At the same time she was trying to puzzle out what on Earth lasagna could be—she pictured chunks of cheese stacked on hunks of bread and garnished with olives—she noticed Sam's face had turned a shade darker.

He obviously felt embarrassed, but why? She went over the last words he'd said. When she got to *I stuck it in the oven when we got home,* the skin on her chest flushed hot with understanding. When *we* got home. He'd implied more familiarity between them than there was.

"Well," he said, heading toward the stairs in a hurry, no doubt trying to move past the awkwardness. "I'll let you get settled. Come down when you're ready. No need to knock." He paused at the top of the steps. "I'll leave the door open for you." He gave her a hesitant smile before starting down.

"Sam?" she called after him and he stopped, doubling

back up to the top step. His smile was nervous again, so she pretended she'd missed his faux pas entirely. "Thank you. I appreciate you letting me stay here. You know, until I get on my feet."

Bare feet, she hoped. The foot harnesses Sadie had given her were pretty, but they hurt.

"Yes, ma'am," he drawled. "It's no trouble at all. See you in a bit."

Her pulse sped up when his smile reached his eyes before he headed down the stairs again. He seemed genuinely happy to be helping her, and she hadn't even used her feminine wiles on him.

Daphne waited until she heard the farmhouse's screen door bang in the distance to flop down onto the bed. The urge to giggle bubbled in her throat. Never mind she was about to fill her belly with food, she had the absolute perfect hiding place. Apollo would never step foot inside a barn. Not in a million years.

Zeus sat in the middle of the porch, right in front of the door; a stoic seneschal to all who approached. His tail thumped twice when Daphne stood before him, indicating that she may pass unhindered. She thanked him with a scratch behind the ears and a smile before continuing on.

She lifted a fist to knock on the frame of the screen door when she remembered what Sam had told her. Entering Sam's space unannounced felt like intruding, but she gripped the small metal handle and pulled the door open anyway. She was too hungry for propriety.

The farmhouse was small, with papered walls and lace curtains, at least it was in what she assumed was the main gathering area. She wasn't sure about the rest of the house, but the smell of old upholstery fabric and even older wood told her she'd find similar.

She inhaled deeper, and, thanks to her immortal senses, she detected both the faint but lingering scent of water-damaged wood somewhere near the foundation underneath the smell of food cooking. She could also smell the greenness of the fresh wood used to replace it. Despite its age and outdated decor, the farmhouse was lovingly kept.

She stepped into the living room to admire a stand-up piano, its top ledge clad in more lace. Sitting on the yellowing doily was an artfully arranged line of framed pictures. Her eyes immediately went to a black and white image of a man and a woman posing for their wedding. The woman's white dress was simple but elegant, and the beads tied into the ends of the long fringes hanging from her chest and sleeves made a V-shaped pattern. Daphne wished she knew what color the beads that made up the necklaces adorning the woman's neck had been. Turquoise? Amber? Whatever they had been, she guessed they'd been spectacular.

She ran a finger along the soft edge of a feather that lay in front of the picture, the markings identical to the one the woman in the photograph wore in her hair.

"Those are my grandparents Meli and Albert Carson," said Sam, entering the room and wiping his hands on a worn apron with "Kiss the Cook" printed on it. When he came to a stop beside her, he pointed to a faded color photo next to his grandparents' wedding picture. "There's mom, dad, and me."

Daphne smiled, understanding Sam's sense of pride for his family. She inspected a picture of him and his parents at his high school graduation, and then, next to that, a picture of Sam as a police academy graduate. He had been less chiseled but just as tall and broad-shouldered.

The young man in the photo stared back at her, sullen and

serious. Alone. She could only guess as to why, and when she looked at Sam, he nodded, obviously trying to keep his smile fond instead of sad.

His parents were no longer living on Earth. Wherever their souls were in the universe at that moment, Daphne hoped they were together. As she debated whether or not it was appropriate to lay a comforting hand on his shoulder so soon after meeting, he closed the subject by plucking a picture of Zeus standing proud in his K-9 officer vest from its place on the piano. "And you already know this guy." Zeus barked from the porch, and Sam opened the door to let him in. "Yeah, yeah. We all know you're the more handsome partner."

Sam returned the photo to its place and nodded for her to follow him. Suddenly aware of the tang of tomatoes and the nuttiness of wheat flour permeating the air, Daphne didn't hesitate. She smelled olive oil as well, and, if she wasn't mistaken, warm cheese, the combination similar to the aroma of the platters of bread and goat milk curd after they had both been warmed in the sun. Her mouth watered, and she fought the impulse to push past Sam, or at least urge him to pick up the pace by stepping on his heels.

The yellow light from the fixture casted a warm glow over the small kitchen. The lemon-colored gingham curtains were cheerful, the white cabinets quaint, and butcher's block countertop well used.

"Almost done," he said as he opened the oven door. When he pulled a metal tray of toasted bread from the oven with a padded glove and set it next to a rectangular glass dish layered to the brim with the bubbling source of all temptation, she thought she might faint.

She inhaled deeply through her nose because she couldn't stop herself, the aroma causing a sharp pang of hunger to stab at her gut. "It smells incredible."

Her gaze wandered to the small table set for two with patterned plates and silver eating utensils. A small white vase corralled a bunch of wild daisies.

"Pull up a chair," Sam nudged his head toward one of the chairs. "I'll fix you a plate."

When they were both seated, and Daphne finally took her first bite, she closed her eyes and moaned, taking extra care to chew slowly and savor the taste.

"I guess you like it," laughed Sam.

She opened her eyes, and when she realized she'd also been swaying as well, her face flushed. "I've never had anything like it before. It's so good. How did you get the bread so flat?"

Sam's mouth dropped open, and his brows crumpled. "They're noodles . . . Have you never had lasagna before?" His tongue probed the corner of his mouth when she shook her head. "Don't take this the wrong way, Daphne, but you don't seem like a small-town girl."

"What makes you say that?" she asked before promptly stuffing another bite of the delicious lasagna into her mouth.

"I don't know. You just seem more . . . worldly, I guess."

Try otherworldly. Since she couldn't open her mouth, Daphne laughed through her nose, searching her brain for a more appropriate human metaphor as she finished chewing. "Well, you sure know how to treat a girl like a princess, so that must make you a prince."

She'd meant to pay him a compliment, but confusion flashed across his handsome face, dark brows angling over hazel eyes.

"You're so . . . Not like anyone I've ever met. You say the strangest things, but I like it. And prince might be pushing it. Try pauper who just makes a really good lasagna."

"Where did you learn to prepare food like this, anyway?"

asked Daphne, using her fork to slice through her square of lasagna with gusto.

"My mom and grandmother. I used to help them make bean bread all the time. I wasn't your typical rough and tumble boy. While other kids were getting or giving black eyes, I was gathering chestnuts for kunuchi." He laughed before taking a bite of his lasagna.

Daphne had no idea what kunuchi was, but she silently thanked the gods that Sam had grown up more interested in cooking food instead of throwing punches.

"Boys aren't so secure in their masculinity where I come from," she said, thinking of a specific someone who used his masculinity as a shield. "It's a shame, really, and I wish there had been more boys that had grown into men like you in my world."

Sam nodded, his smile thin and unsure. The look on his face told Daphne he didn't quite know what to make of her statement. She cringed, hoping he didn't think she'd been patronizing him, but it was hard telling since he was now clearing away the dishes.

She didn't know what to do other than sit there and watch him at first. And then it occurred to her that she could help him. She scraped and stacked the dishes as he rinsed and loaded them into the dishwasher in companionable silence.

After squirting detergent into the dishwasher and closing the lid, Sam said, "I saw you didn't bring any bags with you." Sam dried his hands on a towel before folding it neatly and hanging it on the handle of the stove to dry. "You can't sleep in that. Let me get you something more comfortable."

He headed out of the kitchen, and Daphne followed him, figuring that must be her cue to leave. She sat on the piano bench and waited, wondering what kind of bed he slept in as she listened to the creaking of the floorboards on the upper level. In no time, her lids began to grow heavy. She wanted to stay and talk more, but she probably should get back up to the loft. She'd had a very long first day in the mortal world, experiencing a barrage of human emotions, and she was exhausted.

She stood when she heard him coming down the steps, and he handed her an Anadarko High School T-shirt, a pair of boxer shorts, and some socks when he reached the bottom of the staircase. "You can keep it. It's all too small for me."

His tongue was tracing the corner of his mouth again, making it obvious he was pondering something. She hoped it wasn't about whether or not he should ask her to stay in the farmhouse. Especially since her qualm was now less about being trapped under a roof and more about being entangled in his arms.

Daphne bolted for the door before he could decide which would be more troublesome. She wasn't planning on staying, and it was better to keep herself as detached as possible.

The night air was warm and heavy with moisture, and the soft rhythmic chirping from the crickets made Daphne even more sleepy. When they reached the barn door, Sam slid it open.

"Thanks again for letting me stay," she said, resisting the urge to reach out and touch him. She couldn't stop herself from imagining what his tousled, dark hair might feel like slipping through her fingers, though.

"Not a problem." He reached into his back pocket and took out his wallet. "I'll see if Sadie can take you into town tomorrow. I'm sure she'd love to help get you some proper clothes—and footwear. You'll want boots. Can't be walking around the barn with those." He nodded at her bejeweled feet before pulling out some money and handing it to her.

"Sadie already gave me some."

A half-grin cocked one of his cheeks. "I figured. She's got

a heart the size of Heaven. Go ahead and give it back to her, will you?"

Daphne nodded, hesitating before reaching for the paper rectangles he was holding out to her. She agreed she should give Sadie back her hard-earned money, but she wasn't convinced she should accept Sam's.

It was more than a little sad that mortals needed to rely on money to obtain what they needed to survive. She'd magically had everything she'd ever needed in the Sacred Forest, never wanting for anything, except peace from a certain unrelenting god. If this was the only way she could get that peace, she would take the money. For now, anyway, because she didn't take her debts lightly. She'd pay him back as soon as she could.

Sam broke into her thoughts. "There's no need to pay me back, but if it bothers you, consider it a loan. And I'm in no rush to be repaid."

How did he *do* that, always seem to know what she was thinking?

"And, ah," he continued, "I usually don't lock the barn at night, but as long as you're staying up here, I'm going to start. You okay with that?"

Locked in. The thought made her want to shiver. Her soul had been stuck inside a tree for so long she almost screamed, "*No!*" right there on the spot. But he'd done something Apollo never had—asked for permission. Sam had left the choice up to her, which, oddly enough, drew her to him instead of away.

"Sure," she said. "That sounds like a good idea."

How unexpected. Sam Carson, mere man and non-magic wielding mortal, had the power to weaken her resolve to remain friendless in just four simple words.

Once up in the loft, she slipped out of her clothes and got into bed. Her eyes swept over the loft's support beams. They had been carved, just like the bed posts, to appear as though still wrapped in grooved and knotted bark. She smiled at the leaves and moss twined through the joists above.

But her smile faded when she thought about how she might never see the *real* Sacred Forest again. Resentment that she'd had no other choice *but* to leave tightened her jaw. It had been bad enough Apollo had chased her relentlessly, but after she'd become a laurel tree, she had hoped he would take the hint. He hadn't, and he'd ventured into the Sacred Forest to see her every day after. Most likely to keep tabs on her, but he always came. Without fail. Just staring at her, playing his damnable lyre and singing songs about how they would one day be together again. It had been the worst.

The painful sensation of nails digging into her palms pulled her back to the present, and she unclenched her fists, determined not to be held hostage by memories of the past. A past she wanted to forget. Or at least outrun.

Missing her family, and heart heavy with the need for any solace she could get, she pulled the covers back and slipped out of bed. When she found the clothes Sam had given her, she brought the still neatly folded bundle to her nose. Even with the detergent, his scent was calming. Comforting.

With Sam's T-shirt and boxers on, she crawled back into bed, a smile tipping her lips once more as she hugged one of the pillows. Despite the not-so-great memories this place had stirred up, she found it also had the power to feel just as magical as home.

CHAPTER EIGHT

The rocking of the river boat taunted Apollo's insides. Unfortunately, abs of steel didn't always equate to an iron stomach. He was a formidable god in every way, except when it came to sea sickness. Although sometimes he wished he was, he was definitely not a son of Poseidon. He'd probably get more respect that way.

Apollo waved away a swarm of gnats before continuing to swipe through the Olympus News app on his phone. He'd gotten nowhere with Zeus, of course, and so he'd decided the next fastest way to locate Daphne might be to pay a visit to Peneus. He'd tried to make an appointment, so the river god at least had warning, but of course with no office, no phone, and definitely no answering service, there was no way to contact him other than by rowboat on the Peneios river in Thessaly.

Peneus was as old-school as they came. A true purist. Something, as far as Apollo was concerned, that was a gigantic pain in his gluteus maximus.

"How much farther?" he asked. "Cell reception out here is

atrocious. And why in Hades' Realm do mortals worship these Kardashians? I don't get it."

"It's right up there," answered Calliope from behind him, navigating the boat through the tiny inlet. After a twenty minutes of a queasy stomach and bugs Hades-bent on diving into any exposed orifice they could find, he was thankful she was now steering them closer to the river bank.

"And I have no idea about the Kardashians," continued Calliope, "but isn't it just gorgeous out here?"

Apollo twisted around in time to witness her inhale deeply, that smile of hers breaking out across her face before she pointed excitedly. He was on the verge of telling her to stop being so dramatic, but he didn't have the heart to squash her enthusiasm, and so he nodded, slipping his phone in his pocket instead. A tiny smile snuck its way onto his lips as he held out his hand for the oar.

A dock shimmered into view a short distance ahead of them as Apollo steered the boat toward it. Beyond the dock, a dirt path, flanked by two heavy stone columns, snaked its way up the lushly treed bank. "Thank my fellow gods," he mumbled. "I need to get off this thing before these mosquitoes eat me alive."

Two satyrs stood in front of the stone columns, muscled chests thrust forward, chiseled arms crossed. Their cloven-hoofed legs were covered in thick, shaggy hair.

"Who goes there?" bellowed the stockier of the two. His dark skin was tattooed with even darker ancient symbols, and a gleaming golden ring pierced one nostril.

A slightly taller, tawny-haired one pulled his brows together. His bearded jaw worked back and forth as he leaned forward to get a more accurate assessment of their approaching boat. Scanning its occupants' faces dutifully, he cranked his head toward his fellow guard when he recognized Apollo.

"Ease up now, Darius, 'tis the god of sun and light come calling!"

"Apollo? Well, now, Marius, 'tis all you had to say!" Darius rubbed a hand over one curved horn atop his head before scurrying from his post and onto the dock to moor the tiny boat.

Calliope cleared her throat. "Hey, boss?"

"Yes?"

"Think you could throw them the rope? So they can tie us to the dock? Please?"

Apollo pursed his lips, but it was only for show. Of course he'd help her. He splayed his fingers out toward the thin rope coiled neatly in front of him. The end that wasn't secured to the boat threaded its way out of the pile and, with a sideways flick of his hand, it obeyed his command and shot through the air toward Darius's awaiting grasp.

The sharp movement sent the algae-colored river water rippling out from under the hull. Tiny swells lapped at the side of the small vessel, dredging up the aroma of aquatic life. It smelled wet and slimy, and when the aroma assaulted Apollo's senses, he cursed his weak stomach while resisting the urge to wretch. Holding the back of his hand to his nose, he transported himself onto the dock, just in front of both satyrs.

As Apollo beheld the dock's questionable craftsmanship, he began to rethink his decision to endure the trip and not simply snap his fingers and appear at the throne of Peneus. Calliope had said it would be an adventure, and he'd given in. He'd offered a weak protest, of course, explaining it wouldn't involve defeating opponents or conquering a giant serpent. He'd also argued there wouldn't be, at the very least, a crowd for adulation when they'd finished. She'd just shaken her head at him, smiling that smile of hers, and now he was here.

Curious, the way she thought. Even more curious how

the slightest dose of her enthusiasm, for even the simplest of things, somehow always got him into . . . Well, situations like this. It was no wonder he found her incredibly attractive, and sometimes he wished he wouldn't have gone and gotten himself cursed. More than just sometimes lately.

The two guards knelt in unison at Apollo's feet. Rope in hand, Darius abandoned tying the boat to the dock to pay respect. Chest swelled, chin tipped upward, Apollo accepted their small gesture of worship.

After the appropriate length of adoration, both satyrs rose to their feet, and Darius quickly finished securing the boat before lifting Calliope out of the boat as though she were a mere whisper of a breeze.

Apollo noticed the way she stiffened at the unsolicited help. Her jaw had tightened when Darius, without asking, plucked her up as easily as if she were a pebble on a beach. Apollo saw that it made her uncomfortable, and his muscles tensed in response.

He'd been imagining pinning the satyr to a tree when his eyes settled on her horribly loose and ill-fitting khaki pants and clunky hiking boots. They were in direct and stark contrast to his slim-fitting suit coat and neatly pressed slacks, and he wondered what it was like to be so haphazardly dressed. His gaze drifted down to the flattering indents at her waist, evident even through her fleece jacket, and the thought of her wearing clothes at all disappeared.

Wrestling a writhing Python into a headlock had been easier, but Apollo forced himself to refocus. He had very important business ahead of him. "I've come to speak with Peneus. How far is it to his throne?"

It wasn't that he minded the walk. He rather enjoyed keeping his body in peak physical condition. It was the time. More specifically, how it would be wasted. There wasn't a single moment more he could afford to let slip by, not while Daphne was still missing, and especially not when thoughts of Calliope seemed to be so adamant about wandering into a rather lust-filled corner of his mind.

"Not but a short distance inland, Your Excellence. King Peneus's throne lies at the heart of a land-locked lake a few miles from here," explained Marius, one of his hooves pawing at the ground.

"That won't do. I'll make the journey on my own," said Apollo, making it clear he wouldn't need an escort to take him to the king of the nymphs. "Calliope, you'll remain . . ." He was about to suggest she stay behind when he noticed a tongue slip through the seam of the taller satyr's lips, and how tightly Calliope gripped the straps of her backpack as she nervously shifted her weight from foot to foot. "With me. Take my hand, please." Leaving his assistant alone with creatures whose two most favorite past times included getting drunk and having sex wouldn't do either, especially since it made Calliope visibly uncomfortable.

She latched her palm to his without hesitation, and an instant later they were standing at the entrance of Peneus's throne room deep under the lake. He released her hand, smoothing out his wrinkled pants to distract himself from how soft and warm it felt.

How he liked the way it fit in his.

"Leave the talking to me, Calliope," he said, adjusting the cuffs of his dress shirt. "Just listen and learn, is that clear?"

"Crystal. And you know you can call me Callie, right? I mean, you've only known me thousands of years." Her pinky shot up to her mouth for a quick nibble.

Apollo guided her arm back down to her side. "I prefer to call you Calliope. It keeps things more . . . professional."

A pair of guards with gills slashing their necks and iridescent scales instead of skin pushed the doors open. The throne room was dim, faint rays of sunlight streaming down through the murkiness was the only light illuminating the space. It was like being underwater, but in a glass bubble.

Air-breathing perch, trout, and pike swam through the trees that created a surrounding magical forest, the tallest trunks like pillars lining the perimeter of the great room.

In the center, on a chair made of driftwood and antlers sat Peneus. His salt-and-peppered hair was long and unbound. A welcoming smile split his weathered face and his silt-colored eyes crinkled at the corners.

"Apollo. What brings you out here to visit a soggy, old river god like me?"

"Hello, Peneus." Apollo greeted him with a slight nod.

"Who's this with you?" said Peneus, leaning forward in his pointy throne. "Come closer, my dear girl."

Apollo placed his palm on the small of Calliope's back, wincing when she stiffened. Was she frightened? Appalled? Whatever it was, he didn't like being the source of it. He gently applied pressure, indicating she should take a step forward for presentation to the nymph king. "This is my assistant, Calliope. The muse of epic poetry."

Callie glanced back at him before stepping forward and dipping into a small bow. "I inspire words, music, song, and dance, your Highness."

"Ah, a muse indeed," said Peneus with a wink. "Your voice, so melodious. Such beauty, such eloquence, even in those modern clothes!"

Apollo stepped past Callie, closer to Peneus. "Speaking of beauty and eloquence, I came to speak to you about Daphne."

A twinge of remorse tugged at him when he noticed Calliope's shoulders slump. It wasn't that she was any less beautiful, it was just . . . It was the damned curse. And he wanted it lifted now more than ever.

"Oh, yes, Daphne," said Peneus, sitting back again. "I knew it would only be a matter of time before she grew tired with her lot."

Apollo bristled. "And just what was her lot, exactly?"

He knew what everyone thought, that he was the villain. He wasn't the most personable gods on Olympus, but he was certainly one of the most cursed. He hated that no one seemed to remember that.

"Oh, now don't get high-and-mighty with me, Apollo. We all know the deal. You went and got yourself cursed with the first love/hate relationship, bound by magic and tied into a neat and never-ending bow by time. Haven't you figured it out after all these years?"

"And what is that, Peneus?" snapped Apollo. The part where Daphne hated him was right, but did he truly love her? Or was it more that he was in love with the thrill of the chase? The adrenaline rush of victory.

"You don't mess with the god of love, and you sure as Hades' Realm don't piss him off. Just what in Dante's nine circles did you say to Eros, anyway?" Peneus leaned forward, one eyebrow sliding up. "It must have been pretty bad, seeing as he cursed the golden child of Zeus to chase after my Daphne like a relentless fool." Peneus's hearty laughter rippled through the underwater dome.

Did Peneus really think he was Zeus's golden child? Or was that the joke?

"It wasn't my fault. I was love struck," said Apollo, grinding out the words through gnashed teeth even though they didn't quite ring true in his ears.

Peneus laughed even harder, until tears rolled down his cheeks. "Love struck, indeed!"

"You do know she's missing, don't you?" Apollo squeezed his hands into fists, trying to prevent his simmering rage from turning into a boil. It was his fault, that much was true. He just wasn't sure love struck was the most accurate way to describe what he felt for Daphne.

Peneus's laughter stopped abruptly, perhaps feeling the heat of danger gathering in the air. "Of course I do. She called out to me two days ago. I lifted the enchantment and she came to see me. We talked a good long while. She still wants nothing to do with you."

Apollo took a commanding step forward. "I'm well aware of how the curse works. Just tell me where she is, Peneus."

Peneus stared back at him, defiant. "And betray my daughter's trust? Never."

Apollo tried to unclench his fists, but the flood of adrenaline to his system was making it difficult. Hades' sweaty balls, he was on the verge of losing it.

That is, until Calliope came to his rescue.

"Can you at least give us a hint?" she asked, stepping in front of Apollo and shielding him so he could regain his composure.

His eyes were closed, and he got about as far as three in his countdown to calm when he heard Peneus say, "She's sick to death of his advances, muse," in a harsh tone. The nymph king was getting brave, was he?

Apollo moved to stand beside Calliope, eyes narrowed and ready to intervene should Peneus talk down to her more than he already had.

"Unrequited love is an unbearable beast, I'll give you that," continued Peneus, switching his gaze from Calliope to Apollo. "But I'm not going to tell you where she is. You'll have to figure that out for yourself, so listen carefully. Daphne did come to me, begging—for the second time, mind you—to save her from misery. She told me her last and final wish was to be nowhere. Not here, not there... but *nowhere*. So I granted her that wish and sent her to the middle of Nowhere like she asked." Leaning back into his pointy chair, Peneus folded his arms. "And that is all I'll say on the matter."

CHAPTER NINE

*D*aphne decided sandals weren't all that bad compared to the boots that were squishing her toes. How did mortals wear these things day in and day out? They were so *heavy*.

"Those are too cute, Dee!" squealed Sadie. "I think you just found yourself the perfect pair of shit kickers." She popped another stick of gum into her mouth, her ruby lips moving every which way as she worked it into the existing wad.

Daphne peered down at the embossed leather imprisoning her feet, not so sure they were the perfect anything. "Shit kickers?"

"Cowboy boots." Sadie planted her hands on her hips. "Good Lord, you're a city slicker through-and-through, aren't you?" She reached over, plucked a cowboy hat off a nearby mannequin and dropped it onto Daphne's head. "Don't worry, we'll make you a full-fledged cowgirl in no time."

"Cowgirl?" As far as Daphne knew, mortals couldn't turn each other into cattle.

"Shoot, Dee. Have you been living under a rock or what?"

Sadie pressed her lips together, as if regretting her comment, and switched the dark-brown hat on top of Daphne's head with a smaller, sand-colored one.

"Something like that." Daphne turned toward the mirror for a look, and hopefully an end to Sadie's direct line of questioning.

Sadie continued to chomp on her gum, arms now folded. Apparently she had changed her mind about not broaching the subject because she asked, "That bastard kept you under lock and key, didn't he?"

Daphne adjusted the hat. So much for dodging Sadie's bullets. "What makes you think I'm running from someone, anyway?"

"We may be simple folk out here, sugar, but we ain't dumb. It's written all over your face. Plus, why on God's green earth would anybody come here but to hide? Ain't nothing but trucks and tractors.

Daphne stopped fiddling with the hat and addressed Sadie's reflection in the mirror. If she couldn't do a decent job of lying like a mortal, how was she supposed to hide among them? She tried derailing Sadie's interrogation with the truth.

"It's beautiful here."

"Yeah, if you like the smell of livestock."

"It doesn't bother me. I kind of like it, actually." Animals and their smells were a part of nature, true, but she ought to keep deflecting. "I'm surprised Sam doesn't have more."

"Oh, he used to have a whole mess, cattle mostly, but a few dairy cows, too. Old Bess, Bonnie Boo, Ms. Clover, and the queen bee of 'em all, Marie Antoinette. Couldn't afford to keep the girls after that little gold digger broke his heart, though. He would have given her the sun, the moon, *and* the stars, but she ran off to Texas with that doctor. Living high on the hog these days from what I hear. A real shame she got

half Sammy's money in the divorce." A round of gum snapping rang out like gunshots. "As if she needed it."

Daphne swallowed around the lump in her throat before
reaching down to tug off a boot. "I shouldn't get these, then."
She'd never depended on anyone for anything before, and it
suddenly didn't feel right to start now.

"Oh, spit. I shouldn't have said that." Sadie held up her
hands, batting at the air. "He's fine, Dee, I promise. Sam's
got everything he needs. Better off without her, if you ask
me. Besides, *things* ain't what makes him tick, you know? He
likes helping people, and he's gonna get real ornery with me
if you're walking around in that barn without a good pair of
boots.

Daphne sighed, a flood of some unidentifiable emotion
washing over her. Mortals were some smooth talkers.
"Okay," She stepped into the other boot, "but I'm going to
pay him back. How many of those paper rectangles equals
$159.99?"

"It was an underground bunker, wasn't it?"

Daphne laughed despite the strict orders she'd given
herself not to find mortals enchanting. "Yes, Sadie, I'm hiding
out for a while, but that's all I can say."

"You got it, sugar. I'll leave you to your business, but if
you're in any kind of trouble, you need to tell me, okay?
Speaking of trouble, let's not tell Sammy I told you about his
ex-wife. That was years ago, and he's been doing so good.
Now come on, let's go get you some overalls."

A familiar sensation chipped away at Daphne's determination to remain indifferent as Sadie looped her arm through
hers and pulled her toward a rack of women's clothing. It
took about ten steps, but she recognized it as that warm
familial bond. The kind that, no matter how upset you are at
one another, is always there, like an invisible safety net of
protection you can't see but you can feel, and the disori-

enting sensation she was both home and far from it swirled in her chest.

"Thanks for doing this, Sadie." Tears crept into the corners of Daphne's eyes. She planned on making a break for it, sooner versus later, but if these people kept up this disorienting level of graciousness, it might be harder than she thought.

"Oh, shoot. It's nothing." Sadie held a pair of overalls against Daphne's hips, gauging whether they'd clear her curves. Satisfied the fit was right, she threw a sundress, pair of shorts and some jeans in the cart before heading toward the check out. "Come on, sugar. Let's go."

Sadness turned the warm fuzzy feeling into a cold prickle that raced down Daphne's spine. As much as she was beginning to care about these humans, as much as she wanted to stay, she knew she couldn't. Not ever. And so she'd leave her new boots on the stairs so Sam could at least get some of his paper rectangles back.

"You okay, Dee?"

Daphne's head jerked up, her eyes fixing on Sadie. "Yeah. I'm okay."

"Everything's gonna be all right," said Sadie, stopping to pat Daphne on the back. "You'll see. You've got us now."

As they continued toward the front, Daphne was fairly certain she could survive on her own, out in the woods. It would test both her ability to think on her feet and her planning skills, since the animals and the elements here would be more treacherous than they were in the Sacred Forest. But she was a nymph, with wits and will and just enough wiles to survive in this harsh world full of mortal terrors.

So why did her eyes sting and her heart ache at the thought of doing it alone?

That very thought bounced around Daphne's head during the entire ride back to Sam's place. She let Sadie lead a one-sided conversation the whole way, which turned out fine because the woman clearly possessed the gift of gab. When Daphne saw Sam's truck in the drive, a surge of excitement wound through her. She bit her lip when Sadie parked her Pontiac next to Sam's dusty white chariot so her smile wouldn't crack her face in half.

Sam was sitting, still in uniform, on the front porch with Zeus as they approached.

"You guys working tonight, Sammy?" Sadie called up to him.

"Nope. Our shift just ended. Hawkins is on duty tonight." He tipped his chin at Daphne. "Nice boots."

"Thanks, Sadie helped me pick them out." She lifted a boot-clad foot and wiggled it, to divert his attention away from her blushing cheeks.

Sadie's gaze jumped between the two of them a few times before she said, "Well, shoot. You oughta take Dee up to the Bullpen, then. She's just got herself a cute new sundress, and these shit kickers need breaking in."

Daphne's stomach fluttered. She wasn't sure what the Bullpen was, and when Sam didn't offer more information on the subject, she half wanted to run and half wanted to turn into a tree again.

The silence dragged on.

Make that three quarters for running.

"That's okay," said Daphne. "I'm sure Sam's had a long day and wants to just stay home and relax."

"Nah, I'll take you to the Pen for a bit." Sam got up from a wicker chair that had seen better days. "You going, Sades?"

"Well, if that ain't some kind of fool-ass question." Sadie opened the car door and plopped down into the driver's seat. "You know I love Barney's burgers." She stuck an arm out the window and waved as she backed out. "See y'all there," she shouted out the passenger's side window before turning up the radio and taking off down the driveway.

Sam chuckled. "More like she loves Barney, but all righty, then. Burgers and beer at the Bullpen it is. Just let me go get changed."

"Oh, okay." Daphne clutched the shopping bags full of clothes tighter, wondering if a sundress was proper attire for a night at a pen full of bulls. "Yeah. Me, too."

As it turned out, the Bullpen was not a corral for male bovine, but locals drinking fermented hops. The tiny dive bar was peppered with brightly lit neon signs and various flags hanging from the wood paneling, and just about the homiest little establishment Daphne had ever seen. Her head and shoulders moved to the music playing from some unseen speaker, her feet eager to do the same as she marveled at the muted televisions broadcasting the latest mortal sports competition.

Sam pulled out a stool for her, and she laughed at the sign behind the bar that read, "ATTENTION: Please be patient, even toilets can only serve one asshole at a time."

"Long time no see, Deputy Carson. What's up?" An older woman with greying hair tucked under a baseball cap walked out from the kitchen with a plateful of food. She set it in front of a gentleman sitting next to Daphne. "Here you go, Jud. Anything else I can get you?"

The man shook his head and said, "Hey, Sam," before setting to work on devouring his meal.

"Jud," replied Sam. "How's Judy doing?"

Jud gave him the thumbs up as he chewed his burger heartily.

"Hey, Deputy Carson." A middle-aged man stuck his head

from the kitchen into the bar, raising his metal spatula in lieu of a wave. "Sadie coming tonight?"

"She sure is, Barney," replied Sam, giving Daphne a wink.

A wide smile split Barney's face, revealing a mouthful of crooked teeth.

"Good Lord, Barney. Ask the woman out already, would ya?" teased the bartender, swatting a towel in the cook's direction.

"You tell him, Edna," said Sam before shouting in the direction of the kitchen, "You just gotta rip the Band-Aid off and go for it, man."

Edna pulled a bottle of beer from the cooler. The cap dropped into a bucket as she deftly pried it open on a bottle opener bolted to the bar. She set it down in front of Sam then looked at Daphne. "What can I get you, sweetie?"

Daphne looked at Sam for guidance, seeing as the Bullpen didn't likely serve nectar or ambrosia.

"This here is my friend Daphne Brooks. She's helping me with the farm." He turned toward Daphne, touching his knee to hers. "Burger? Bud Light?"

Daphne eyed Jud's burger, her stomach going queasy at the thought of actually eating one. "Just the Bud Light, no burger."

"Always did like that name," said Edna, pulling a draft of Bud into a glass. "Pretty, and old, too. Greek, isn't it? Means laurel tree, if I'm not mistaken."

"That's right," replied Daphne, the painful memory of her limbs stretching into branches making her chew on her bottom lip.

Edna tossed a square napkin down before setting the beer on it. "We got veggie burgers. You want one of those instead?"

Daphne nodded, thoroughly pleased at her luck. Sam had left her a note that morning there were bagels on the farmhouse kitchen counter. She'd had two, but had somehow managed to forget to eat lunch. She was famished. "That sounds good."

Sam looked at her, jamming his tongue into the corner of his mouth as was his way when he was trying to decide something. "You know what, Edna? Let me try one of those veggie burgers, too."

"Barney!" barked Edna. "We need two veggie burgers. And don't forget to use a different spatula." She turned toward Sam. "It's about time you got back into the game, Deputy." She chuckled as she wrung out a rag over the sink under the bar. "I'm calling this one right now." Edna snort-laughed as she wandered away to wipe down tables.

Sam shook his head, a tiny smile playing at the corner of his mouth. "This town . . . Full of matchmakers, I swear." He took a sip of his stout. "So, Mysterious Miss Brooks, it's my duty to ask, I'm not harboring a dangerous criminal, right?"

All Daphne could think to do was stare at her glass of Bud Light.

Oh, and run. But that wasn't an option at the moment.

Sam took another sip of his beer. "Your silence is saying more than you are. Is it aiding and abetting? Should I run a background check?" He arched an eyebrow at her. "That is if I already haven't."

"You could . . . But you wouldn't find anything." Not unless he Googled *the myth of Daphne and Apollo* and actually believed it—that she—was real.

"Okay, well, I'm just doing my due diligence. I took an oath to serve and protect, you know."

It was a nice thought, but there was no way to protect her from Apollo, which was why she was currently second guessing why she'd thought staying with Sam was a good idea in the first place.

Thank the gods their conversation was cut short by a

squeal from Sadie as she walked through the door. "This is my *jam*. High-step those shit kickers over here and *dance* with me, girl." She ran over and grabbed Daphne by the elbow, pulling her off the stool and over to a small dance floor where a few people were doing choreographed moves in a line.

Daphne obliged, and it didn't take long for her to learn when to clap and when to shake her hips. Her sundress belled with each twirl, and her giggles grew more carefree with every shuffle. The feeling of complete inner peace took over, and the realization how much she'd missed dancing all that time she'd spent rooted to the ground hit her like a double heel dig.

Dancing was the soul's physical expression of happiness, and it seemed it provided the same sheer delight for mortals as it did for nymphs. She looked around the dance floor, at the crooked, wide smiles and red, sweating faces, the beautiful flaws and limitations that made them so perfectly human, and she suddenly longed to never have to leave.

When she caught a glimpse of the half-smile on Sam's face as he watched her dance with his people under man-made lighting instead of the moon, she was taken with him. She smiled back, wishing there really was a way she could stay, right there, in that very moment. Forever.

CHAPTER TEN

*A*pollo looked out his office window and down at the busy city streets below. Normally, with a flick of his thumb and middle finger, the businessmen and women would fall to the ground. It was a game he liked to play when he felt inadequate, which was most of the time. They thought they'd simply tripped on an uneven crack in the sidewalk, and whenever they tried to get up he would knock them down again. But the mean and childish game had lost its luster, so he simply watched them.

"So Zeus won't help at all?" asked Calliope, interrupting his thoughts. They found a new place to go, however, which was directly to the image of her perched on the sofa, knees bent and legs crooked to the side, writing in that beat up old notebook of hers with one hand. In the other, she held the mocha he'd brought her from Siren Coffee on his way into the office.

"Too busy." Apollo turned away from the window, sliding his fists into his pockets and discovering she was in the exact same position in which he'd just imagined her. "It doesn't matter. I'll find her just like I do everything else. On my own."

Calliope looked up from her writing. Setting her pen and notebook aside, the brows above her blue eyes pulled together as she untucked her legs and scooted to the edge of the couch. "Of course you will, but you won't have to do it alone. I'll help you."

His relief rushed to the surface in waves. Careful not to let it show, Apollo bit the inside of his cheek and nodded. After sinking into his office chair, he loosened his tie and undid the top button of his crisp, white dress shirt. Calliope's eyes went wide. If he wasn't mistaken, which he wasn't, she was holding her breath, too.

He unknotted his tie and slid it off entirely before undoing a second button. Did she still find him attractive? Did she think about him like he did her?

"You haven't gone to see Orea yet." She gulped, her voice tightening.

Apollo wondered what it would take to make it so tight it cracked.

Undoing a third button before leaning back in his chair, he nestled his elbows into the back of the arms so there was no mistaking just how strong and wide the expanse of his chest was.

"You should really do that soon if you, um, have time?" The pitch of her voice climbed higher with each word.

"Okay, but I insist that you come with me." The ruddiness high on her cheeks confirmed she most assuredly did still find him attractive. The ache low in his groin warned him if he didn't stop he might lose control.

Control he couldn't afford to lose, especially right now.

Callie was beautiful, and that lovely head of hers was overflowing with intelligence, but, as maddening as it was, he was compelled—by a powerful curse cast by that little shit Eros—to forever chase one woman.

Daphne.

Springing forward, he propped his elbows up on his desk. All the desire from a moment ago deflated, dissolving into frustration and guilt over having tried to use Calliope to bolster his wounded pride. He needed this curse broken, and sooner rather than later. Lacing his fingers together, he rested his forehead on them and sighed.

"Can I pour you a nectar?" Callie's voice finally cracked, making him feel worse than he already did. He shook his head, looking up just in time to watch her walk over to one of his many display cases.

"I know how hard this has to be for you. I could go talk to Orea alone, if you want, so you can stay here and get your bearings."

Callie gently placed his lyre on the desk in front of him. The corners of his mouth quirked up, and his mood followed suit, lightening at the thought of playing.

And at the thought of her knowing him so well.

"Thank you for offering, Calliope, but I should probably be the one to go talk to her." Apollo picked the instrument up off his desk and tucked it lovingly against his arm and shoulder. "Maybe that old goat, Peneus, told her where Daphne is." His smile grew wider as he strummed the lyre. "Or maybe I just have to use some of my infamous charm. You know, seeing as it works so well on nymphs."

Apollo second-guessed his decision—the suede oxfords he was wearing might be too casual for official business meetings. He'd decided that morning there was no sense ruining his good shoes, especially if he was on a mission to see every Tom, Dick and hairy satyr on Mount Olympus, but now he suppressed a groan. If he kept agreeing to traipse through the wilderness every other day, he just might have to invest in a pair of gods-awful hiking boots.

"Who is it we're looking for again?" he asked, deciding there was nothing he could do about his choice now but go with it.

"A woodland nymph named Orea." Callie snapped the spout on her water bottle shut and slipped it inside the mesh holder on the side of her backpack. "You really don't know who she is?"

"Other than what you've told me, no idea." He tucked his phone into the back pocket of his khakis, neatly pressed, of course, because he wasn't a heathen.

Not yet, anyway.

Calliope hooked her thumbs onto the underside of the padded shoulder straps and cleared her throat. "Good morning, everyone! May we speak to Orea, please?" She looked around, waiting for an answer, but only whispers from the surrounding beech, ash, and pine whirled on the breeze.

A smile reached Apollo's eyes as he rolled up one of his sleeves. She really was adorable. "You need to speak to them with authority, Calliope." Smoothing the second sleeve into place, he hoped they would respond better than the last time he'd been there. He folded his arms over his button-down and puffed up his chest. "Faithful and devoted residents of the Sacred Forest, this is Apollo, the god of sun and light. We need to speak to Orea. Immediately."

The wind instantly picked up, lifting the prickly branches on a group of black pines, and a nymph stepped out of a nearby ash tree. Apollo grinned triumphantly at Calliope.

"You called oh great god of sun and light?" said Orea, her voice flat and monotone on purpose. Her arms were defiantly crossed, and a wreath of woven twigs bearing tiny shimmering leaves adorned her head. Glossy dark hair hung in thick ropes over her shoulders and down her chest. The thin, gauzy material wrapped around her hips barely covered what her hair couldn't reach.

"Hello, Orea," said Apollo. "We'd like to ask you a few questions about Daphne."

"Daphne?" Orea's arms fell to her sides before sliding back up to her hips. "Why would you want to talk to me about *her*?"

The disgust on the nymph's face was evident. It didn't take a genius to see that, and with her mouth clamped shut like it was, she didn't seem too keen on volunteering information, especially to him. Apollo looked at Calliope for guidance.

Calliope stepped forward. "She's missing, and we really need to find her. We thought you might know—"

"We?" scoffed Orea.

Apollo fixed a heavy glare on the nymph, and she shrank under its weight. No nymph was going to be rude to his number one muse.

"We just want to ask you some questions. We'll be out of your hair in a few minutes, promise." Calliope offered Orea a comforting smile.

Orea sighed, gesturing toward the ash tree. "Fine. Come in, and I'll tell you all I know, which isn't much."

The long-legged nymph turned and promptly disappeared through a hollow the size of a door that hadn't been in the tree before, and Apollo gestured for Calliope to enter first.

Callie smirked up at him and whispered, "Probably best if you let me do the talking this time. Clear?"

"Crystal," answered Apollo, biting back a grin as Callie slipped into the darkness of the ancient tree.

She was toying with him, using the very words he'd said to her before their visit with Peneus. He couldn't argue, or get mad, because she was right. The nymph would probably divulge what she knew to someone who hadn't ignored her for three centuries.

Plus, Calliope's brazen attempt at being insubordinate was highly amusing.

He passed through the entryway and found himself in a paneled foyer, with a magnificent chandelier made of branches, rubbed free of bark and fitted together to form a tiered circle, hanging overhead to light the space. Fireflies swirled in and out of the knots and gnarls of wood, their glowing light reflecting off the polished dark wood floors. Orea didn't bother stopping, expecting them to follow her down a narrow corridor into a wide-open space that defied logic—from the outside, the trunk of the tree looked to be no more than five or six feet wide.

Orea gestured to a group of chaise lounges in the parlor, strategically arranged for conversation. "Please, have a seat." After settling herself down onto the comfiest looking one, she lifted her chin. "So, how is it that I can help you?"

"Daphne is missing," said Calliope, settling down onto the next comfiest-looking one, "and we need your help finding her."

Apollo's stomach muscles clenched. Calliope was being careful with her choice of words this time. Kind was more like it. Daphne wasn't only missing, she was hiding from him. He knew it, and so did Calliope.

"I did hear that. Are you sure she's missing?" asked Orea, shooting Apollo a pointed look. "Maybe she just doesn't want to be found."

Apparently Orea knew it, too. Did she have to say it like that, though? As if she was *trying* to piss him off.

"Whether she wants to be found or not is of no concern," responded Apollo, and a light touch on the arm from Callie prompted him to loosen his fists.

Orea tipped her shoulders up, shrugging off Apollo's

angry tone. "Look, I haven't talked to Daphne in forever. How would I know where she is?"

"But aren't you two cousins?" he asked, much calmer than he'd been just a few moments ago thanks to Calliope's Midas touch. "I thought you were inseparable."

Orea gawked at him. "Just because we're related doesn't mean I'm her keeper. How would I know where she went? I mean, we *were* inseparable, but things ended up a bit strained between us for the last three thousand years or so . . ." Orea narrowed her eyes at him. "You have no idea who I am, do you?'

Apollo flicked his gaze over to Calliope. He did, but wouldn't have if his trusty assistant, who he now realized pretty much thought of everything, hadn't told him. "I know who you are."

An awkward silence filled the air. Why wasn't the nymph saying anything? Was she waiting for an apology?

When she still said nothing, his anger began to rise, and he licked his lips to make it easier for the words to slide out of his mouth. "You're the nymph who didn't get the honor of being chased by me."

Calliope sighed heavily, and Orea looked like she wanted to rip his throat out. He couldn't blame her, really. His conscience knew the insult had been completely uncalled for. It was his pride that hadn't gotten the memo.

"You have a lot of nerve, you know that?" Orea's eyes flashed black, and she bared her teeth when she hissed at him. "I don't know what I ever saw in you. Now that I see you up close, you're not quite as impressive. Not as *strong*."

Apollo's nostrils flared in response, and his lungs filled with air in preparation for another round of insults. She'd found a sore spot and had pressed. Hard. What did a half-naked woodland nymph know about how strong he was, anyway?

Callie placed her hand on his knee. "Apollo." The pressure from her fingertips was light, but hard enough to keep him in his seat. "I think we can all agree that Orea understands what it's like when someone you love doesn't love you back, but this is not her fault . . . or Eros's."

But he *didn't* love her, that's what no one understood. The curse had never been about him loving her, only him getting rejected by her over and over again. Eros might be a young god, but he was a master at casting clever curses. Apollo had simply been chasing Daphne for so long that everyone, including himself, assumed it was because he loved her. Until now. The thinking he loved her part was just icing on the personalized punishment cake.

But the real cherry on top? Apollo couldn't risk being contrary to what everyone thought to be true. If he did, he couldn't keep blaming Eros for making him appear feckless and weak. So his choices had been either to admit to being a loser outright, apologize, and change his ways, or keep the facade intact and suffer the secret in silence.

Yep. Eros was a gods-damn curse savant.

"She's right," added Orea. "Eros really does have every-one's best interest in mind. I'd still be chasing after some-thing that was never meant to be if it wasn't for him."

"Is that so? Well, lucky you," replied Apollo. He was being petty now, he knew, and didn't have to look at Callie to know she was glaring at him with those big—and probably supremely pissed off—blue eyes of hers.

"Speaking of Eros," continued Orea, "Have you—"

"You're out of your mind if you think I'm going to ask that little shit for help." Everyone needed to stop suggesting he go to Eros. It was really starting to irritate him.

"Okay, then. Have you talked to Peneus already?"

"He said she asked to be sent to the middle of nowhere, whatever that means," said Apollo. "That's all he would say."

"He loves speaking in riddles, so there's probably a clue in there somewhere, but that's all I can tell you. I don't have the faintest idea where on Earth Daphne would be.

Apollo lifted his eyebrow at Calliope when she decked him in the arm. Whether he'd agreed to let her do all the talking or not, it was highly inappropriate to punch your superior in the bicep. It didn't hurt, but still.

"Give me your phone," said Calliope.

"Why?"

"I need to Google something."

"Where's *your* phone?"

"At the bottom of the river in Thessaly. It slipped out of my pocket when I got into the boat and I haven't had time to get a new one because a certain *someone's* been taking up quite a bit of my time lately. Just give me your phone, will you?"

He fished his phone out of his back pocket and punched in his passcode before handing it over. Was she really upset he was taking up so much of her time?

After some swiping and tapping of her own, he watched Calliope go from wondering to wide-eyed. "Oh my gods," she whispered, one of her fingernails finding its way between the edges of her teeth. "That's got to be it."

Leaning over, Apollo pulled her hand away before she could mow her fingers down to stumps. She smelled like lemons, and he said, "Stop being so dramatic, Calliope," so he wouldn't say something else and sound like an idiot. Or a jerk. He had a knack for that.

She flipped his phone around and held it out so he could see the red pin on the map she'd pulled up. He swallowed, seeing the marker but not grasping the meaning of its location.

"I'm not being dramatic," she said. "I just figured out where Daphne is."

CHAPTER ELEVEN

*W*ithout warning, Callie's jaw popped open. She would have preferred if it had stayed clamped tighter than a steel trap, but the confused look on Apollo's face had sprung the lock. "Nowhere. That's where she is."

Apollo raked a hand through his hair, the silky, golden strands parting easily. "Okay, sure, she's nowhere, but nowhere could be anywhere, and she has to be *somewhere*. The question is where. The universe is vast, the dimensions infinite."

Her big mouth opened again. Yep, the one she wished she could keep shut, but the slight furrow of Apollo's eyebrows jacked opened the gods-damned thing even wider. No surprise there. "She's in the last place Peneus thought you'd look. Nowhere, Oklahoma."

Orea threw her head back and laughed, the scratchy sound funneling through the air like dry leaves. "Oh, that is *too* good."

Callie frowned, preparing for the next round of Apollo's facial expressions that would break her. Sure enough, he leaned forward, his brows angling even deeper.

"Oklahoma?"

Like a charmed cobra, Callie swayed as more unbidden words came out, her mouth clinching the deal and relaying information she knew would start a chain of events she wouldn't be able to stop. "A place down on Earth. It's a tiny incorporated community in southern North America."

Stop singing like a canary, you idiot!

Low and behold, Apollo manifested a paper map, neatly folded in his lap, just as one of her traitorous fingers tapped the location. Not surprising, since she knew he was going to do it. She'd anticipated his next move and then had acted accordingly—that's how in-tune she was to him. Thank the gods Clio hadn't been around to witness it. She'd have had a field day.

"Peneus never thought we'd figure it out," said Callie, trying to focus on finding a way out of the crater she'd just dug. "But that was the riddle. He literally sent her to the middle of Nowhere."

In addition to more laughing, Orea now clapped with sheer delight. "How *clever* you are, Uncle Peneus."

The creases on Apollo's handsome face smoothed, and his blue eyes flared brighter as he ran his fingers through his golden hair, this time combing the strands back into their previously neat and orderly position. "My gods, Calliope. You're brilliant."

Callie's chest swelled, a burst of laughter from the tickling in her stomach begging to be let out. She bit her lip so a fit of giggling wouldn't escape. By gods, his warmth felt so good when he chose to bestow it. It almost made her mouth's betrayal worth it.

His praise cooled into a cold sweat as something else began to fill her with . . . what? Dread?

No. Regret. Knowing where Daphne was meant the chase would resume. Apollo would undoubtedly begin to pursue her again, and Callie had handed him the key to doing that on a silver platter. Apollo always got what he wanted, and what he wanted, now more than ever, was Daphne.

Always Daphne.

Callie smacked her knees. "So, uh, I guess that settles that."

Orea pursed her lips as Callie rose to her feet. "Well, I'm glad I could be of assistance," she said, looking up at Callie with an arched brow. "Although I'm not sure you needed much."

Callie heard the silent message in Orea's bark-colored eyes as loud and clear as if the words had come out of her mouth. *"I've been in your shoes, muse. He's not going to change."*

When Orea finally stood as well, she switched her gaze from Callie to Apollo. "Thanks for stopping by, but now if you'll excuse me, I have wine to drink and satyrs to fuc—fraternize. I do wish you luck on retrieving Daphne from the mortal world." She turned to lead them back through the foyer. When they were almost to the archway, she pivoted gracefully. "A word of warning, if I may? Although they have no powers to speak of, mortal wills are strong. They are formidable of mind, if not body. And, quite frankly, a giant pain in the ass."

Orea dipped into an exaggerated curtsy as Apollo strolled past, but her hand landed on Callie's shoulder once he disappeared through the door. The nymph squeezed gently, her eyes filled with an equal measure of pity and warning as she whispered, "Walk away while you still can."

Sunny days were normally Callie's favorite, but right now the sun's brightness was almost unbearable. Its rays burned through the leaves, casting cheery patches of pure delight on the ground. The temperature had risen, too. As if she needed another reason to sweat.

Apollo's mood had elevated significantly after their meeting with Orea. Callie's, on the other hand, had plummeted, taking a nosedive straight to Hadesville. Even though she was trying her best not to let it show, she was preoccupied with wanting to kick herself senseless.

"Good work, Calliope."

"Thanks, boss." Apollo walked just ahead of her, so she smiled weakly at the back of his head.

He slowed, adjusting his pace so he fell in-step beside her. "How about lunch? My treat."

"Sure," she replied, even though she wasn't hungry. She'd opened her mouth, and there was no taking it back. There was no,*"Oops, I'm sorry. I didn't mean to tell you Very Important Stuff because, oh hey, I might be completely denying that I still have feelings for you."*

Her only option now was damage control. If she could make it through the next twenty-four Olympus hours without the inevitable happening—he was going to ask her to go down to Earth with him, she'd bet her journals on it—she might be able to keep lying to herself.

Maybe she could feign an emergency—a family emergency. She had eight siblings to choose from, so that would be believable, right? Because who questions a family emergency? She ran her tongue along her teeth as she trudged along, knowing exactly who would question a family emergency.

So, scratch that idea.

Perhaps she could beg Zeus to give her a side project, like venturing into the fiery pits of Tartarus to see if any of its inhabitants needed a glass of ice water. Apollo wouldn't challenge his father's orders . . . Scratch that, too. That would be the first thing he'd do.

Gods, what a freaking mess.

Callie sighed as they entered the cave leading to the elevator that would take them up to the Atrium at the top of Mount Olympus. Clearly lost in his own thoughts, Apollo didn't seem to notice, which was fine by her. In fact, she was glad he hadn't said much during the trek through the forest. For one thing, she didn't know what to say. For another, she no longer trusted her mouth at this point. Surely it was for the best he hadn't noticed her aura dim.

The cool, damp air inside the cave became humid and stifling when Ares stomped in behind them. He glistened with sweat in the torchlight, dirt clinging to the exposed skin of his muscled arms and thighs, and the smears of blood left trails as they dripped. He tamped the dirt with the butt of his spear and whistled lightly, as if death and destruction was all in a day's work. Which, being the Executive Director of Combat, it was.

"Long day?" Apollo rocked onto the balls of his feet and folded his arms across his chest, protecting his ribs should Ares decide he wasn't in the mood for conversation. Even a spectacular victor like Apollo was no match for the sheer brute strength and unabashed violence of the god of war. There was only one person for whom Ares ever lowered his guard, and that was Aphrodite. Ares purred like a kitten whenever he was around the goddess of love. Everyone did.

"You look a bit worn out," remarked Apollo, pushing his luck. Rather bravely, thought Callie, considering she was shivering like a leaf simply standing in the presence of such a destructive force. "Doesn't the war machine practically run itself these days?"

Ares grunted. A low, gravelly sound emanated from deep within his chest. His lips peeled back, revealing blood-soaked teeth.

Oh, how comforting. The god of bloodshed was laughing.

When the elevator dinged and the doors slid open, both gods let Callie on first, which was not really as reassuring as one would expect. As soon as the doors closed, Ares took off his helmet, his inky shoulder-length hair soaked and dripping with gods knew what. The elevator music droned on as the pulley system shuddered to life and the ancient lift began its slow ascent upward.

One of her fingers migrated to her mouth. Good gods, as if the otherworldly juggernaut couldn't afford a more modern lift. Apollo tilted his head at her, and she stopped mid-nibble.

Callie glanced at Ares out of the corner of her eye. Violent, yes, but no eyesore, that was for sure. Muscled, but not bulky. Full lips and brooding dark-blue eyes. No wonder Aphrodite had been attracted to him. Their son, Eros, had definitely inherited his good looks from both sides.

That's it . . .

The answer to her most recently developed problem hit her like the pommel of a sword to the temple. If she could convince Apollo to go see Eros, to somehow talk the god of love into going down and bringing Daphne back up for him, then she could dodge the part where she would have to go through with helping Apollo chase Daphne. It would be devastating knowing they were together, but Callie would get over it. Eventually. If she couldn't, well, she'd ask her mother, Mnemosyne, to wipe her memory free of Apollo.

There was one teensy problem. She didn't really want to forget about Apollo, or their time together.

Okay, two teensy problems. Apollo would never go talk to Eros unless he was forced to.

After what felt like an eternity, the elevator doors opened. Ares' armor clattered as he exited, and Callie crinkled her nose as she walked through a pocket of divine-sweat-tinged-with-mortal-fear scented air that swirled around him. She held in a groan when she spied three of her sisters at a table outside the cafe. It took a nano-second for Clio's gaze to zero in on her, even less time for the words *dickhead* to form on her lips.

Callie gulped down a lungful of air, hoping her fear and anxiety went with it. She wasn't exactly sure how Apollo was going to take the next words out of her mouth. "You know, boss, I really think you should go talk to Eros."

Apollo tossed an annoyed look over his shoulder. "What? No." His sigh was heavy, but he continued toward the enormous gilded doors of Life Industries as if nothing was wrong. "That is not an option, Calliope." He said, his lips barely moving through his fake smile. "Why would you even suggest it?"

Careful to avoid Clio's eyes, Callie forced the smile on her face to hold. She'd worked for Apollo long enough to know appearances were everything, and although she didn't like what she was about to do, it seemed like the best way— maybe even the only way—to get out of her current nightmare. "Well, normally I wouldn't, but . . . I've been hearing rumors."

Apollo stopped dead in his tracks. "Rumors? What rumors?"

Her stomach churned, but, bingo. He despised gossip. It led to rumors, which were almost always based on hearsay, and if there was anything that could tarnish a shiny reputation in the blink of an eye, it was hearsay. And if there was anyone's shiny reputation Apollo worried about, it was his own.

"Well, you know, that maybe you're not as great as you once were." Good gods, she hated bending the truth. He was still great, and she hadn't actually heard anything, but she was desperate for a way out of going to Nowhere, Oklahoma.

Besides, just because tongues weren't wagging yet didn't mean they wouldn't be soon.

"Gods dammit," said Apollo, resuming his already brisk pace at an even faster clip. "I really am going to have to pay Mr. Cuddles a visit, aren't I?"

CHAPTER TWELVE

Apollo walked straight past his office and continued down the covered arcade of the Hall of Olympians at a hurried but even pace. He'd tried convincing his father to help, to no avail. He tried gossiping with his mother. That hadn't worked either. Orea and Peneus had been little to no help. As always, Calliope had been the one to come through for him, but she'd only solved half of his problem. He knew where Daphne was, but not how to get her back to Mount Olympus.

And now, just moments ago, Calliope had alerted him to another problem. The rumors were starting to make their rounds. Just thinking about what that could do to the reputation he'd painstakingly built over the centuries had his stomach roiling. He'd been dreading something like this and, well, now here it was. He needed this chase over, as quickly and as quietly as possible.

He scrubbed a hand down his face. He knew where Daphne was now, and that was definitely a step in the right direction, but it might not matter. She'd just keep right on running if she saw it was him coming for her.

That's why he needed Eros to go get her.

And then the matchmaker needed to lift the curse.

Yes, a visit to the god of love was in order, but he wouldn't beg. Begging was something he couldn't bring himself to do, especially when it came to Eros. He'd have no problem engaging in a slight bit of coercion. Light bullying, if necessary, but groveling?

Apollo straightened his cuff links before imparting two curt raps on the door. A woman's voice, gentle as the whisper of butterfly wings, came from the other side. "It's open."

"Dearest Fates," muttered Apollo, figuring a quick prayer to the only beings more powerful than gods wouldn't hurt. "Please give me the strength, even more than I already possess, not to throttle this little shit."

Apollo squared his shoulders and stepped inside what used to be Hermes' old office before he started working from home. Olympian, UPS man to the gods, patron of a lot, mostly to do with traveling and boundaries, sure-footed and quick-witted Hermes was Life Industries' renaissance man. In fact, he was good at almost as much as Apollo.

Almost.

Nonetheless, Hermes was a god Apollo could respect. It also didn't hurt that they were siblings. Well, half, anyway. Sometimes Apollo wished he could be more like his younger half-brother. It might be nice not caring what people thought for a change.

The office had previously been full of precious relics collected from around the world, but now the cloying scent of flowers, thick and heavy, made the inside of Apollo's nose tingle. They were everywhere—on display tables, in decorative buckets and in coolers—and butterflies bounced overhead. Framed posters featuring ridiculous inspirational quotes about love and other such nonsense hung on the brick walls. There was even a sign that read *Follow Your Heart*

Flowers & Gifts hanging over a cash register that was sitting on a sales counter.

Eros and Psyche, Life Industries' Co-Coordinators of Hearts. The dynamic love duo. More like two peons in charge of the worst job imaginable. Binding hearts. Leave it to them to ruin a perfectly good office.

Apollo fought the urge to use his power to wipe the whole love explosion clean. "A flower shop? Really?" He held a finger to his nose so he wouldn't sneeze. It was the last place he wanted to be, and their questionable taste in office decor—and the pollen—was making it worse.

"What can I say, we like flowers." Eros eyed him warily from behind a desk tucked along the back wall.

Apollo detected the surprise on both Eros and Psyche's faces, even though they tried to hide it. "I never would have guessed," he mumbled.

"Hello to you, too." Psyche stood up from her desk, which was the twin to the one Eros sat behind—all over-the-top curves and ornate scrolls—and came around it to stand in front of him. Her butterfly wings glinted when they caught the track lighting just right. "What brings you to see us?"

"Daphne is gone," Apollo informed her, skipping any more pleasantries and getting right to the heart of the matter. "She's gone down to Earth and I need one of you—Don't care which, quite frankly—to go and get her. After you get back, I want this ridiculous curse broken once and for all. I'm tired of this love/hate nonsense." Turning toward Eros, he pointed a finger. "I want *you* to shoot a golden arrow into Daphne so we can finally be free. You owe me, matchmaker."

"No. He doesn't," said Psyche, tilting her chin down and fixing both of her golden eyes directly on him.

Taken aback, Apollo cocked his head at her. "Excuse me?"

"You heard me." She responded dryly. "You've been a giant asshole to Eros for ages now. So, no, he's not going to go down to Earth for you. Neither am I." Psyche pointed at him like he'd done to Eros, driving home the fact she wasn't intimidated by him in the least. "You're going to go down there yourself, and you're going to convince her to come back all on your own. Then—and only then—will we break the *spell*."

Apollo tried to cover up a wince by dragging a long breath in through his nose. Psyche's words stung, and the slap to his ego's face made his jaw set. It didn't take long for his pride to join the party, and he sent a narrow-eyed glare her way. Luxurious chestnut hair and pretty gold eyes aside, she'd found a direct path to his last nerve.

"She was shot with a leaden arrow by your precious lover boy, here." Apollo swung his arm dramatically to make a show of jabbing a finger at Eros again. "The curse—and it is a curse as far as I'm concerned—makes it impossible for her to give me the time of day, let alone want to come back with me, you know that."

Psyche folded her arms. "Po-tay-toe, po-tah-toe . . . and impossible? Hmm, like your ego, perhaps? I guess you messed with the wrong god a few centuries ago then, huh?"

Apollo continued to glower at her, not sure what to do next. His outburst and subsequent demands were supposed to instill fear, illicit compliance. Yet, she showed no sign of doing either.

And was that a faint but determined smile curling her lips?

Eros smirked. "I'd think twice about making her mad, my friend." He tapped a finger to his temple. "Mind like a steel trap, even stronger will. Don't even get me started on how stubborn she can be . . ." He whistled through his teeth, emphasizing the high level of stubborn he was talking about. "I'd just take my lumps and get to packing for a trip down to Earth if I was you."

Apollo's nostrils flared. Mr. Cuddles was really enjoying this. "I'm not your friend, I'm your superior, and I demand that you follow my orders." His pride was in control now, the words coming out automatically.

Wings unfurling to their full height and width, Eros drew up his chest. "You're not my superior."

Apollo scanned his fellow god up and down, making note of his trim physique. Eros was nowhere near as tall or muscular as he was, but the matchmaker definitely had a bit more cut to him than Apollo remembered. He had to admit, the god of love's wings were impressive, to the point that Apollo wished he'd been born with a pair. He also noticed that Eros had lost his cherubic rolls. He must have gotten a gym membership.

The thought incensed Apollo even more. "I'm better than you, at pretty much everything, so I'd say that makes me your superior."

As soon as the words left his mouth, it was like they were back in the Sacred Forest all over again, reliving the moment that had started this whole thing. The unfortunate part was he'd already shifted into autopilot. Once his pride was in charge, it was hard to take back control.

"No, you're not," Eros shot back. "You suck at patience, you're horrible where kindness is concerned and you're arrogant, but nice try. We're not going through this again because I'm done letting you get to me. You're barking up the wrong tree, man."

Apollo narrowed his eyes at Eros. "Do as I say, matchmaker, or you'll be sorry."

Eros snorted. "What are you going to do? Get me fired? Been there done that. Destroy me like you did Python? News flash, I've been up against a worse snake. I survived Hera, remember? I may not rule over as much as you do, but I rule over something that matters. You don't intimidate me anymore. I'm a god, same as you."

"And the only one who can break the spell," added Psyche.

Apollo couldn't stop his top lip from curling, now that his need to be the ultimate victor had arrived on the scene. My, wasn't she clever? What she was doing with an idiot like Eros, he didn't know, but Apollo could certainly appreciate her cunning. She'd backed him into a corner quite nicely.

What was it about love he couldn't seem to conquer? He was between a rock and a hard place, the exact place where his ego, pride, and need to win had absolutely no leverage. The love duo had nothing to lose at this point, and they weren't likely to budge.

"Fine," said Apollo. "It's probably better I go down and bring her back myself anyway. I want it done right, after all." The butterflies flitting about the room suddenly stopped, floating in mid-air as if someone had pressed pause. "But you must give me your word that when I do, you will lift the curse." Apollo tried one last attempt to make himself feel powerful.

"Don't you dare," whispered Psyche.

"He won't," Eros replied, calling Apollo's bluff. "Because he's better than that. Aren't you, Apollo? Deep down you want to be loved for who you are, just like the rest of us. Believe it or not, I feel for you. I really do. Unrequited love is tough. It hurts. So you have my word, I'll lift the spell. On one condition."

Apollo sighed, and the butterflies began to flit around their heads once more. No, he wouldn't mess with them, even though a few more blows to his ego had just been delivered. The urge to punch the ever-living shit out of Eros made his muscles tighten, but he refrained, choosing instead to impart a warning. "You're pushing it, matchmaker. I am the son of Zeus, and he . . ."

Eros shook his head and laughed. "You're really going to try and play that card? Please. If Zeus was going to help, you wouldn't be here right now."

Apollo ground his teeth, daggers of irritation slicing through his remaining patience. He wasn't used to conceding to anyone. In fact, he couldn't recall a single instance, not one, least of all to such an insufferable twit. But Eros was right, gods damn him, and Apollo was determined to prove him wrong. He *was* loved. And if not loved, at least he was adored. "What's the condition?"

"She has to tell you she loves you." Eros flicked his gaze over to Psyche, his partner in crime in this hot mess, and she sent him a mischievous smile in return. "Out loud."

"Ooh, I like that," said Psyche, giving Eros a vigorous nod of approval.

Apollo sucked in his cheeks and inspected his fingers as if the hangnails he didn't have were more of a concern to him at the moment than convincing a woman who hated every single thing about him that she loved him. Apollo had no other choice but to accept the challenge, so he fixed his eyes directly on Eros and forced himself to smile. "Not a problem."

CHAPTER THIRTEEN

*D*aphne stopped weeding to lift the hair sticking to the back of her neck. When Jimmy had mentioned garden plots, it turned out he'd meant small field. Oh, and Oklahoma summers were *hot*.

She pulled her hair back and secured it with a rubber band before checking on the radishes. They had come along nicely over the three or so weeks she'd been here. The tomato plants, laden with tiny yellow flowers, were already waist high. She made a mental note to ask Sam where he kept the garden stakes as she made her way over to the large galvanized water bin and submerged the watering can, filling it up again.

Delilah stood near the fence stoically, watching her work.

"Come on," said Daphne. "You can't keep giving me the cold shoulder forever. What do you say you tell me your troubles, and I'll tell you mine?" The horse swung her head up and whinnied before looking away.

Daphne wiped a wet hand on the seat of her overalls as she walked the short distance over to the fence. She leaned against the top rail and hugged the half-full watering can. "I'm sorry she left you, girl, but you've got to find a way to carry on." She cocked her head to look up at the majestic beauty. "At some point, you've got to give someone else a chance."

Delilah blinked and turned her head the other away, giving Daphne the horse equivalent of an eye roll. It succeeded in making Daphne feel like a hypocrite.

"I had my reasons, okay? You try living your best life as a tree. Anyway, haven't you ever just needed a break?" Daphne sighed when no answer came. "So, any tips on how I can make some money? You know, where I come from, we had everything we needed, and I think I like that arrangement better. Of course, there are also flesh-eating monsters to watch out for so I suppose it's a trade-off."

Her days of leisure in the woods came to mind; nothing to fill the endless hours but dancing, singing, painting, and feasting. Oh, the feasting . . .

She'd been pretty good at all of those things back in her world, especially painting. In fact, once the residents of the Sacred Forest had caught wind of her talent, she'd barely had time for much else. Her mystical, watery landscapes had been a hit.

A smile touched her lips, and she sat the watering can down, its contents sloshing as a plan formed in her head. She owed Sam, not just figuratively, but literally. Acts of service like tending his vegetables might be a way to pay off the intangible things he'd provided for her, but she owed him for *actual* things. Just because she'd hadn't needed to worry about debt in her world, didn't mean she should dismiss it in his. "Be right back."

The easel and blank canvas were small enough for her to carry under one arm, and she grabbed a cup out of the cupboard before stuffing a few brushes and some tubes of paint into the front pocket of her overalls. She could barely contain her excitement as she descended the steps and walked into the yard, or her pride at coming up with such a perfect solution to her debt problem. She would paint, and then sell her art at the market for those paper rectangles.

"What do you say you show me where the water is, huh?" said Daphne, slowly stretching out her arm. "I know there's water back there, and wouldn't it feel nice to frolic a bit?" Her fingers twitched, reaching further still, but Delilah just stared at her. "I promise not to run if you do."

The mare regarded her for a few more seconds before pushing her muzzle the slightest bit toward Daphne's hand. When she was allowed to make a connection, Daphne smiled triumphantly as she stroked the soft hair along the horse's neck.

When Delilah pulled away, Daphne thought their truce had come to an end before it had even begun, but when the horse trotted over to the gate, she grinned. "Good, because these things are killing me."

She pulled off her boots and dropped them next to one of the fence posts before flinging both footie socks in either direction. Daphne popped the latch and swung the gate open for Delilah, who stepped through and waited patiently for her to shut it.

Sampson stuck his head out of the stall window, blowing out a snort.

"Sorry, Sampson. Just the girls," said Daphne, climbing to the top rail of the fence and sliding onto Delilah's back. "Lead the way, sister. These overalls need to come off, too."

Zeus barked at her from the bank. If he'd sniffed her out, that meant Sam wasn't far behind. Daphne's heart danced in her chest as she bolted out of the river and onto the grassy bank to grab her overalls. The water felt nice, and she was a bit sad her basking had been interrupted. To make up for it, she pictured Sam in the water with her, at night, with the moonlight reflecting off the droplets on his wet skin.

Almost as immediately as the image popped into her head, she wiped it clean, cursing herself for letting her mind wander into dangerous territory at a time like this. She hurried into her tank top before shoving a leg into the overalls, and she barely had time to pull them over her hips before Sampson appeared on the narrow trail with Sam on his back.

"You're skinny dipping *again*?" He laughed down at her, holding the reins in his left hand as he hopped off Sampson. "You must really like the water."

Like gentlemen, man, dog and horse turned their attention toward her unfinished painting while she finished dressing. It took several attempts, but her shaky fingers finally succeeded in getting the straps of her overalls hooked.

"Wow, you can paint one helluva watercolor."

The appreciation in Sam's voice felt warmer than the rush from the sweetest nectar, and she reveled in it—until another feeling streaked through her, hot and prickly.

Her eyes flicked to the easel, and her vision tunneled. She'd taken something that wasn't hers. "I hope you don't mind." Her gaze left the easel and, as if it had a will of its own, landed on Delilah munching on a patch of thistles.

Make that two things she'd taken without permission.

Sam's grin succeeded in quelling her rising panic. "No, no. Not at all. I did say help yourself to anything."

The burning in her belly subsided. At least enough so she could venture to ask, "So was it you who . . .?"

"Liked to paint? Yep." Sam shrugged. "Turns out I'm better with a hammer and nails than I am with a paint brush.

I thought maybe taking up the arts would make me more . . . Refined. It's all good, though."

Daphne's heart cracked wide open, flooding her whole being with sympathy. That was just about the saddest thing she'd ever heard. How could anyone abandon this man? And more refined? She'd never met anyone as comfortable with who they were than Sam, and if that wasn't the very definition of refined, then she didn't know what on Earth was. A fierce protectiveness wound its way through her, and she struggled to stop a whimper of pity from escaping. It bothered her to think that Sam hadn't been enough for his ex-wife.

Or maybe it was a tiny grunt of frustration since she wasn't supposed to care. That was his business, and she had her own to mind.

"I saw Delilah was gone," said Sam. "And Zeus noticed you left your boots at the scene of the crime. Neither of us can resist a good investigation."

And there went his laugher again, sparkling brighter than the sun glinting off water.

But there was something lurking just beneath the surface of his calm demeanor.

Feeling more connected to him with every day that passed, Daphne picked up on it right away, and it was much stronger than the three emotions—lust, guilt, pity—she'd just experienced in rapid succession a minute ago. It was fear, and the panic was still rolling off of him in waves even though he was smiling. "I'm sorry, I don't know what I was thinking," Daphne began to explain. "She promised not to run, so I thought . . ."

"It's okay. Now that I know I don't need to file a missing person's report, dinner is at six. Hope you like hominy." He patted Delilah's flank to let her know it was time to go. "Ready?"

Daphne's heart thundered when he held out his hand. He was going to help her up onto Delilah. He was going to *touch* her.

The thought should have given her the strong urge to run the other way. Instead, it had the opposite effect, and she moved toward him as blindly as a moth to a flame.

"But the easel," she offered a weak protest.

"I'll get it." He motioned for her to come to him.

It was a fluid, graceful movement, and it made her feet move automatically. She locked her knees together so she wouldn't wobble when he positioned himself behind her, which, as it turned out, was another movement that did things to her. Namely, getting the butterflies in her stomach fired up again. She put a steadying hand on Delilah's side just as the tiny hairs she didn't even know she had came alive with the electricity jumping between their bodies. When he placed his hands on her hips, the charge intensified.

"Ready?" He squeezed, gripping her waist tighter. "On the count of three, okay?"

Daphne nodded her head, since words were out of the question.

"One, two . . ." His deep voice soothed her like a gentle wind. "Three." His guiding hands slid down her thighs, and the feeling was exhilarating, like the static in the air right before a lightning storm. As soon as her belly lay on Delilah's back, she grabbed onto the horse's mane and swung a leg over. Her arms shook from the exertion, but the warmth of his hand sliding over the back of her thigh and traveling down its path to rest on her calf set her skin alight.

He gathered up the painting supplies and handed them to her before mounting Sampson in a few strong and swift motions. He made a clicking noise, and with a slight tap of the reins Sampson headed in the direction of the farm.

Daphne barely squeezed her heels and Delilah was off as well. Always on duty, Zeus brought up the rear.

The pounding in her chest was just beginning to slow when the thought hit her. Sam hadn't come all this way to tell her when and what he planned on eating that evening. He'd thought something bad might have happened to her. Considering it wasn't exactly a secret she was running from someone, an abusive lover as far as he knew, he'd been more than a little worried.

A new emotion coursed through Daphne, and it made her stomach do a flip. Did he feel protective of her, like she did him? And was it possible she felt more than sympathy?

Also, what in Hades' Realm was hominy?

Her stomach fluttered again—no, rumbled—and the butterflies settled into a burning sensation that grew with every second she thought of food. When her belly settled into growling furiously every thirty seconds, her eagerness to eat became more pronounced.

After running up to the loft for a quick change of clothes and to finger comb her wet hair, she bounded onto the porch and into the farmhouse. The smell wafting from the kitchen nearly knocked her over, and not in a good way. It seemed as though hominy involved searing animal flesh, and the strange look on Sam's face when he noticed the open-mouthed expression on hers nearly had her beating him with her fists.

Daphne swallowed hard, mind racing to think of a reason why he'd prepare her a meal that included meat. He *knew* she didn't eat it. When she saw the huge bowl of seasoned corn, along with chopped onions and chilies, a sauce—tomato, it looked like—and an array of beans lined up on the counter, she relaxed. Her gaze quickly moved on to the rounds of fried bread and her mouth began to water.

Sam whistled as he spooned the crumbled meat over the

kibble that was already in Zeus's bowl. "Chuck wagon's here, boy." Zeus came tearing into the kitchen, all but crashing into the center island in his excitement at the unexpected treat. Sam lifted his hand in a stay motion. "Just let it cool a bit." Zeus gave him a pitiful whine as he sat, but licked his chops and patiently obeyed his partner.

"Sorry if you thought that was for . . ." Sam shook his head, clearly disappointed in himself. "I should have warned you that I sometimes brown up some ground beef for Zeus," Sam said as he mixed the corn and beans into the tomato sauce.

"Oh no, it's all right. Really," said Daphne. And it was. He was only human, after all.

"I've got Bud Light in the fridge. Can I get you one?"

"Sure." She couldn't help but smile at the fact she'd thought Sam had forgotten. It was a bit ridiculous of her now that she thought about it. The man was the most perceptive being she'd ever met. His attention to detail, especially where her likes and dislikes were concerned, had a way of making her feel as though she were walking on the clouds that surrounded the peak of Mount Olympus. Not that she'd ever actually had the pleasure of walking on clouds, but if she had been born a goddess, she imagined this is what it would feel like.

After sticking the pot on the stove, Sam grabbed two bottles of Bud Light from the refrigerator. "Want to go sit on the porch while we wait? There's a nice breeze."

Daphne nodded, her head feeling light and her limbs heavy. She felt at ease and unsettled at the same time. Calm, then nervous. Yearning to run, but wanting to stay. Human emotions were full of strange paradoxes.

Sam sat on the porch swing, and when she started to take a seat on one of the old wicker chairs, he said, "I built this swing for two. Look, there's even a place to put our beers."

He pulled down the built-in holder from the back slats of the swing.

Daphne sat next to Sam, sipping her beer and swinging her bare feet. "I've been meaning to tell you, this farmhouse, the loft, this whole place is amazing."

"It is pretty amazing, isn't it?" Sam looked out at the landscape, to the thick grove of trees in the distance then up at the endless sky above. "I sometimes envy my ancestors for getting to live off the land, but then, well . . ." He shook his head, a mix of grief and anger flashing across his face, and he took a sip of his beer. "So, are you a camping or "glamping" type gal?"

Her face grew hot. She didn't know what either of those things were. Plus, she wanted to hear about his ancestors. They sounded like her kind of people. But she didn't want to press on what was obviously a sore spot.

"Camping?" She'd been asking because she was genuinely curious, but he'd taken it as her answer.

Sam nodded his head. "Figured. You have that *sleeping out under the stars* look about you."

Daphne couldn't contain the happiness bubbling up from somewhere deep down inside her, and an incredulous laugh burst out of her. She'd been doing it a lot lately, having unexpected feelings that caused her to make strange noises. A giddiness, like she was tipsy on nectar wine, always accompanied these fits of auditory disturbance, and her current bout made her so lightheaded she practically fell off the swing. "I love sleeping out under the stars. I've wanted to do it so many times since I got here, but I thought you'd think I was strange."

"For sleeping under the stars? That's not strange at all. My grandmother was Cherokee, so it makes perfect sense to me. Being one with nature just feels right." A deep chuckle rumbled his chest before he proceeded to make her limbs go weak again with that broad smile of his. "The skinny dipping, the star gazing . . . Are you sure *you're* not part Cherokee?"

She grinned like a fool, quietly soaking him in. It was all she could do as a sudden longing to be everything he was instead of part nymph, part tree, part *not-from-this-world* tugged at her heart. Add part fool into the mix, since she was supposed to have been gone by now.

"You know, Zeus and I usually do a property check at least once a summer. I was thinking about doing it this weekend. We ride out to the fence line, check to make sure everything's all right. It's only six or seven miles past those trees." He pointed to the woods lining the back of the pasture. "But Zeus and I like to make a camping weekend of it. We usually leave Saturday morning, stay overnight by the river, then head back Sunday afternoon. Seeing as you and Delilah are BFFs now, would you want to go with?"

Daphne jumped off the swing. There was no way she could sit still, not with how much joy was buzzing through her. "Oh my gods, I would love to go with you!"

Zeus barked at her excitement, dashing toward her and hopping up on his hind legs so she could grab his humongous paws and dance him in a circle. "Did you hear that, Zeus-y? We're sleeping under the stars this weekend."

Elation overtook her and, without a thought of consequence, Daphne reached for Sam.

"Hold on, hold on," he said with an amused chuckle. "Let me put my beer down, nature girl."

After setting his bottle down, he let her pull him to his feet. It wasn't long before he was twirling her around, and she was pirouetting in place. When she stood on the balls of her feet to throw her arms around his shoulders, he went stiff. His body language told her he was surprised that she'd suddenly latched onto him. To be honest, so was she, but when she didn't let go, he eventually relaxed and laughed.

The sound was music to her ears, comparable to absolutely nothing else in the world—this one and hers.

"God, Dee," he said, wrapping his arms around her. "If I'd have known you liked camping so much, I'd have asked you sooner."

pollo held the back of his hand to his nose. If the air, thick with the smell of motor oil and desolation, didn't put him over the edge, the musty stench of mortals might send him racing back to Mount Olympus. It was bad. Even worse than he had been anticipating. The pollution they'd caused in the short time they'd inhabited the Earth was nothing short of staggering.

He stifled a groan before dropping his hand and pretending he wasn't bothered. Well, *as* bothered. He was very bothered, for multiple reasons. He was sure he'd already be back on Olympus if it wasn't for one thing: They had not ascertained the nymph as of yet.

"Oh, come on, boss, it's not that bad." Calliope meandered ahead of him as they perused the Caddo County Vintage and Craft Market. "I just wanted to look around for a minute."

Why it was called a "vintage" market Apollo could easily guess, but the "craft" part? He saw nothing but row after row of tables filled with worthless junk. He rolled his eyes at the sheer amount of costume jewelry being passed off as family heirlooms. Had these people never seen a nice silver bowl ringed in gold?

"Oooh, this is nice," said Calliope, picking up a handmade journal.

Apollo sized up the seller sitting behind a table. He was young and looked bored, not paying attention to much other than his mobile device. Irritated at having to be down on Earth in the first place, walking among creatures who were clearly no comparison to the likes of gods, Apollo took the bright yellow leather-bound book from Calliope's hands. He flipped through the blank pages before turning it over to inspect the back. The craftsmanship was clumsy, and the stitching shoddy at best. She deserved better.

"Nice? That's debatable." He set the journal on the table and nodded politely at the irreverent lump of flesh before ushering Calliope onward. "Fortunately, we have other, more interesting matters to discuss, like how hot pokers to the eyes would be more enjoyable than being subjected to this place. Do they honestly consider this a market? Where are the spiced meats? Olives? Wine? There's not even a single goat for sale." Apollo made an exasperated sound. "It seems as though proper markets were abandoned along with the hecatomb."

"Speaking of public sacrifice, what should I call you down here? And how long has it been since you've visited the modern world?"

Apollo set down a turquoise ring he'd been inspecting. "Well, Calliope, I'm glad you asked. Not since the sack of Troy, so it's certainly been a while." He shrugged his shoulders. "War, death, famine . . . other than the advent of plastic, it seems as though the human world hasn't changed much. Oh, and I've decided to pose as a physician. Dr. Paul Brighton at your service." He bowed with a flourish.

"Cool," she said, a hopeful smile inching her cheeks upward. "Then maybe you can call me Callie?"

"Not happening, Calliope."

Her smile fell, and she gave him the slightest hint of an eye roll, but Apollo blocked it out. If things got too casual, he might be tempted again. And he couldn't afford the distraction.

"Oh, come on, boss. Lighten up a—"

His hand flew up. "Shhh."

There she was, standing near an ice cream truck. Why she was wearing such awful boots he couldn't fathom, but he was sure they, and the hideous hat on top of her head, were part of her disguise. What a clever nymph, that Daphne.

She might be clever, but he was cunning.

He waited a second for the fierce supernatural pull to draw him to her, but it didn't come, which was strange and slightly disconcerting. Perhaps it worked differently down here. No matter. He'd approach Daphne with or without that undeniable magnetic force that usually overpowered him.

He continued toward her, taking care to keep each step steady and sure. One step, two. Three, four, five. The pull would happen any second now . . .

Still nothing.

An uneasiness in his gut coiled tighter. Where in Hades' Realm was it, that *feeling*?

But the hair, the curves; it was her, he was certain, even as he placed a hand on her shoulder and tried to sound as confident—and less desperate—as a god of his importance should feel.

"Daphne."

The woman spun around, her face registering first terror then anger as she smacked his hand away with a loud *thwack*. A stocky bearded fellow next to her turned around at the sound.

The man's face instantly flushed. "Hey dickhead, get your hands off my wife before I kick your ass."

Apollo took a step backward, but it was only to assume a fighting position. The man may have surprised him, but he hadn't caught him off guard.

It didn't take long for the small twinge of shock to grow into a swell of anger. Apollo felt it gathering strength and tried to stop the black cloud of fury from forming, but did this mortal man honestly think he could best him? With a kick to the ass? He bit back a maniacal laugh. He could say, with the highest confidence, this man was picking the wrong fight.

Apollo leveled a warning glare. He really didn't want to have to decimate the idiot, especially in front of Calliope. He should at least try and talk some sense into him. "You'll do no such thing."

Or, you know, make demands. Whatever.

"The hell I won't." The man dumped his wallet and keys into his hat before handing the whole lot over to his wife.

Apollo could tell he had been in finer fighting trim before the years had stolen his youth and high fructose corn syrup had hijacked his physique. In a rare instance of pity, he actually felt sorry for the man. Brawny as he was, his ample beer belly was going to impede what little chance he had at winning. Depending on how hard-headed he turned out to be, maybe even at surviving.

Calliope stood behind him, not saying a word. Although she may not have been speaking, Apollo could feel her anxiety vibrating in the air. It made his stomach churn with indecision, and he found himself in a rather uncomfortable position—torn between backing down and charging full speed ahead.

"Please. I'm warning you." Apollo tried talking sense into

the man again. "It isn't wise to challenge me in a contest of strength."

"Who the fuck does this guy think he is?" The man asked no one in particular.

The woman wasted no time stoking the fire by throwing her two cents into the flames. "I don't know, babe, but I'm pretty sure you can take him."

With his wife's encouragement, the man charged like a bull. Apollo lifted his hand, raw power crackling in the air, and the faint outline of his enormous silver bow appeared. The adrenaline coursing through his body hadn't ramped up even an eighth of his magic yet, and he nearly laughed out loud at that fact. It was going to feel *so* good to obliterate this guy. He only wished there was a way to make the thrill of it last longer.

"Boss, don't!"

The urgency in Calliope's voice stopped him cold. He blinked, his bow shimmering and waving in and out like a mirage. The small break in concentration was just long enough for the man to land a punch to his jaw. It didn't hurt, of course, but he knew the man had to be in some serious pain.

"Goddamn, brother." The man cradled his rapidly swelling hand close to his chest. "You made of stone?"

Calliope stepped in between him and the bull-headed idiot daring to fight him. Apollo's heaving slowed when she placed her hands on his chest.

"It's not worth it." Her voice was less frantic and more steady now. Calming.

He looked into the twin pools of blue staring back at him, begging him to stop, and somehow, even with the man chanting *fuck that hurts, fuck that hurts, fuck that hurts* in the background, that's all it took for winning this particular fight to lose its appeal.

Apollo nodded. "You're right, Calliope. That's not what we came here for." He put his hands on her arms and gently moved her out of the way. He addressed the still chanting man, whose hand had already swelled to twice its original size. "I mistook your wife for someone else."

Not an apology, but it was the best he could do under the circumstances.

The man eyed him warily, his bad hand—most likely broken in several places, possibly shattered—tucked gingerly against his sternum. His good hand was, not surprisingly, clenched into a fist and at the ready should the situation turn ugly again.

"Damn straight it was your fault, buddy," said the woman, who, upon closer inspection, looked nothing like Daphne. She handed her husband his wallet, which he promptly stuffed into his back pocket. "And for the record, I wouldn't go around touching women you don't know if I was you." She set the hat on her man's head before putting her arm as far around his sizable girth as it would go and leading him away. "Come on, babe. Let's go. You're gonna need to get that looked at."

Apollo watched the two mortals walk away. The man's good hand flew into the air, his middle finger raised. Apollo was fairly certain it was the rudest of human gestures, used to get the last word and/or provoke fisticuffs. He clamped his teeth around his bottom lip so his inner victor couldn't sling another insult and restart the fight. He proceeded to bite harder, until he tasted blood, because as Calliope had stated, it wasn't a fight worth winning. Obliterating some nobody human down on Earth wouldn't win him any points with her, and, right now more than ever, he needed her on his side.

"That was a close call," sighed Calliope, sounding tired as she rubbed her forehead. "That would have totally been a huge mess."

The damage his teeth had done to the inside of his lip had resulted in blood finding its way into the corners of his mouth. He dabbed at it with the back of his hand, refraining from words as the deep gash repaired itself.

It was just as well he didn't speak. He didn't know what to say, anyway. Half of him agreed. The other half was too busy sulking.

"Well, I suppose we should find accommodations for the next few nights, then," Calliope continued, blowing out more exasperation. "There's a motel down the road that didn't look too bad. Do you want to magic there or . . .?"

"Let's walk," said Apollo, scrubbing a hand over his face. "I need a bit more time to collect myself."

Get in, find the nymph, get out. The job was simple. He needed to stay focused and keep his eye on the prize. The right one.

His head throbbed, and he suddenly felt like one of Calliope's sighs sounded. Bone-tired. Good gods, he'd forgotten how draining the mortal plane of existence could be. That nymph, Orea, had been right about one thing: Mortals were a giant pain in the ass.

They left the Vintage and Craft Market and started down the dusty road that led into town. They walked for a few minutes in silence before Apollo halted. Calliope stopped as well, looking around, he presumed, to make sure he hadn't found more trouble to get into.

"What is it now?"

He was only going to say that he changed his mind about magicking them to the motel, but he found her vigilance when it came to protecting him so endearing, his heart swelled. The feeling was accompanied by an overwhelming urge to laugh. And he suddenly wanted to make her laugh, too. Or at least see her smile.

He didn't bother to answer her question, but simply

snapped his fingers instead. His expensive dress shoes disappeared, replaced with a pair of cowboy boots. Another snap and his tailored dress pants turned into jeans, complete with leather chaps and a belt with a gigantic belt buckle. His dress shirt was now a plaid button-down.

He grinned, and when he snapped his fingers once more, Calliope stood there in the most over-the-top outdated western get-up he could conjure—a long denim skirt sporting a patch of embroidered roses, cowboy hat and boots, and a collared chambray shirt with rope fringing across the front.

"You can't be serious," she said, folding her arms.

The angry look on her face made his palms go sweaty, but he ignored it. Why would she be mad at him for trying to lighten the mood? He shrugged away the uncertainty and forged ahead with his attempt at humor. "You know what they say . . . When in Rome."

"This isn't Rome, and you know these clothes are from, like, the wrong decade, right?" She grabbed the straps of the striped Kate Spade travel duffel that had appeared beside her with a huff.

"Oh, I know," he replied, taking his eyes of her for just a second, so he could pick up the black leather Versace weekender bag next to him. He broke out into a full-fledged hot and prickly sweat when he looked up and saw her stomping away. "But you look so fetching in them?"

CHAPTER FIFTEEN

Apollo had finally adjusted to the air, but now it was the silence between him and Calliope that was growing uncomfortably heavy.

"What do you think of this?" he began, trying to engage her in conversation to warm up the cold shoulder she was giving him. "When I find her, I will firmly—but nicely—tell her she has to go back to Mount Olympus. Or maybe I should just go the stern route and say, *'It's ridiculous for you to stay down here on Earth, we're going back immediately.'* What do you think?"

"Sure, boss." Calliope's irritated tone teetered on the verge of being downright angry. "That sounds like a good plan."

She couldn't still be peeved about his joke earlier, could she? He had only done it to try and lighten the mood. To let her know he was sorry for almost blowing it. Except, he supposed he technically hadn't said he was sorry for anything.

He sighed, and she rolled her eyes at him in response. Not in the patient, playful way like she normally did, either.

He'd switched their clothes to something more fitting for the present day almost immediately, but she still seemed upset. He had the sneaking suspicion it had more to do with that mortal's near-death experience and less about his poor attempt at being funny.

All right, fine, he didn't just have a feeling, he *knew* the reason why she was upset was *because* he'd almost wasted that guy, and then had tried to disguise a non-apology as an apology. But it wasn't like her to carry on this long. She usually got over such trivial things more quickly. He nibbled on his bottom lip, wondering how long she was prepared to keep sulking. She was the only person who could talk sense into him, and he couldn't afford for her to be angry.

Also, he didn't *want* her to be angry. But he didn't know how to make her *not* angry.

Just apologize for real, you idiot.

"Of course it's a good plan," he continued, holding the door to a run-down motel open, hoping things would miraculously go back to normal on their own. "But do you think it's a good *idea*?"

Calliope turned sideways, avoiding eye contact and passing through as though he was a certain snake-infested gorgon and looking at him might turn her to stone.

He followed her to the front desk, the feeling he'd finally gone and pushed her to her limit growing stronger. He should get it over with and offer her a more direct apology, for not taking this acquisition seriously, but how could he manage that with his throat tightened like this? Besides, that would mean he'd have to convince his pride to ease up. Not an easy task, considering it was currently holding all words hostage, especially "I'm" and "sorry."

In his defense, he never walked away from a fight, and she *knew* that. Hadn't it been his right to accept such a challenge? Hadn't that man deserved everything he almost got?

Apollo's shoulders slumped under the weight of the answers: No, and not really. He was just trying to find ways to excuse what he'd done, and he knew it. The truth was his actions had upset Calliope, and he had to try harder to not let his victor rise to every punch thrown his way. She was on his side, his partner in all of this, and as much as his pride and his victor would swear up and down it wasn't true if pressed, this acquisition might fall through without her.

Worship he understood, and he had no problem wrapping his head around admiration, if it was for him, of course. It was humility that was confusing. Respect that was hard to comprehend. Apparently, teamwork was a two-way street, and if they were going to retrieve the nymph with any amount of success, he had to start acting like a team player, not an arrogant fuck who dressed up his assistant like a doll for a laugh.

The petite, young woman at the front desk tore her eyes away from the mobile phone she was trying to hide behind the counter as they approached. When her blue-eyed gaze landed on him, it widened. "I got this one, Tonya." She yelled into the back room, nearly getting tangled up in her own two feet and falling onto the floor when she stood up from her stool. "Hi there. Need a room?"

"We do," said Apollo.

"Just one?" The girl's eyes flicked toward Calliope. Hope arched her brows when her gaze returned to Apollo. He could practically hear her praying to her monotheistic god that they needed two.

He glanced at Calliope, who was gnawing a fingernail while looking anywhere but at him. He was tempted to say they only needed one room, but he'd already taken too many liberties for one day. Plus, the aggressive way she was chewing on her cuticle made it perfectly clear one room would not be a good idea. "Two. Right next to each other if you can manage it."

The girl smiled as her fingers flew over the keyboard at a blinding rate of speed, clearly thinking she might have a chance.

A second woman came out of the back room. Her gray hair and pronounced crow's feet emphasized how sick and tired she was with the hand that life had dealt her. "What'd you say, Amanda—oh, hello."

"I said I got it." Amanda practically snarled as she threw a harsh look Tonya's way.

"Calm down, Mandy. I'm just doing my job. What rooms are you giving them? I'll get the keys."

Apollo handed over his Life Industries corporate card, and after a few more minutes of accelerated tapping on the keyboard from Amanda, the printer clanged to life. She slid the paperwork toward Apollo before informing Tonya, "It's *Amanda*. Now please get the keys for 12A and 12B."

Careful to use his new alias, Apollo penned it with great flourish before accepting the keys Tonya held out to him. "Entitled Millennials. Think they know everything," muttered Tonya under her breath before pasting on a smile. "Continental breakfast starts at eight—"

Amanda interrupted Tonya's spiel. "Ah, breakfast starts at seven, actually, and if you need anything at all just ring me here at the front desk. I'm working evenings all week."

"Thank you, ladies." Apollo wasted no time turning toward Calliope and leaving the Millennial and Baby Boomer to finish duking out their generational grievances in private. "So you don't think force is going to work, then?"

"Probably not," Calliope mumbled around her thumbnail.

Apollo dipped his toe further into the Pool of Apology and tested the Turn It Back On Her Waters because, quite frankly, he was desperate and starting to go through Nice Calliope withdrawals. "You're acting like a disgruntled goddess. What's the matter?"

She stopped biting her nail and tilted her head at him. His mouth went dry at the site of her flared nostrils, and his heart hammered in his chest. For Fates' sake, what in Hades' Realm was wrong with him? How did he always manage to say the wrong thing? Better yet, why couldn't he even get a simple apology right?

Her eyes narrowed to slits. "I'm sorry," she said dryly. "In case you hadn't noticed, I take my job very seriously. I don't use my magic on you, so please don't use yours on me. I don't want to be down here any more than you do, okay?"

He nodded. Using people to make himself feel better was a bad habit of his. It was why the Pool of Apology was freezing and the foot he'd managed to insert in his mouth tasted awful.

He handed over her room key before picking up both their bags. When they reached the door, he held it open. His revelation made a difficult apology even harder, so he tried approaching from a different angle, at least for the time being. "Are you hungry? We should seek sustenance."

She gave him a thin smile and started off across the parking lot.

Hmm. A smile, but it was weak, and there'd been no verbal response to accompany it. Poseidon's soggy balls, she might be even more upset with him than he suspected.

When they reached their rooms, he nodded his head toward the diner across the road. "How about we go check that place out after we get ourselves settled?"

"Sounds good," she murmured, fumbling with the lock.

He found himself wanting to reach out and touch her, to lay a hand on her shoulder and ease her discomfort. To say he was sorry for being such a total jackass. But he took too long thinking about it, and when she finally got the door unlocked, she didn't so much as glance his way before slipping inside.

Apollo followed suit, pushing away the urge to follow after her. He needed to apologize, with actual words. If they were going to find Daphne, he needed her to be working with him, not against him. The thought of losing her help scared him.

He frowned, biting the inside of his cheek as he stepped into his room. Or, maybe it was the fact that, for the first time he could remember, he really felt the need to say he was sorry, and it was frightening.

On top of that, he was having trouble keeping rogue images of them together out of his head. They were both already stressed, and this was not the time to create more, for either of them. He knew what could happen when they both needed to let off steam, and it would just complicate matters.

But it was even more than *that*.

Something much bigger than bringing back Daphne. He couldn't quite put his finger on it yet, but it was there.

He pushed the pesky existential thoughts out of his mind and set his bag on the suitcase stand. After surveying his surroundings, he wiped a finger through the dust on top of the television. Wholly unsuitable for a being of his divinity. Irritation expanded his chest as he wiped the dirt from his finger. This sojourn into the mortal world was so inconvenient, on all levels, and he didn't know who he blamed more: Himself or Eros.

His thoughts turned to Calliope again as he unpacked, and his shoulders relaxed. When all was said and done, he was grateful she was down here helping him. She always knew what to do. He was the muscle behind his numerous victories, but somewhere along the way, she'd become the brains, and he wasn't sure his long list of achievements over the centuries would have been as great without her.

The sound of a dripping faucet suddenly got louder. Apollo flipped on the light of a tiny room and inspected the smallest bathhouse he'd ever laid eyes on. He had occasionally indulged in bathing and oiling in his youth, during some clandestine trip down to Crete when he'd gotten bored, but how modern mortals enjoyed bathing in such a cramped space was beyond his comprehension.

He waved his hand, and the faucet stopped its incessant racket. Another wave of his hand and his motel room transformed into a spacious luxury suite.

Much better.

Satisfied, he moved on to more important things. Things like thinking of Calliope as he regarded his appearance in the expansive mirror, inspecting his perfect posture and admiring his trim and muscled physique. How was it even possible for her to be mad at him? And, honestly, how could Daphne not return his affection?

Oh, yeah. He was an ass. And also, he was cursed.

He stared at his reflection without blinking. What was the mortal saying? Beautiful on the outside, ugly on the inside? He resisted the urged to smash a fist into the glass. Unfortunately, ugly was all he had to work with at the moment. What Daphne truly thought of him wasn't important in the grand scheme of things, and when he convinced her to go back to Mount Olympus and the curse was finally lifted as promised, perhaps then he could work on the beautiful on the inside as well as the outside part.

But right now, all that mattered was being free.

And making Calliope happy again. He wanted that, too. Luckily he didn't have to wait to right that wrong. He could start now, by refraining from engaging in any more physical altercations from here on out. And also by offering her a proper apology. It might hurt his pride a little, but that was fine, he owed her a pound of flesh.

Besides, once the curse was broken, it wouldn't even matter. He could work on changing that prideful part of himself once he wasn't spending all of his time trying to win over a nymph who hated his guts. Sweet Persephone, he could hardly wait to put that part of his past behind him.

To do that, however, he needed a plan.

"Well, hot shot? What are you going to do?" he asked his reflection.

His reflection didn't answer, but his brain piped up with an image of Calliope's smiling face.

When his reflection finally spoke, it said, "Say you're sorry."

He nodded, intent on following through with his own advice. And since honesty was always the best policy, he decided he would also simply explain to the nymph the ultimatum he'd been given. If she stopped running long enough to listen, that part should be easy.

The hard part would be going against the very thing he stood for by convincing her to lie.

CHAPTER SIXTEEN

*H*ad he actually called her a *disgruntled goddess?* Yeah, no. She was a freaking *muse*, one that didn't even want to be down on Earth with him in the first place. Especially now that she'd found out he wasn't taking this *Mission: Totally Possible* of his more seriously. Did he not realize that he'd almost ruined the entire operation? And did he think dressing her up like a doll for his amusement was *funny?*

There had been some expensive toiletries, and even more expensive designer clothes in the bag, though.

She shook her head, frustrated at herself for even thinking such a thought. She'd much rather be back on Mount Olympus being ordered around, or maybe experiencing those hot pokers to the eyes. Anything would be better than playing second fiddle to a nymph.

But she'd opened her big mouth and gotten herself into this mess, and now she was stuck trying to make the bed she'd made for herself somehow more comfortable to lie in.

She flung the now empty bag onto the bed and looked around. Not the best, but not the worst. Hopefully, once they located the *target* they wouldn't be here that long. Oklahoma was a decent sized area to search, but since Callie had pretty much pinpointed what's-her-face's location, in *theory*, it shouldn't take them all that long to find her.

"Almighty Zeus," she muttered, knowing her prayer would most likely go unheard. "Please have mercy and let us find that lowly nymph ASAP."

The moment the words left her mouth, she cringed. Calling the nymph lowly was a low blow. It wasn't the nymph's fault she had been in the wrong place at the wrong time, and things always happened for a reason, didn't they? Maybe this whole thing was the kick in the laurel wreath Callie needed to get on with her life.

If Daphne had stayed a tree, things would have carried on business as usual. Apollo would have continued to visit the Sacred Forest every day, and Callie would have woken up and gone to work thinking there'd be a snowball's chance in Hades' Realm that she and Apollo would actually end up together.

And she wouldn't be here now, having to admit that her sister was right.

With a heavy sigh, she decided seeing the glass as half full was the better option. Seeing it half empty was making her supremely grouchy, and she didn't like this pessimistic side of her. At all. "Sweet Persephone, rescue me from this mess," she amended her prayer as she dug her journal out from beneath the pile of designer clothes.

She busied her hands by putting the clothes back into the bag, but her mind insisted on ruminating over the depressing thoughts clambering around in her head. The possibility of Daphne seeing the light was much greater than it had been when she had branches for limbs, and gods only knew, Apollo always got what he wanted. Which, if she stopped and thought about it, wasn't saying much as far as she was concerned.

He doesn't want you, Callie. He never did, and he never will.

Her sister was right. The sooner Callie could get that through her thick skull, the better. She needed to get this over with, help him convince Daphne she loved him so they could all get on with their immortal lives.

Oh, enough was enough. She abandoned her bag and exited her room to knock on Apollo's door.

"Enter."

She did as instructed, and like magic, her depressing thoughts vanished the minute her lips quirked up at Apollo's decked-out room. Luxury apartment was more accurate. It could hardly be classified as one room anymore, seeing as there were now several.

She shook her head as she reached for the Do Not Disturb sign so she could hang it on the door knob. Gods, he was incorrigible. "You might want to change this back whenever we leave, as an extra precaution, or else housekeeping will have quite a shock. Not to mention we'll have to ask my mother to alter their memories. That's always a pain."

Why couldn't she stay mad at him? Without thinking, she inhaled deep, pulling in the comforting scent that always accompanied Apollo. It was hard to describe, but he smelled like warmth. The closest thing she could liken it to was sun-kissed skin, bleached driftwood and lush, tropical sea breezes.

"Don't worry." He strode over to the door and, of course, she followed close behind like a duckling. "Housekeeping won't be a concern. Are you ready?"

Once out in the parking lot, Apollo traced an outline of the door with his finger and, sure enough, when Callie peeked inside the window, the room had gone back to its original dingy, late 1990's explosion of burgundy with contrasting mauve accents.

After walking across the street, they entered the diner and settled into a booth by the window. A server came by to drop off two waters, setting the red plastic cups down on the paper placemats before promising to come back. Callie's stomach growled, and Apollo's smile reached his eyes. Annoying as it was, their mortal shells needed sustenance.

She took a sip of water, forcing the dull and tasteless liquid down. It was nothing compared nectar. "So, I've been thinking."

"Yes?" Apollo scanned the menu. She wasn't sure why since she knew he wasn't going to order anything. Quail eggs —his favorite—weren't popular around these parts.

"I like your idea about being direct, but what if you tried a different approach?," she asked. "What if you woo her?"

Why was she suggesting this? And was she referring to the nymph . . . or herself?

"Woo her? That's interesting," said Apollo. "I don't think I've ever needed to try and woo anyone before."

His gaze landed on her before dropping back down to the menu in his hands, and that was all it took for the memory of their three nights and one long afternoon that eventually turned into a night together, of what he did to her with those hands, to flash through her mind. When it did, the sequence of events was still so vivid her cheeks warmed considerably.

She took another sip of water, refusing to dwell on how gentle his touch had been. It didn't matter anymore. It had probably never mattered to him at all. "Well, maybe you try it now. And you can start with *asking* her to spend some time with you, so you can get to know each other."

"I don't ask, Calliope. I tell," remarked Apollo, still scanning the menu.

"And how's that worked out for you?"

He looked up, his eyes holding her captive again.

Oops.

"Point taken," he finally said.

Apollo went back to searching the laminated piece of paper for a halfway suitable meal. "All right, then. Once we find her, I'll ask her if she'd like to spend some time together. What on Earth does one do while getting to know each other, anyway?"

Their server came over, pen and pad of paper at the ready. "Howdy. What can I get y'all."

"Bring us eggs, all the olives you've got, and do you have goat cheese?"

"I . . . can check?" said the young woman, her bubbly demeanor fizzling rapidly. "Do you want that in an omelet?"

Her furrowed brow was hard to miss.

"That would be great," Callie said with a reassuring smile, handing the menus to the girl and waiting for her to leave before explaining the mechanics of courtship as if she had any kind of experience with it. "It's called a date, I believe, and I don't know. Talk? Maybe you can ask her what her favorite color is."

"Are you sure? I know your favorite color, and I didn't even have to ask."

Callie's heart picked up, so she took another sip of water. It seemed her physical reactions were more pronounced down here. "How do you know my favorite color?"

"Well, you wear yellow at least three times a week, you favor canaries, and your outlook, therefore your aura, is always sunny."

"Oh." Now her heart was really pumping. He'd noticed and had called her out quite thoroughly on top of it. "Well, that's probably because we've worked together for so long."

"No, it's because—" Apollo stopped. "Yes, that's how I know. Now, what other ideas do you have?"

Callie nibbled on a thumbnail, giving her cheeks some time to cool. Once her skin was back at a normal temperature, she tucked both hands under her legs to keep her fingers out of her mouth. Was there anything more torturous than this? "Okay, after you find out as much as you can about what she likes and dislikes, maybe you can get her a gift. You know, something from the heart."

Apollo lifted an eyebrow at her. "You're starting to sound like Eros."

"Eros is a good god. Why do you hate him so much?"

Apollo gave her a thoughtful look. "I don't hate him, I suppose." He bit the inside of his cheek as he contemplated his stance on the matter. "I just . . . Feel he might still have the wrong impression of me. I'm not the same god I used to be. Or I'm trying not to be, at least."

Sweet Persephone, why was he opening up to her now? It made all the barricades she was trying to put up, with the express purpose of keeping him out, more like flimsy walls. Crumbling ones at that.

"Look, I know Zeus abandoned you and Artemis when you were young, but you don't need to prove your greatness, to Eros or anyone else." Her gaze dropped to the floor for an instant before she peeked back up at him. Almost as immediately, it landed on her water glass. "Especially not to me." She clasped her hands together in her lap. That hole she'd dug? Yeah, it was getting deeper, and if there was ever a time she wanted to bite a fingernail, it was now.

The waitress came by to deposit their plates. "Everything look good? Okay, great." She turned and high-tailed it before either of them could respond.

Apollo picked up a fork, and after a long pause inspecting the food on his plate, he said, "I don't think these are quail eggs." He taste-tested a few bites. "Definitely not quail. Chicken, maybe? Anyway. What else should I do, then?"

She stabbed at her omelet as disappointment jabbed at her already tender feelings. That's it? She'd let her guard down to comfort him and he'd decided to ignore it? Well, she wanted him to feel the sting of rejection, too, then. "Try being a little more selfless and a lot less selfish."

Apollo straightened, his head jerking back in disbelief, jaw stopping mid-chew. He swallowed his mouthful of food. "Do you really think I'm selfish?"

She shoveled another bite into her mouth and chewed, buying herself more time before she answered. "What I meant was maybe try giving her something you know *she* likes, not something *you* think she likes."

Apollo's stare was blank, his eyes darting from table top to napkin dispenser to the extra bundle of silverware as he sifted through his mental notes.

"You can't think of anything she likes, can you?"

"Not off the top of my head, no."

"Okay, well, how about music? Everyone likes music. Your lyre playing is beautiful." There went her eyes again, down to the ground. "So is your voice."

"Yes." Apollo nodded. "That could work. Have I told you lately how brilliant you are?" Without warning—and by gods she needed warning if she was going to have any chance at keeping it together even remotely successfully—Apollo's face beamed bright as the sun. "You know, I really have no idea what I'd do without you." Apollo gave her that look as he slid out of the booth. The look of awe, of pure, uncensored appreciation. The one that was her downfall. Every. Damned. Time.

"In fact, you've inspired me not to wait any longer. No time like the present to start looking, right?"

"What about . . .?"

She'd been about to try and convince him that they should start their search in the morning when Apollo grinned, his eyes darting toward her plate. She looked down at her half-eaten omelet. "Yeah, it didn't taste as good as it looked."

"Right?" he said. "Goat cheese really would have made the dish. But, no, look under your plate."

Callie lifted the plate and discovered a credit card with the Life Industries thunderbolt logo emblazoned across the front. She'd only been waiting for a company card for ages. It made traveling so much easier when she came down for one of her inspiration sprees. "Oh my gods, really?"

"Of course," said Apollo. "It's long overdue. And I'm sorry for poking fun at you. We are a team, and I promise to take my part in this just as seriously as you are from here on out, starting right now. Why don't you go back to the hotel and relax while I do a preliminary search to see if I can locate our nymph."

Our nymph?

His apology softened her glare, and it even made her belly flutter, but Callie could barely stop herself from rolling her eyes as she slid over the vinyl seat. She wanted nothing to do with Daphne, and she wished Apollo didn't either, but he couldn't know that. As far as he was concerned, there was no other option but to locate her and drag her kicking and screaming back to Mount Olympus. "Okay, boss, you're forgiven. But how about we meet up later and go over next steps . . ."

When Callie looked up, Apollo was already halfway to the door. She pursed her lips, and unleashed the eye roll she'd kept under wraps earlier. Of course he was eager to find the nymph, and sooner rather than later. What in Hades' Realm else had she expected?

CHAPTER SEVENTEEN

The scorching Oklahoma sun beat down on Daphne. She didn't mind, though, because she was at what was quickly becoming one of her favorite places in the world. The Caddo County farmers market.

"Thanks for the ride, Judy," she said before proceeding to unload a few dozen baskets of vegetables from the back of the pickup truck. It belonged to Judy Pitkins, one half of the adorable old couple that lived a mile down the road from Sam.

"You bet, Dee." Judy wiggled her fingers at her before heading to her table to arrange jars of preserves next to the metal tabletop rack adorned with handmade wind chimes and dream catchers.

The brim of her cowboy hat protected Daphne's face. Her arms, however, got the full brunt of UV rays as she carried the large baskets over to the permanent vegetable stand Sam had built several years ago.

"Remember to drink plenty of water, missy. She's a hot one today." Judy called out to Daphne when she walked by with the last bushel of radishes.

Sweat dotted Daphne's upper lip as she made sure the tape holding the "ART FOR SALE" sign to the front of the table she'd set up next to the vegetable stand was secure. She took off her hat to swipe at her forehead with the back of her hand before using it to fan herself. Hat replaced atop her head, she settled into a folding chair. After hooking the heels of her boots on the support bar, she took a long sip of her vanilla iced latte and leaned over to arrange the small watercolor paintings for optimal viewing.

It was her third time at the market. She'd sold a lot of vegetables, sure, but she'd gotten a lot more than money in return. She'd made friends, and she'd even made sixty dollars of her own so far selling paintings. True, most folks just wanted to look, but if she struck up a conversation, asked them about their lives, they tended to do more than that.

Their smiles were all different, crooked ones just as precious at the straight ones. Their bellies jiggled when they chuckled. Their eyes sparkled when giggles turned into laughs, the corners crinkling into beautiful lines, showing signs of good times and bad. And with each person who stopped by her table, she fell a little deeper in love with the human race.

On the other hand, while it felt amazing to get to know them, to hear their stories and grin at their gossip, she'd probably have the money she needed to pay back Sam for the boots sooner rather than later. Once she paid him back, there was really no good reason to stick around.

She was getting too attached to Sam, which was not the plan.

She inhaled a lungful of dusty air, resigned not to think about that just yet, and opened the romance novel Judy had lent her. Absently shaking the ice in her clear plastic cup, she continued to read about rakish dukes falling in love with independent ladies. She bit her bottom lip as her eyes raced across the page, devouring each word and trying not to miss a single one while also trying to get to the good part, the part where they . . .

"I've often wondered what radishes tasted like," a voice interrupted her reading.

It was deep and smooth. Regal in pitch and tone. Familiar.

Daphne bolted upright, heart pounding hard and fast like the hooves of a wild mustang. She wanted to take off like one, too. The book in her hand bounced off her leg before falling to the ground, as a book tends to do when the person holding it loses feeling in their fingers.

"I jest. I prefer Ambrosia." Apollo peered down at her with those striking blue eyes of his. "Hello, Daphne."

An alarmed huff rocketed from her throat, followed by a scratchy whisper. "How? How did you find me so fast?"

His gaze dropped to the card table for an instant. "It wasn't that difficult."

Daphne's head throbbed against her temples in time with her frustration. *Why? Why? Why?* "Why can't you leave me be?"

"Come now, Daphne." Apollo tapped his fingers on the table twice, as if he had no time or inclination for ignorance, but was trying to remain patient. "We both know the answer to that."

Her cheeks grew hot, and her lips pressed together. He was being patronizing, and the fists at her sides itched to thank him for it by landing a solid punch.

Apollo took stock of her tightly balled hands, the firm set of her jaw, the daggers in her eyes, ready to be deployed "I know you dislike me." There was an uncharacteristic air of uncertainty in his words. "But I think it's just because you don't know me. We've never really gotten a chance to get to know one another."

Daphne launched the daggers. Was he serious? She knew

exactly who he was, a relentless bastard. What else was there to know?

"The real me," he finished hastily.

"Is there a real you? The mighty Apol—" She caught herself and stopped. The young woman at the table to the right gazed out over the market, pretending to be oblivious to the commotion, but Daphne knew better. As much as the residents were growing on her, this was a small town, with a close-knit community of folks who made it a point to know every birth and keep track of every death. Who knew who was dating and who'd just broken up. And who was fighting with whom. Caddo County was one giant grapevine.

"Paul," offered Apollo.

Daphne snorted. "Paul?" Clever, but he was still an asshole. "Worshiped and adored for his brilliance."

"And strength," he added, his eyebrows lifting. "You know, because I've single-handedly won . . ."

Did he really think she would finally, after all these centuries, be impressed?

"Ugh." Daphne groaned. She was the furthest thing from it. "My gods, you are the worst."

"I'm not . . ."

Was that hurt flashing in his sky-blue eyes, darkening to storm-cloud gray as he spoke? His golden aura heated, glowing like the sun, and Daphne cringed.

"The worst at anything," he finished. "Please don't make this harder than it has to be. I've changed—or at least I'm trying. Look, I have a plan. All you have to do is trust me."

"No thanks."

Apollo's face hardened, the sky suddenly darkening and a strong gust of wind blowing through the market. The middle-aged woman in the next booth jumped up and laid her arms across her baskets of green beans to prevent them from blowing off the table and scattering over the ground.

"What are you doing?" whispered Daphne.

"Something I don't want to do but most assuredly will if you don't cooperate." The wind began to whip, and fat drops of rain pelted the ground. "This whole town will suffer if you continue running from me."

When Daphne folded her arms, intent on calling his bluff, a sickly looking rat scurried between her feet and staggered toward Judy's booth. Another appeared, and then another, until there were dozens zig-zagging throughout the market.

She scowled at him the moment she understood. He would punish her by raining plague down upon the people she cared about.

"Fine, what do you want?" she said, frantic.

The rain lightened to a drizzle, and the sun peeked through the clouds again.

"A date," said Apollo casually.

"A what?" Irritation and fear warred for dominance, making her words come out as a hiss.

"Everything okay, Daphne?" called Judy from across the way.

Daphne leaned back in her chair, sucking in a breath and glaring up at Apollo as she pushed it back out. "Everything's fine, Judy. Thank you."

Gods, she despised him. He never could take no for an answer, and he always pushed her right to her limit. It would appear nothing had changed over the centuries.

"It's called a date," said Apollo. "Apparently, it's a meeting where we get to know each other. But I also have something important I wish to discuss with you."

Daphne clamped her teeth onto her upper lip. There was no way in Hades' Realm she wanted to agree to spending even one minute alone with him, let alone have a discussion, but what other choice did she have? Apollo would hold true to his word and make everyone in this town suffer just to get his way.

She cursed the Fates under her breath.

"I will go on this date thing with you, but I get to choose the time and place."

"You have three days." Apollo didn't look at her as he delivered his mandate, but at the watercolors arranged on the corner of the table. He picked one up, inspecting it with interest. "You know, to decide. These are quite good, by the way. I didn't know you painted."

Of course he didn't. He didn't know anything about her. Never had and, if she had anything to say about it, never would. Daphne's mind raced. Her worst nightmare had come true. Apollo had found her. Now what was she supposed do?

Whatever you do, don't think about . . .

Too late. Sam's hazel eyes popped into her head, and the way they crinkled at the corners when he smiled. Of all the things there were to admire about the man, his eyes were her favorite. How the brown and gold and green mixed to produce a color so captivating she'd never know.

Admiration for Sam quickly turned to anger at Apollo, and it burned a path through her. This date thing was an elaborate ruse. Apollo didn't want to spend time with her. He wanted to control her. To win the game of cat and mouse started so long ago. She was one hundred percent positive he'd magic them back to the Sacred Forest the minute he got her alone.

If she agreed, however, at least she'd have a few days to figure out how to say goodbye before she was forced to go back. She'd also have a head start if she took off running again.

Furious, she rolled her eyes before snatching the painting from his hand. "Stop trying to flatter me. You've gotten what you came for. Now can you please go?"

The painting was something she'd done with Sam in mind. The thought of Apollo touching it made her stomach turn. What if he felt the emotion she'd poured into it? What if he could somehow sense who she'd been thinking about and then go looking for him? So he could crush the competition. He was a powerful god, and a petty one at that.

The revelation that Sam's life was undeniably at risk now kicked her square in her already churning gut. Yet, she didn't have time to fully process it because Apollo reached for her. It could have only been to shake on it, to make her word binding, who knew, but she shrank from him.

The muscles over his jawbone bunched, and he withdrew his hand. "Three days, Daphne."

It wasn't nearly enough time to say goodbye to Sam—and Sadie, Judy and Jud, Edna, Barney—because that's basically what it amounted to, and Apollo's needless reminder injected venom into her words. "Am I supposed to *thank* you for your generosity?"

His rigid stance softened as he scrubbed a hand over his mouth and chin. "You are so petulant."

"And you are so pompous," she spat, her blood reaching a boil.

He leaned over the card table, gripping the edges hard, the heat of his anger wafting on the humid afternoon breeze. The sudden force of his movement made the table bounce, upsetting the watercolors and sending them fluttering to the ground. Something that looked a lot like guilt swept across his face as he watched them fall.

But that was impossible. Apollo didn't have the first clue about guilt, let alone what it felt like. A cynical laugh bobbed in Daphne's throat. The only thing he knew how to do was feel sorry for himself. She folded her arms, and he released the table just as quickly as he'd seized it, the spots where his palms had been wrinkled and on the verge of a melted vinyl mess. Her gaze moved from one rippled spot to the other, prompting him to examine them as well.

The air in his lungs rushed out through his nose as he straightened, and as his head tilted toward the sky he closed his eyes. After collecting himself, he waved a hand over the table top, the man-made material smoothing out to its original state. Then he bent down to pick up the watercolors and placed them back on the table.

"It's a date then," he said before he turned and walked away. And for the first time in their complicated history, Daphne wanted to run after him.

So she could strangle the bastard.

CHAPTER EIGHTEEN

Sweet Persephone, he'd done it. Barely, but that wasn't the point. All that mattered was Daphne had agreed to this date thing, without his having to use force. Well, *much* force, anyway. He wouldn't lie when he told Calliope the news, but he didn't see the harm in glossing over that part. What was more important was the look on her face when he told her he'd actually located and then convinced the nymph to go on a date with him on his own. He could barely wait to see that megawatt smile light up Calliope's face when she found out.

Apollo almost burst out laughing as he turned the ignition on a sleek Audi R8. He'd seen a dealer commercial playing on the television in the motel lobby. All he'd had to do was think it into existence, and it had been waiting for him outside the motel that morning. He was riding such a high right now—the engine's substantial horsepower, the fact he had big news to share with Calliope, locating Daphne almost as easily as it had been to conjure the car—and he felt invincible.

The R8 purred as he left the parking lot, a satisfied smile

still on his lips. He would loop Calliope in on his plan to first explain the situation to Daphne, and then convince her to go along with it. Once he got Calliope's input, he was sure they could figure out exactly what he had to say to talk the nymph into saying she loved him out loud.

It was a means to an end, and the thought of it actually working made the hair on his arms rise. His skin tightened when a surge of adrenaline coursed through his veins, but Callie's face, complete with pursed lips, popped into his mind, and his elation deflated.

Hack.

He shook away the thought. He'd deal with it later. Right now, he had to do whatever it took to be rid of the curse. The only thing he should be thinking about was mapping out the best course of action for his date with the nymph.

Apollo ran his fingers through his hair, trying to switch focus, but his mind insisted on exploring all the ways he was a fraud. In particular, how sad it was he had to resort to trickery in order to get the nymph to cooperate. The biggest winner on Mount Olympus was actually a total loser. No one really liked him, they just all pretended they did. He huffed a short, frustrated breath. He should have respected the god of love's power a little more.

Okay, a lot more.

He tried to shove the thought away. Now wasn't the time to examine his mistakes.

No, really. Why *had* he felt the need to pick on Eros that day?

Apollo gave in and flipped through his mental Rolodex of most troubling questions. Almost immediately, he landed on Dionysus. Then Hera, and the words he'd found out she'd said, through the gossip mill of all places, which went a little something like, *"Leto shall give birth nowhere on terra firma nor water."*

Well, guess what? His mother had persevered and, even being chased by Python, had finally found a place to deliver on the island of Delos. Artemis had come first, and then helped their mother bring him into the world. When he'd found out how the whole thing had gone down, what his mother had gone through at the hands of Hera, and indirectly, a kowtowing Zeus, that's when Apollo had vowed to prove to the bastard just how big of a mistake it had been to choose Hera over his mother.

His hands gripped the steering wheel hard, turning his knuckles white. So, basically, his anger and resentment had pretty much started the day he was born. It was all there, the events he tried to ignore but couldn't. The irrefutable evidence that proved he'd never be good enough. That he'd always be a pathetic loser.

Apollo slammed the door shut on the painful memories, and as his surroundings slowly came back into focus, he realized the R8 was idling in the middle of the road with him still in it. He blinked a few times, discovering he had no idea where he was or what had happened other than he'd blacked out on a deserted country road down on Earth somewhere in a place called Oklahoma.

The road before him seemed to stretch on for an eternity. He was tempted to take it, so he could escape all of this . . . whatever it was he was feeling.

For the first time in his life, he understood why Daphne always ran, and he shifted the Audi into gear, jamming his foot down on the gas pedal until he was flying down the open stretch.

60 MPH.

A torrent of emotions threw themselves against his chest.

75 MPH.

His jaw clenched so hard he heard a tooth crack.

110 MPH.

Anger and hurt jettisoned from the depths of his wounded soul, and when he roared, the windows shattered, spraying tinted and tempered glass onto the asphalt.

He slammed on the brakes, and the car screeched to a halt. "Fuck!" He pounded his fists into the steering wheel. Naturally, it crumpled into the dashboard.

"Why doesn't anyone love me?" he bellowed, hating his insatiable need to be revered, but not knowing how to quench his endless thirst. He despised how just thinking of his father could expose him so easily, drag such painful realizations and hurtful truths into the light. And he was angry that he couldn't control them. Defeat them. It would be so much easier if they were tangible monsters, ones he could pummel with his fists. Rip apart with his bare hands and cast aside or drag up a mountain.

He wanted to be nothing like his father, with his imperious one-track mind. At the same time, Apollo couldn't help but obsess about the one thing that never seemed to be enough, just like his father did. In Zeus's case, it was a lust for women. In his, a deeply ingrained need to be the best. To always be the victor, at any cost.

Whatever the vice, he was just like his father, and it drove him right into a vicious circle he wasn't strong enough to break. A fact he tried to hide by overcompensating. For everything.

Spent and drained, he flopped his head against the headrest. Calliope, with her lemon-scented ivory skin and unbelievable blue eyes, floated into his mind and his shoulders relaxed. Just thinking of her, and her infectious can-do attitude, reassured him. Like everything else, he could pull this off with her by his side. She was always so positive and patient, and he . . . Could be such an insufferable dick sometimes. It was a wonder she hadn't thrown in the towel long ago.

He looked down at the passenger seat, bits of glass strewn across the black hand-stitched leather, and sighed. What would Calliope think of his outburst?

That was a bit much, don't you think, boss?

With a wave of his hand, the glass—and his throbbing tooth—reassembled itself in an instant, and the steering wheel popped out into its original state, like nothing ever happened.

Like he hadn't just lost his shit.

In all fairness, he'd just thought through some really heavy stuff.

He shook his head, flinging the rest of his unanswered questions to the corners of his mind. There were too many of them to deal with, especially when he should be channeling all of his energy on figuring out how to get the nymph onboard with his plan.

Lying was something *he* would never do, but it was the only conceivable way he could think of to get Daphne to go back to Mount Olympus and declare that she loved him, out loud, so Eros would lift the curse.

Hypocrite.

Apollo swallowed the bile creeping up his throat, his uncertainty about whether or not he was going to be able to pull it off tasting far less than palatable. Originally, he'd wanted to curse broken for his own selfish reasons. Mainly, so his reputation as a strong and formidable god would remain unblemished. Come Hades or high water, as long as it would have ended with him as the victor, that would have been good enough for him.

But now . . . now there was more to it. A lot more, and continuing to play the victim wasn't going to prove anything, to anyone, much less convince them to lie for him. He had to be completely honest with the nymph, or else it would mean she had been unfairly dragged into this mess because of him.

And poor Calliope, she shouldn't have to put her life on hold because he was an unlikable ass and refused to admit it. She always put him first, even though he didn't deserve it.

Thoroughly exhausted, Apollo turned the car around. He'd known the truth all along, hadn't he? The god who claimed he never lied was the biggest liar of them all. It made him want to rage out of control; set his victor loose to leave a path of destruction in his wake.

Except, he wasn't sure that would make him feel better this time.

The only thing he *did* think would work was carefully packing his bruised and battered emotions into their respective boxes then going back to the motel to find Calliope. She would know what to do next.

She understood the deepest, darkest parts of him, without him even having to explain. And all he wanted right now, more than anything in the universe, was to hear the soothing sound of her voice.

CHAPTER NINETEEN

*D*aphne swallowed the saliva pooling in her mouth. Whatever Sam was cooking tonight smelled divine. Honestly, was there anything he couldn't do? Excellent investigative skills. Talented carpenter. Amazing at handling animals *and* people. Plus, he knew his way around a kitchen. Sam Carson, as it turned out, was good at everything. The man had the Midas touch, and after what happened earlier that afternoon, she could use some gold, especially for what she was about to do.

She admired the way the muscles moved under the button-down hugging his broad shoulders as he stirred whatever it was inside the large pot on the stove. The heavenly combination of tomatoes, peppers, onions, garlic—and bay leaves?—made her stomach growl.

She continued to watch him as he worked, inching her gaze lower before dragging it back up when he lifted his bottle of beer off the counter for a drink. Maybe she could satisfy more than one appetite before she slipped away into the night. He really was a fine-looking specimen.

"What's on the menu tonight?" she said, trying not to think about leaving. Or him naked. "It smells delicious."

"Ratatouille. After I'm done putting it together, it should be ready in about an hour."

Her stomached clenched. "Rat-a-what?" She gulped down air to keep her insides from lurching. She doubted it actually had rats in it, but even just saying the word in a kitchen made her queasy. It also reminded her of Apollo's threat.

Sam laughed through his nose as he tapped a wooden spoon on the rim of the pot before setting it down and taking another drink. He turned around to face her, leaning against the counter next to the stove. "It's a stewed vegetable dish. Ratatouille is a French word derived from *another* French word meaning "to stir up." He grinned wide. "Don't worry, the recipe doesn't call for vermin."

She sighed. He was so damn alluring. It really was a shame she had to run. She bit back a groan as she took a sip of the Bud Light he'd poured for her, and Sam turned off the stove and slid the pan onto a back burner so the contents could cool.

"That should do it for this." He punched a few buttons on the oven, then plugged in the blender before heading over to the refrigerator. Zucchini, more tomatoes, and an eggplant tumbled into a colander in the sink. He flipped on the faucet and let the water run over the vegetables while he got out a cutting board.

Gods, she hadn't imagined meal preparation could be this laborious. Then again, why would she have? She'd never needed sustenance when she was in the Sacred Forest. Partly because nymphs were generally too busy frolicking to eat. Mostly because soil and sunlight had been all she'd needed for thousands of years.

But now that she was here, she not only had to eat, she wanted to. Partaking in these mortal rituals, like working for a living and eating food to stay alive, well, it was growing on her. Plus, having a man to cook all her meals? She could get used to that.

Well, she could have gotten used to it. Damn Apollo for finding her so quickly, and curse this date nonsense. It left her no choice but to cut her losses and fly like a harpy out of Hades' Realm. There was no way she could make it through ten minutes with that pompous ass, let alone another three centuries.

Speaking of the devil, Apollo would definitely not do something like prepare a meal for her, or any sort of unselfish act for that matter. It was beneath him, or so he thought. He had wars to win, victories to claim, and snakes to wrestle. The god of every damned thing didn't have time for the simple things in life like Sam did.

Sam, who made her feel like she was walking on sunshine, not getting burned by it. He made her feel happier and more content than he should, and it made her sad because caring for Sam would eventually turn out to be all for nothing.

Daphne stifled another groan. There had been nothing else she could do but agree to spend time with Apollo, and it incensed her. He'd given her three days, but she doubted he would actually wait that long. From what she'd witnessed that afternoon, he still had about as much patience as a Kraken for a boatload of sailors. Her mind was made up, she had to leave tonight, but how was she going to bring herself to say goodbye in the next few hours?

An overwhelming wave of panic hit her, and it was so strong her stomach almost turned. She could always say nothing, just enjoy the evening and each other then slip away while he slept. As she watched Sam finish drying the vegetables and start cutting them into thin coins, her heart ached.

He'd already gone through that once. She couldn't be the one to put him through that again.

Neat stacks of zucchini and eggplant dotted the counter, and Sam deftly sliced through a second juicy tomato in no time. "Something on your mind?"

Her gaze settled on his long fingers. Calloused but beautiful. She'd always thought of mortal men as lumbering and clumsy, both mentally and physically. Not Sam. He was the farthest thing from either, and she was beginning to think her quest for freedom may have been doomed from the start. She'd run from the clutches of an egotistical god right into the kitchen of the most down-to-earth man in existence.

Pain and regret twined in her belly. She had to broach the subject now, or she'd never have the courage to go through with it. "Yeah . . . Can I ask your opinion about something?"

"Sure, Dee. You can ask me anything."

The term of endearment made her want to laugh and cry at the same time. She inhaled sharply, determined to keep from doing either.

"Do you think people can change?"

Why was she stalling?

"Sure, I think people can change, but only if they really want to. Sometimes it's better not to get your hopes up. I've learned the hard way that most times they just don't want to. Some people are too selfish to even try."

"Okay, well let's say they *tell* you they've changed? Should you believe it?" The heat in her cheeks spread to the tips of her ears. She already knew the answer. "Should you give them a chance to prove it? Asking for a friend."

"For a friend, huh?" He tried to smile, but she could see it took effort.

She knew what that faltering smile meant, and her stalling made her feel worse. She needed to rip off the bandage and get it over with. Stop this connection that was happening between them before it could get any deeper. There was no way she could spend the weekend under the stars with him now. She was already too attached. If she waited any longer, the bandage would take a whole lot more than skin with it.

"Sam, you're . . ."

"Working you too hard?" he said, laughing nervously as he sliced vegetables. He'd felt it, that something was off, and now *he* was stalling. The sick feeling in her gut grew, making her head spin. His grin faded, and he stopped to give her his full attention.

"No, your kindness has been amazing."

But she would rather leave than put Sam in even an ounce of danger. If she stayed, Apollo would remove all obstacles in his way, no questions asked. And sooner rather than later. Right now Sam was an obstacle. A big one. One she didn't want to get hurt—or killed. "But I'm going back to . . ." She couldn't say where she'd end up, she just knew she had to go, and unfortunately, her mouth automatically spit out the first location that popped into her mind. "Texas."

Good gods. Why Texas? Of all places, why had she said *Texas*? That's where his ex had gone off to with that doctor.

Sam's bottom lip disappeared between his teeth as he inspected the chopping board in front of him. When he finally lifted his head, his hazel eyes were full of something she was beginning to feel, too, and it almost knocked her off the stool.

"When?"

Tonight. After you fall asleep. "Tomorrow morning."

The broken look on Sam's face just about brought her to her knees. She hadn't said it, but he'd put two and two together that their weekend wasn't going to happen.

"You know I can't let you go back to a bad situation, Daphne."

Despite the good intention behind his words, the tone of his voice ignited another emotion. Anger. This was hard enough as it was, so why was he making it more difficult? It's not like she wanted to have to run again. "I have my reasons, okay? I'm sorry I can't tell you what those reasons are but I can't stay."

Gods dammit. She thought she'd have more time. Yet, here she was, angry at someone who, it was becoming abundantly clear, she didn't want to leave behind. In fact, she'd go so far as to say that she wanted to spend every waking moment with him. What made it worse? He would never know it because she would never have the chance to tell him.

Sam bent down to pull a baking dish from a cupboard. "Can't or don't want to?" He pursed his lips as he set the dish on the counter, his handsome, rugged features darkening.

She matched his intensity. She had to, or she'd crack and end up changing her mind. "Can't. Believe me, if I had a choice, I'd stay, but it's not possible. Please understand, Sam."

"Is it money? Is that it?"

Her heart plummeted. That's what he thought she cared about? Useless paper rectangles? He was way off base and headed in the completely wrong direction, but she couldn't correct the course he was on. Instead, she had to be strong enough to sacrifice what *could be* to prevent what she knew *would be* if she stayed.

She dodged his question. "I just can't stay, okay?" It wasn't about money, but if that misconception would slice deep enough to sever their connection, then she would let him believe it.

Sam nodded his head, arranging the vegetables around the edge of the dish. "I really wish you wouldn't do this. We haven't known each other long, but I—"

"I know you wish it could be different, Sam. So do I."

He stopped arranging to place his palms on the counter and bow his head, a war obviously waging inside him. When he sighed, the sound clawed at her heart so deeply that, before she could think of the consequences, she'd slid off the counter and went to him.

The hammering in her ears drowned out the thumping in her chest as she stood there, just looking at him, wishing things could be different. When she circled her arms around his waist and laid her head on his back she could feel how hard his heart was pounding, too. Her head spun with so many what if's it made her dizzy.

Was this what living life as a mortal felt like? Because she currently felt like dying.

Screaming obscenities at the Fates was a close second.

He placed a hand on one of her forearms, a silent admission that he was dealing with the same barrage of emotions. When Daphne felt his muscles tighten, it made hers stiffen as well. She could feel his hesitation, his uncertainty, and it was torture. While she wanted him to turn around and ask her to stay, she also didn't want him to say anything at all. To leave it alone and let her memorize the feel of him as she held him.

But he didn't leave it alone. He turned around.

"Is there anything I can do to convince you not to go?"

Her throat tightened, and the air in the room seemed to vanish. She was a nymph. He was a mortal. She was determined to leave, for both their sakes, but he very clearly wanted her to stay.

It couldn't happen.

He pulled her closer, and when he looked into her eyes, her resolve began to crumble.

It shouldn't happen.

But she'd never felt anything like this before.

She tilted her head up, drawn to him by an undeniable force, and he moved toward her, his earlier hesitation gone, the battle won, even though the war was far from over. When their lips met, she was helpless against it, against him. When Sam slid both hands to cradle the sides of her head, gently pulling her to him so he could deepen his kiss, she knew it was going to happen. She was going to stay with him as long as she could.

The tingle of cool water rippling over warm skin was invigorating, but his mouth on hers was unlike anything she'd ever experienced. It was more blissful than dancing in the moonlight dressed in nothing but wild abandon. More satisfying than the tickle of grass beneath her feet and the twinkle of stars above her head. If she thought she'd felt complete before, she was mistaken.

She pressed closer, matching his urgency. How could she not spend the time she had left with him? The longing to wrap herself around him grew stronger, weakening her.

Sam gifted her with smaller, less rushed kisses, too. On her lips, her cheeks, her temple, where he murmured, "I don't need to know your past to want to be in your future," before resting his cheek on the top of her head. "Give it the weekend. If you want to leave after that, I won't say a word."

Arms circled around his waist, head resting on his chest, she closed her eyes and breathed him in, reveling in the safety and comfort he so effortlessly gave to her. Yet, the world continued to spin out of control, right along with her head.

He'd said every word she'd needed to hear. So she held on tighter, desperately trying to figure out a way to never let go.

CHAPTER TWENTY

*C*allie stood outside Apollo's motel room door gnawing on what was left of her nails. This was it. She was going to tell him. Had to tell him, because although she'd been a big talker, promising the universe when all she had was her heart to give, she couldn't bear to go through with helping Apollo squash their relationship out of existence, even though it was only a working one.

Because if she thought Clio would let her work for him after that, she was crazy.

Her knock was light, and she waited for the *"Enter"* that would inevitably follow. Instead, footsteps, slow and measured, came closer and the door opened.

Apollo was dressed more casual than usual—flat-front gray chinos, light blue button-down, one side tucked in, the other side strategically left out, sleeves rolled up—and it made his golden hair even brighter and his tanned skin even smoother. "Hi."

She silently cursed that perfect French tuck for toying with her, making her knees weak as she peered up at him. "Hi."

To add insult to injury, his smile dazzled. It always did, but this evening's display was blinding. That was very bad news. The good news, however, was he seemed genuinely happy to see her, so she smiled back, even though she'd told herself not to.

Gods, she was hopeless.

He opened the door wider, and she slipped inside. Like before, his room was luxuriously appointed, but this time it was laid out more like an apartment, with a granite and stainless steel kitchen open to a spacious sunken living room. Large glass doors opened up to a veranda, with misty mountains in the background, not a skyscraper in sight.

Must be nice to have such power, to be able to physically manifest whatever one wanted. She could only inspire hearts, he could literally stop them from beating. Oh, and turn a motel room into a mansion. That, too.

"I found her," he said in a rush.

Callie's stomach clenched. "You did?" She pulled it in tighter so its contents wouldn't find its way up her throat and onto the floor. "How did it go?"

His smile was hesitant, and if she wasn't mistaken, more akin to a grimace. Although, she couldn't be sure of much in her panicked state.

"She agreed to a date." His gaze slid away as he turned toward the step that led down into the living room. "She needed a little convincing, but that's neither here nor there."

Callie followed him into the room and took a seat on the sleek leather couch, promptly shedding her bag from her shoulder and crisscrossing her legs beneath her. How else could she act beside one hundred percent unbothered? "Oh, that's great. When?"

Please say never . . .

"In three days. Would you like a drink?"

Callie swallowed hard as he walked over to the cabinet

stocked with liquor and filled a shaker with ice. He'd never offered her a drink before. "Sure, what is it, though?"

She hoped he'd say nectar of the gods. A surge of other-worldly strength would be wonderful right now.

"Something called a dirty martini. It sounded interesting. You like olives, right?" He popped one into his mouth before pouring some of the brine into the shaker.

"Uh huh." She swallowed again before nodding slowly. Even the way he chewed disarmed her.

Did she say hopeless? She meant *completely* hopeless. She was supposed to tell him she was tapping out, yet here she was, making small talk and having a drink.

Maybe that was good, though. Maybe this meant it would all be over soon.

"Hopefully she doesn't try and take off before then." Ice and vodka tumbled together as he shook. "She tends to be a bit of a wild card, if you know what I mean."

Please let her run . . .

Apollo handed Callie a delicate, wide-brimmed glass with a large green olive speared by a toothpick floating along the rim. "You're supposed to save the olive for last, I guess, so it can soak up the alcohol." He shrugged, clearly unsure why mortals liked to torture themselves.

Callie took a sip of her martini. A hefty dose of saltiness subdued the sharp sting of the alcohol. She took another drink before setting her glass down on the end table and dug a notepad out of her bag, and another sip before diving back in for a pen. Apollo sat in a chair opposite the couch, cocktail in hand, and rested his feet on its matching ottoman.

Despite a rather quick heart rate, which was starting to concern her, the momentary silence they fell into was easy. Comfortable. They'd been in this position before, many times. Him across from her, her with notepad in hand, ready to take dictation for some letter or memo he wanted to send to the partners. But this time, she could see it, the thought so clear and fully formed she wondered if it was a prophesy; this was their house on Mount Olympus. Apollo and Calliope, god and muse, together forever.

Head spinning a little, she cleared her throat. "So what happens next?"

She knew what happened next. The date. Helping him win Daphne over.

"Well, I suppose now we figure out how to convince her she loves me."

He unleashed that smile again, and the urge to finish her martini in one gulp was so strong, the pen in her fist almost snapped in half.

Please don't say it like that . . . like you mean it.

He kept smiling at her, all of his perfect, gleaming white teeth showing, like he was trying to say something without actually having to say it. Wait a minute. Had he been happy to see her, or had he been beaming because he was proud of himself?

Son of a child-eating Titan, he actually thinks he got this far on his own.

"You know what? It looks like you've got everything under control." Maybe it was the alcohol talking, but suddenly it was *really* too much to bear. "You don't need me," she said, shoving her things into her bag and hooking the strap around her shoulder. "I'll go back to the office and hold down the fort."

There, she'd said it. And it had felt *good.* Well, for the two whole seconds before she regretted it. She didn't *actually* want to leave. The problem was, she didn't want to stay and help, either.

Apollo shot upright in his chair, the cloudy liquid sloshing around the edges of the glass in one hand, the other gripping the arm of the chair so hard and fast she flinched. "Callie, no.

You can't leave. I need you . . . I need you here, with me. Please. I can't do this without you."

Callie. He'd called her Callie.

And was he begging?

The phone, which, oddly enough, he'd left an old school rotary, rang and scattered her thoughts. He pushed out of his chair to go answer it.

"Hello? Yes, thank you. I'll be right there."

Callie shot him a look, confused as to where he was going.

"I'll be right back. Don't go anywhere, okay? I won't be gone long. Promise."

Once Apollo scooted out the door, she hauled her note-taking supplies out of her bag again and started making a list of things to do on a date. Apparently, she was a glutton for punishment.

There was sharing a candlelit meal. A trip to the cinema, holding hands in the dark. Snuggling for warmth under a cozy blanket while gazing at the stars . . .

She heard the doorknob rattle, but before she could get up, the door swung open and Apollo waltzed into the room holding a flat box. The smell of warm bread, tangy tomato sauce, and melted cheese made her mouth water.

"You ordered pizza?"

"I'm trying to—how did you put it?—live a little. Even though I am a god and living has nothing to do with it. I take it you're pleased."

"Oh my gods, yes. I've been dying to try pizza. It smells amazing."

He set the box on the coffee table and lifted the lid, revealing the most tantalizing mortal food she'd ever laid eyes on.

"Ask and you shall receive, my muse."

He turned to transfer his martini to the coffee table. Thank Zeus he didn't see her cheeks go pink.

And then he actually sat on the floor.

She slid off the couch slowly, cautiously, wondering if this wasn't some kind of other dimension she'd found herself in. Apollo was already eating a slice of pizza. Voluntarily.

The suspense killing her, she took a slice and bit off the end. First, what an ingenious way to eat. Second, the flavors mingling in her mouth were beyond compare. She took another bite, then another. Before she knew it, she was happily chewing her way through a third slice.

"So, obviously," said Callie. "Take her out to dinner. People bond over . . . food." Both their gazes dropped to the one slice of pizza that had managed to survive their ravaging.

"Okay, dinner," he agreed. "What else?"

"Music. We've established you're incredible at playing the lyre." Maybe she could do it. Maybe she could settle for being in the friend zone forever. The thought of not being around him at all seemed worse.

"I do love music, but I'm still not convinced. I've played for her many times. She always just stood there."

"Well, she was a tree. Of course she was just going to stand there. Maybe she'd appreciate it more if you put some lyrics to it. You have a beautiful voice, you know."

"You've heard me sing?"

Callie nodded, her teeth catching her bottom lip and biting down hard. She thought it was one of the most beautiful sounds she'd ever heard.

"Okay, well, as good of an idea as serenading her is, the last time I checked, songs had words. I may have a beautiful singing voice, but I'm atrocious with the words part." He eyed her bag laying open on the couch. "Do you know anyone who is good with words?"

"Apollo, don't." Before she could even reach for it, he'd magicked himself into the chair with her bag in his lap and her journal in his hands. Her heart thundered when he opened it, and her stomach plummeted when she watched his eyes move across the pages, a ghost of a smile haunting his lips.

"You're very good." He closed her journal and returned it to her bag. It sat on the couch again as if it had never left, a lyre simultaneously appearing in his hands. "Would you help me write a song?"

She wanted to say no. In fact, she wanted to scream at the top of her lungs that she'd actually prefer to have Medusa turn her to stone over writing a song so that the god she'd been crushing on forever could sing it to a nymph. "Sure, I'll help you write a song for Daphne." The words came out mumbled, as though she had a mouth full of marbles.

Her sister was right—she couldn't say no to Apollo.

He sat, quietly regarding her, and then a smile curled his lips. "I have a better idea."

Oh gods. What now? Did he want her to write a love poem, too? A song was torture enough. She'd be damned if she was going to—

"Would you like to go on a date with me, Calliope?"

All her thoughts vanished. "I'm sorry, what?"

"I said, 'Would you like to go on a date with me, Calliope?'"

"No, I know that's what you said . . . I just . . . Like, a practice date or something?"

His smile twitched. "Um, yes. Of course." He cleared his throat. "A run-through so you can assess my performance. That's exactly what I was thinking. Good idea."

The thoughts that had flown out of her head came rushing back, bringing with them one very important question. *Do you really want to torture yourself like this?*

She knew the answer, and she hated how easily it came to

her. Yes, she loved Apollo, okay? Yes, the torch she carried for him had never gone out. Yes, it had always been burning, no matter how much she'd tried to extinguish it, and yes, it was so out of control right now she could do nothing but say yes, yes, yes.

Maybe there *was* a chance in Hades' Realm he felt the same, and maybe this date was the perfect way to find out.

"You're wrong, boss. I don't think it's a good idea . . ." She reached for the last slice of pizza. "It's a great idea."

CHAPTER TWENTY-ONE

pollo's knuckles hovered mere inches from the door. *Knock already,* he commanded his hand, but it disobeyed, adjusting his collar instead. Positive his mortal shell was only attempting to shake whatever human trapping was plaguing him at the moment, he attributed the slight flutter in his gut to hunger and lifted his hand again, determined to act like a grown-ass god and knock.

"Apollo?" Callie's muffled voice came from behind the door, making him jump. She must have felt his loitering presence. As for him, he wasn't quite sure what he was feeling, except that he liked it when she said his name.

When the door opened, all thought flew out of his head except one: Exquisite. Her russet hair, free from its usual spot gathered at the nape of her neck, fell in soft waves around her face. She wore a simple cotton sundress—a soft, pale yellow—but her curves succeeded in making it look like the most expensive fabric in the universe. And the conch shell pink of her lips . . . The cloudless blue of her eyes.

Okay, he knew exactly what he was feeling. He just needed to ignore it.

Callie stiffened her spine. "Enter," she said, doing her best impression of him.

Her smile sent his heart racing, succeeding in reminding him why he'd been attracted to her all those years ago as he stepped over the threshold and into her dingy motel room. Not that he needed much reminding. "You look lovely.

"Thanks. So do you," she replied, but then clamped her lips together, as if to stop any more than the obligatory greeting from coming out. Just when he thought her reply was only reciprocal, meant to be nothing more than hospitable and gracious, an approving noise resonated softly in her throat. "That was very good. Complimenting a woman on her appearance lets her know that you've noticed the trouble she's gone through to look and feel attractive."

His response hadn't been planned. It had been genuine and the compliment he'd offered had come out easily, and he thought she should know that. "That's good to know, but—"

"I'm ready," she interrupted. "Let me just grab my purse."

"Very well," said Apollo, holding the door open for her while Callie fetched her bag from the dresser. It was probably better she hadn't let him finish his sentence. It wasn't prudent to mix business with pleasure.

His gaze fell to her ankles, their delicateness accentuated by the thin ribbons of her espadrilles tied around them. He'd held those ankles once. While he'd kissed his way up . . .

So much for prudence.

He tried swallowing, but his throat was rather dry. His lust swelled, but a rush of guilt immediately put a damper on it as he tried conjuring images of Daphne, the woman he was supposed to be thinking about. When the only thing he could picture was a tree, he nodded and turned on his heel, before any more memories of Callie's glorious body could infiltrate his mind.

Not a great time for his libido to make an appearance.

And definitely not a good time to be thinking of his assistant without clothes on. Honestly, what was he thinking was going to happen? This was just a practice date. She was too good to ever be with a pretender like him.

Under control once more, he glanced back at her when he pressed the key fob and the Audi's headlights flashed. "Nice, huh?"

"Yeah, I saw that. It's . . ."

"The best," he finished her sentence for her.

She stood there, lips pursed, arms folded and staring him down as he opened the car door. He'd been uneasy with the way he'd gone about things yesterday—the getting the nymph to agree without force but really using force thing. Talking next steps over with Calliope, about what to do on the date and all that, had made him feel better, but with the way she was looking at him right now, he couldn't help but wonder if he'd crossed the line by asking *her* out.

"Sure," she finally said. "The best, but you do know that some women aren't impressed with material things, right?"

Apollo eased out the breath he'd been holding. There was a slight rush of air at the end he was thankful Calliope didn't catch. He inhaled another as she slid gracefully into the passenger's seat, swinging her legs in after. They weren't long, and they weren't short, either, but finely shaped as far as appendages went. They were perfect, he decided.

Then, from out of nowhere, he began to wonder if his plan to tell Daphne the truth would speed things along or drag them out. He hoped it would speed things up, definitely. The thought circled around his head for a few turns before he pushed it to the back of his mind. Calliope deserved his full attention.

"Of course." He leaned down, looking into her eyes. Why hadn't he told her how pretty they were before? "But I got it for you. Because you should have the best." He closed the door and began the walk around the back of the car. *I got it for you? Because you should have the best?* Sweet Persephone, could he sound any more patronizing? Or was it idiotic? Either way, he wanted whatever he said to not make him sound like an ass—pompous or stupid.

He wanted to get this date thing right. It seemed important.

The engine's fierce, low rumble sounded like he wished he felt. Powerful. Right now all he was feeling like was a Kraken out of water. The prospect of being alone with Calliope hadn't ever rattled him before. They were together constantly. They'd seen each other every day for centuries.

But this was different, and being on Earth was affecting him more than he thought it would. It was making him face his demons, deal with the emotions he normally locked away. Down here, he went from totally confident to completely unsure. Full of pride and ready to fight one minute, humbled by a few words from Calliope the next. It was so odd how elation could turn to worry and doubt at the drop of a hat. And remorse, well, that was the most confusing feeling of them all.

If he could learn how to navigate those feelings down here, to be more flexible and go with the flow more easily, perhaps he—all of them—could finally be rid of the curse.

He pulled out of the parking lot and headed to the restaurant he'd picked out. It wasn't up to his standards, and would take them a half an hour to get there, but there were no five-star restaurants even remotely close, and it had been given 3.5 out of 5.0 stars, so it was as fancy as it was going to get. Unless he used his magic to give the place a makeover. Or perhaps magic them to Paris . . .

No. No magic tonight. He didn't want Callie to think he was taking the easy way out.

He smiled, realizing what the fluttering in his stomach—

and now his chest—was. It was excitement, pure and unadulterated. He'd asked Calliope to spend time with him and she'd said yes. Even though she thought it was work-related, and supposed to be practice, it was more than that to him. It was time he got to spend with her outside of work, hearing that laugh, seeing that smile. He had a feeling he only knew half of what being a muse was like, and he wanted to know. Everything. Knowing her inside and out, he decided, made him feel like he was winning. Not by force. But for real.

When the hostess asked for his name, he threw out his chest. "Apol—" The squeeze at his elbow was just hard enough to stop him. "Paul. My name is Paul. So be sure to give us your best seats." He caught a look from Calliope. "Please."

The squat middle-aged woman, apparently impervious to unbelievably handsome men, gave him a look before tilting her head to take note of the number of people waiting for a table. "Sure thing, Paul. I'll get right on that."

Apollo clenched his teeth and zeroed in on the woman, using just enough magic on her so that she tottered slightly and had to steady herself on the hostess podium. "Actually, sir, I can seat you right away."

She quickly gathered two menus and beckoned them to follow her, even though the three couples waiting behind them clicked their tongues and grumbled their displeasure. Apollo's grin faded when Callie rolled her eyes and huffed.

"You'll catch more bees with honey. Plus, it's always good to show you have patience."

"I don't know that I have much."

"You don't say."

The hostess showed them to their table, which was tucked in between two huge planter boxes filled with tall grasses. "Is this okay, sir?"

He glanced at Callie, who was admiring the glittering fairy lights strung between the roofs of the two brick buildings with delight. "It's perfect."

The hostess set the menus on the table. "Your server will be right with you."

She hurried away as Apollo pulled Callie's chair out for her. When he sat down, he looked across the table at her expectantly, for an assessment of not only the timing, but the quality of his gentlemanly act.

The color high on Callie's cheeks confirmed he'd done the right thing at the right time. Now what? Ah, that's right. Making conversation.

Apollo waited until the young man filling their water glasses finished. Once they were alone again, he began the next test. "Since I already know your favorite color, why don't you tell me something else you like to do. You know, when you're not keeping my calendar."

"Or picking up your dry cleaning?"

"Hey, at least I get my own coffee."

"In the morning, but your afternoon cup is all me. Which reminds me, Hephaestus said he could pave—Oh, never mind." She swallowed hard as she shook her head, her face blushing a deep crimson.

"Yeah, I guess there's no need to . . ." He bit the inside of his lip. He didn't want to talk about Daphne or the damned curse.

"I write poems, you know, when I'm not . . ." She trailed off, obviously thinking of a delicate way to put what she was about to say next.

"Doing shit for me," finished Apollo, grinning at her with one eyebrow raised.

Callie's giggle bordered on incredulous laughter. "I don't think I've ever heard you swear before, boss."

"Don't think of me as your boss tonight." He raised his

eyebrows at her.

He admired the way Calliope's skin flushed, until he realized the innuendo he'd just made.

"I didn't mean it like that. . ."

"I know what you meant," said Calliope, blushing even deeper.

"Not that I wouldn't, you know, want to. Have sex. But, we shouldn't . . . Because . . ."

"Come to think of it, I don't think I've ever heard you trip over your words, either."

"I seem to be doing a real bang-up job of it tonight, huh?"

Calliope laughed, and he pressed his lips together. Initially, it'd been to stop any more bad puns from coming out, but it ended up being to keep himself from grinning like a fool.

"No, please. Keep them *coming*," she said, laughing harder.

The sip of water he'd taken almost went down the wrong way, but he saved it from sending him into a choking fit just in the nick of time. "How dare you! It almost went down the wrong *hole*."

Calliope leaned to the side, doubling over in a fit of giggles, and he couldn't help but chuckle as he wiped away the water that had dribbled down his chin with the back of his hand. Ah, gods, how embarrassing would *that* have been? Helpless and gasping for air in front of the entire restaurant. Knowing Calliope, she probably would have really enjoyed it.

The part that confirmed the reason why he needed to be free of the curse now more than ever? He probably would have liked it, too.

CHAPTER TWENTY-TWO

Callie fiddled with a loose thread on the strap of her purse as Apollo pulled into the motel parking lot. He cut the engine and pulled the keys out of the ignition before turning to face her.

"Well, how did I do?"

Seriously. Why did his eyes have to sparkle like that?

And how did he do? Well, let's see. Oh, that's right, he passed with flying colors, just like she thought he would. An A+ for not bringing up the nymph, not even once. Instead, he'd asked her what it was like growing up as a muse. How it felt to inspire so many people. The best part was he'd listened intently to every word. No interruptions. No corrections. No condescending questions. In fact, there hadn't been any awkward pauses in conversation all night, even on the car ride home. Until now.

The moment of truth, when she learned whether or not she had changed his mind.

"Um . . . you did really great."

"Don't sound so convincing, Calliope." He gave her a sly grin before opening his car door.

He must have seen her reach for the handle because he disappeared, reappearing at her side of the car the next instant. When he opened the door and offered her his hand to help her out, she let him, even though she was perfectly capable of exiting the vehicle on her own.

The butterflies in her belly went crazy. She'd been trying all night to decide whether to do what she was about to do next. "I have something for you," she said over her shoulder. She started to bring a fingernail to her mouth, to her anxiously awaiting teeth, but dropped her hand and bit her lip instead.

"Oh?" Apollo trailed close behind. So close, in fact, that if she turned around, they'd collide.

She imagined turning around and kissing him, but instead of throwing caution to the wind and acting on impulse, she dug her room key out of her purse. If that was going to happen, it was going to have to be initiated by him. Her fingers trembled as she unlocked the door. It was a given that he'd come into her room. She'd just said she had something for him, after all.

She tossed her purse onto the bed. "I thought of you when I saw it," she said, struggling to keep her voice even. "It's just a little something."

Had she really just said it was only a little something? Her heart pounded as she reached into the closet and pulled out an acoustic guitar with an enormous yellow ribbon tied into a bow around the neck. She'd seen his eyes light up before, but there hadn't ever been a time she remembered seeing them as luminous as they were now.

"For me?" His words were barely above a whisper.

"Yeah, and it's a Gibson Hummingbird, which is—"

"The best. Calliope, I don't know what to say."

"Thank you is customary." Her whole body flushed. "I

mean, you can't very well serenade someone in the twenty-first century using a lyre, now can you?"

He smiled as he stepped closer, gently cupping her face and brushing a thumb lightly across her cheekbone. Was this it? Had she succeeded in making him forget about the nymph? She'd know in approximately one second if the guitar had either turned the tide or the whole thing was going down like the Titanic.

She held her breath.

His lids lowered as he glanced at her lips before finding her eyes again. "Thank you . . . for everything."

When he leaned down and kissed her forehead, she wanted to cry. Or die. Maybe both. No, definitely both. It had been a good night, but not good enough to win Apollo's love.

"Good luck, boss." Her words ached to come out strangled, but she somehow made them sound cheerful. "I hope you win her over."

No she didn't. Callie wanted him to choose her. At the very least, she wanted to suddenly have the courage to tell him that he was making a huge mistake. Barring that, what else could she say? She'd led the god of sun and light to water. She just hadn't been able to make him drink.

Apollo looked away, down at their now joined hands, and nodded.

She looked up at him, at his beautiful face, and pretended her heart hadn't just shattered. "Good night, boss." She let go of his hand, careful to keep her movements smooth, her voice light.

He stood there for a moment, his mouth opening and closing before sliding a hand—the one that wasn't holding the heartfelt gift she'd just given him—into a pocket and walking over to the door without word. When he shut it behind him, she clamped her own hands over her mouth to muffle a sob.

The bedsprings creaked and groaned when she dropped down onto the lumpy mattress. She willed herself to get it together, but her tears insisted on streaming down her face as she untied her shoes and slipped them off. The urge to lay back and curl up into a ball overwhelmed her, but she fought it. She knew this had been coming. There hadn't really been a chance he'd change his mind, had there?

She wiped her eyes, taking a pair of pajamas out of her bag and sniffling as she laid them out on the bed. When she caught a glimpse of herself in the mirror on the way to the bathroom, the reflection succeeded in making her feel worse. Perfect skin, large blue eyes, enviable hair.

Her sister had been right from the beginning. About everything. They were muses. Their sole purpose in the universe was to inspire souls to create wondrous things, sometimes to the brink of madness. And Callie had. She'd stirred so much in so many, just not the one soul she truly wanted to inspire.

Callie slipped out of her dress, put on her pajamas, and tied her hair into its usual spot. After removing her makeup, she splashed cold water on her face and brushed her teeth. Afterwards, she took her journal from her bag and pulled the covers back. Write. Pour her feelings onto paper. That's what she would do, what she always did.

She opened the journal to one of the last few blank pages left. She'd have to get a new one soon, so this one could join the volumes of other journals filled with musings and poems. She had so many, yet not enough.

The knock on her door was light, but loud enough to make her heart thud in her chest. She slipped out of bed and went to the window to pull back the curtain.

Apollo, with a pile of blankets in one arm and the guitar she'd given him in the other hand, nodded at her. She twisted the lock and opened the door, the thudding ramping up to hammering.

"Hey," she said, trying to sound casual. "What's up?"

"It's so nice out, I thought you might like to join me." He tipped his head upward.

Stars. He wanted to look at the stars.

She shouldn't. Like, *really* shouldn't. She was already devastated enough, and gazing at the stars with him would lead to more disappointment. But she felt the pull, that persistent gods-damned *pull* that wouldn't let her say no. Why was she such a glutton for punishment? Wasn't her heart already broken enough?

"Um." Clio's disapproving groan rang inside her head, reminding Callie she needed to try and resist. "Practice is over. You're going to get her back."

"I know." His gaze dropped. "I mean, I know practice is over. I could just use a bit more company right now is all."

The torch she'd just stuck into the sand sputtered back to life. Okay, it reignited in a blazing ball of fire.

"Sure," she said, against her better judgment but unable to stop herself, and followed Apollo into the parking lot toward the R8. He leaned his guitar against the wheel so he could spread a thick blanket across the shiny-even-in-the-dark hood. He held out his hand to help her up, and of course she took it.

He picked up his guitar and walked onto the hood in one swift and powerful step. He settled himself next to her with all the grace of the great god he was.

"Thank you again for my gift." He began to strum. It took her a moment, but she recognized the melody. Beethoven's Moonlight Sonata. "I love it."

All she could do was nod and smile. She couldn't bring herself to say you're welcome out loud. Instead, she curled into the blanket he'd wrapped around her shoulders and leaned against the windshield.

Apollo stopped playing to point upwards. The stars were out in full force, beautiful as always. "Sly Corvus. That old crow thought he was so slick." He looked at her, his eyes glassy pools in the night. "Did I ever tell you about that? About what that shit did?"

"No," murmured Callie, exhausted. "Tell me, though. What did that shit do, boss?"

He began to play again, the chords a somber backdrop to the story he was about to tell. "Okay, so I was preparing a sacrifice to my father, and I asked Corvus to go fetch me some water from a mountain stream. It had to be pure, you see, nothing but the . . ."

"Let me guess, nothing but the best."

Apollo chuckled. "How'd you know? Anyway, Corvus decided both the water and I could wait. He stopped to eat some figs, but they weren't ripe yet. As you can imagine, waiting for them to ripen took a while."

"Uh oh. No one makes the mighty Apollo wait. *What* was he thinking?"

"Precisely. So when he comes back, he's got this snake in his mouth. And you know how I feel about snakes. When I asked him where the water was, and what took him so long, what do you think he did? I'll tell you what he did, he blamed it on the snake."

Callie gasped in exaggerated disbelieve. "He didn't."

"He did. And, Callie, I was furious. I mean absolutely livid. Who did this crow think he was, trying to pull one over on me?"

"So what'd you do?" she asked, even though she already knew.

"Turned him as black as the lie he told me."

"And?"

"I cursed him."

"A curse, huh?" She let out a tired laugh, which sounded more like a, "Hmm, hmm, hmm."

A curse. Just like Eros had cast on him. Out of anger. She sighed, wondering if the mighty god of sun and light would put two and two together. When Apollo went quiet but his strumming grew louder, something told her he had indeed realized the hypocrisy.

"I gave him a perpetually sore throat, too, so he could never eat figs again," he continued, quieter, less animated than before. "And then I put him up there." He stopped playing so he could point at a cluster of stars.

"Don't you think that was a bit harsh?"

"He lied to me," answered Apollo matter-of-factly. "I needed to make an example of him."

He stopped strumming again, allowing the crickets to take center stage, and they both listened to the tiny maestros play their little hearts out.

"I meant what I said about you being talented." He was speaking so low now Callie almost didn't hear him. "I wish I was better with words."

She nodded.

Hold on, was he *admitting* he wasn't the best at something?

"You're good with words, too." She snuggled further into the blanket, not able to stop herself from boosting his ego. She'd been doing it for centuries.

He smiled, and the sad, tortured look in his eyes almost talked her into throwing her arms around him. She looked up at the stars instead.

He eased himself against the windshield next to her. "Not as good as you are, Callie. And you don't have to tell me I am. Okay?"

Callie was glad that when the tear slid down, it was on

the cheek Apollo couldn't see. "Okay," she whispered. *Anything you say, boss.*

CHAPTER TWENTY-THREE

*D*aphne gazed up at the stars. A fond smile curled her lips when she thought about how every nymph in the Sacred Forest would be dancing that night. They always gathered to set their intentions under the new moon, then again during the full moon, to send them on their way out into the universe. She almost had the urge to get up and dance herself. She didn't, but she did send up an intention: *Please let there be a way.*

They'd ridden for most of the day, stopping to check different areas. After setting up camp near a wider part of the river on the far end of Sam's property, they'd had their dinner —fry bread and beans from a can—and were now enjoying the evening's display of twinkling points of light just beginning to appear in the twilight.

She couldn't seem to stop smiling, or laughing, and she'd told Sam tonight's dinner had been the best he'd cooked so far. He'd laughed, too, his eyes like polished amber in the last vestiges of the sun before it set. They listened as the cicadas sang to the irregular beat of the crackling and popping fire, and the easy silence between Daphne and the man at her side was just what she'd needed to forget about her troubles for a while.

"What's on your mind, Dee?" The orange glow seemed to light his stubbled cheeks and chin from within. Hat tipped low, hands resting on his stomach and his legs stretched out in front of him, crossed at the ankle. Content to just be in the moment. Happy to live a simple life.

"You know what's on my mind," she said.

"Then don't run back, stay."

"He'll come for me." There was no use pretending Sam didn't know that she was hiding from someone. They'd danced around it long enough. He just didn't have to know that someone was a god.

"I'll protect you."

A pop from the fire echoed in the night around them. One of the logs shifted, sending a shower of embers upwards like a sparkler. She wrapped the blanket tighter around her shoulders. She could stay like this forever, with this man, under this sky.

"He'll hurt whomever gets in his way," she finally said. "You know that, right?" Or destroy them, that was probably a more accurate way to put it.

"I hate that he scares you so much. No man should ever make a woman feel that way."

"He's never hit me, if that's what you're thinking." Even as the words left her mouth, she knew they were a poor attempt at diminishing the seriousness of the situation.

Sam sat up, giving her his full attention. "Regardless, he's hurt you in other ways, and it's not okay."

"Well, yes, but . . ." She shook her head at the irony of what she was about to say. "The relationship was doomed from the start, but because of things that are out of my control. I'm stuck, Sam."

Delilah nickered softly, adding her two cents to the

conversation before moseying off toward the riverbed where Sampson and Zeus were hanging out. Suddenly, Daphne longed to be there, too.

Actually, she wouldn't mind being *in* the river.

"I feel you on that one." Sam sighed. "Does a number on your mind, doesn't it? Makes you think you're not good enough, and then you find yourself, like you said . . . stuck. You want to leave, run away, but you can't because you're unable to move past the reality you've created for yourself."

"Exactly," whispered Daphne.

"And you stand, frozen, because you think you're all alone, and you'll never find anyone else who will love you."

"Exactly."

He scooted closer, resting his forearm on a bent knee. "But it's a myth, isn't it? We're not really stuck, you and me. Not unless we've already decided we are."

She smiled, her eyes focusing on the two turquoise feathers set in silver that always hung around his neck as she soaked up the sound of his voice. Yes, it was a myth, in more ways than one, and oh how she wished she could tell him how right he was about everything.

"You know what we need, Sam Carson?"

He leaned over and tucked her hair behind her ear. "What's that, nature girl?"

His touch ignited the nymph blood in her veins, awakening her desire, and she abandoned her suggestion for a dip in the river. She suddenly didn't need the blanket anymore, either. It slipped from her shoulders when she turned to face him, her wild abandon sparking to life.

"To get out of these clothes."

Why not? She felt heart-pounding joy when she looked into his eyes, shining like stars in the night sky. When the firelight danced in them like that? Her joy turned into pure ecstasy. The strength of his jaw, the line of his long, broad nose, the curve of his heavenly full lips, they made her bones melt when he slid even closer.

"I might like the sound of that."

Her head whirled like a dervish spinning out of control when his fingers slid along her neck to cradle the back of her head. And when he leaned in to press his lips to hers, the spinning made her dizzy.

His kiss was slow and gentle, and she responded in kind, relishing the tenderness. But a nymph could only handle so much, and soon the ache pooling low in her belly drove her to circle her arms around his neck and deepen the kiss. He leaned into her, the urgency in his sigh causing her to draw him down on top of her.

Being weighted to the Earth like this felt divine.

Their hands set out on a journey together, her exploration of hard muscle encouraging him to discover the hills and valleys of her soft curves.

She sighed when he cupped her face in his hand, kissing her lips then tipping her chin up so he could do the same to her neck. She tangled her fingers into his hair as he undid the buttons of her shirt. He pushed the fabric away, tracing the line of her clavicle before pressing his lips to the hollow of her throat. It didn't take long before he was lavishing his kisses on the ample swells of her breasts. A sensitive peak grazed the silky fabric of her bra, puckering against the night air when he reached inside and pulled it free.

The warmth and wetness of his mouth on her hardened flesh nearly undid her.

She wanted him, now, which made her fumble with the buttons of his shirt, unable to think of anything but his smooth, bronze skin on hers. The hard muscle of his arms and shoulders flexed as he removed it, and she sucked her bottom lip into her mouth to stop herself from whimpering. If she didn't know better, she'd think he was part god.

She shivered, the ache low in her belly growing. His hand roamed over her thighs. Over, under, and when she opened up to him, between. He took his time, exploring the delicate folds there before finally venturing inside with his fingers while caressing the most sensitive one with his thumb. The slow circling of his touch threatened to burst her at the seams.

There was no doubt about what was going to happen. What she wanted to happen.

She returned the favor and undid his Wranglers, reaching inside and taking him in her hand. The sound he made was urgent, an intake of breath that made her aching sharpen. She stroked him with a tempo to match his touch. Slow. Teasing. Delicious. Their breaths mingled, tongues seeking to connect through lips barely touching.

She wanted him, and whether it was wrong or right didn't matter. Nature had kicked in, for both of them it seemed, and she didn't want to wait any longer. She'd protected her chastity long enough. She'd gone far too long thinking she could never know the pleasures of the flesh and not be missing anything. She was so very wrong. He would be the first to be with her. The first to share in a bond she never thought she wanted.

"I want us to be together." She pushed his jeans down over his hips. As he finished the job, she shimmied out of her own jeans and tossed them aside.

The tip of him pressed against her, and the swollen folds gave way easily. Readily. She looked into Sam's eyes as she slowly pushed her hips upward, taking him in. Welcoming him. Forehead on hers, he met her with a gentle thrust downward. His small gasp of pleasure unleashed the whimper she'd held in earlier, and when he was fully inside her, she nearly cried out at the feeling of completeness.

They moved, slowly at first, until they found a rhythm.

When he lifted her hip, so that he could move deeper inside her, she hooked her leg around the back of his thigh, drawing him closer. She ran her hands over his chest and over his stomach, feeling every rigid muscle he was using to work his way further inside. She gripped his waist, urging him to crash into her faster and harder, again and again. When her need for him crested, she arched her back, raising herself so her nipples grazed his hot skin, the sensation sending sparks down to the place where their bodies moved in the most satisfying dance of her life.

Her ache exploded into a shower of sparks, and she did cry out then, holding him close as wave after wave of her climax left her trembling against him. Sam shuddered, moaning into her lips as he kissed her, his release leaving him shaking and spent right along with her.

Moments later, as she laid in his arms, fitting against his body like they were made for each other, hearts beating as one and their breathing keeping time with one another, it was so simple. She wanted to stay here with Sam. She just didn't know how to make that happen. If her father had the power to turn her mortal, she would have already called out to him by now.

A shooting star streaked across the night sky, the answer coming to her as she watched its glowing tail fade. She needed to convince the god of sun and light that his desire had faded. That the curse was only in his head, and he didn't want her anymore because she wasn't worth the chase.

She needed to convince him she had already been turned into a mortal.

CHAPTER TWENTY-FOUR

The next morning, the sounds of the market drifted lazily on the breeze—people talking, laughing, and haggling over prices. Butterflies tickled Daphne's insides whenever she thought about Sam, keeping her floating above her worry. She couldn't recall ever feeling this wonderfully happy, this perfectly content, even in a magical place like the Sacred Forest. And she'd found it here, on Earth with a mortal.

Now all she had to do was put on the biggest show of her life to keep it that way.

When the guitar chords floated into her ears, she thought nothing of it. In fact, she tapped her foot in time to the melody. Until they got louder—and she heard that voice.

Daphne froze, an icy chill rippling through her, even on a torturously humid, eighty-degree day. He did have a beautiful voice, she'd give him that, but it was also the most terrifying sound she'd ever heard.

No, not yet. I still have one more day.

A crowd gathered around him as he made his way toward her. Her breathing went shallow when she saw the looks of adoration on the faces of women in the booths across from her . . . and caddy corner and, oh Hades' wrath, on either side of her.

She inhaled a shaky breath. She needed to stay calm, so she didn't blow her new cover. Things always escalated very quickly with Apollo. She doubted her father knew what a Mortality Request even was let alone able to get one approved so quickly, but telling Apollo he had, and that her mortality was already a done deal, was all she could think of to buy her more time. The other, more immediate problem? Trying to pull one over on the very god who abhorred deception. But it was the only way she knew how to do what must be done: Convince him the request had already been approved.

She cleared her throat, preparing to spin her web, and put up her hand for him to stop. Miracle of all miracles, he actually listened to her for once.

"That was lovely, thank you." Not welcomed, though.

He smiled, no doubt encouraged by the fact she hadn't taken off running yet. Oh, she wanted to, but only into the arms of her mortal lover. But she'd gotten them into this mess, and she was determined to get them out.

She spied her first obstacle to doing just that as her eyes flicked to a blonde with teased and sprayed hair, chomping on a wad of gum. If she knew Sadie, and the folks of Caddo County for that matter, and how fast word traveled, Sam would know a stranger was serenading her within minutes.

Sadie had come to a halt twenty yards in front of her and was giving Apollo some serious evil eye. She knew. Enemy number one had found Daphne. She started pressing buttons on her phone.

Make that seconds. Sam would know in seconds.

Which meant Daphne had to play it cool. Sam would come to her rescue, no doubt. And if he tried to save her, things might end up worse. She squared her shoulders, steeling herself for what she knew had to be done, even though it could end in disaster—and not just for Sam—but the old thoughts came rushing in, eating away at her confidence.

Poor, helpless nymph. Poor, helpless nymph . . .

She shot up from the table, before the thoughts could consume any more of her nerve. "We need to talk." She brushed past Apollo and walked over to a grassy area outfitted with several picnic tables. Of course he followed her. She could feel the hair on the back of her neck raise.

"Are you ready for our date?" He lifted his brows in question. "Shall we start now?"

She whirled around. "No. Look, we're not going on a date, okay?" She needed to be firm, but more than that, she needed to be convincing.

Apollo sent her a thin smile. "Why not?"

"Because I'm not worth it."

Apollo's jaw loosened enough to fall open. "What do you mean?"

"I had my father put in a Mortality Request weeks ago. It just came through, so you can stop chasing me now."

Her nerves ramped up, and she started to tremble. Fates have mercy, if he figured out she wasn't telling the truth . . . She took a deep breath to recalibrate. She was fine. She hadn't actually lied and said she was mortal, only implied she wasn't worth chasing.

"Peneus put in an MR for you? Nonsense. He doesn't have an admin. He doesn't even have a phone. How could he have possibly scheduled a meeting? Besides, my father wouldn't . . ." He trailed off, sounding unsure if anything she was saying had an ounce of validity to it.

It was working. Oh, gods, it was working.

"It doesn't matter," said Apollo, shaking his head.

Scratch that, it wasn't working.

But it wasn't over until it was over, and even though she'd broken out into a cold sweat, she kept the ruse going. "What do you mean it doesn't matter? Of course it matters. I'm just a plain old mort—person. How would it look if someone like you ended up with someone like me?"

Apollo bit his lip, as if actually choosing his words carefully before speaking. "Not good, but I meant it doesn't matter because we're still cursed. We have no choice but to go through with the date, Daphne. There is no other option, for either of us."

"There *is* another option. We can both just . . . not." Daphne shrugged her shoulders as if the solution was simply that easy. It wasn't, but, by gods, she really needed him to think it was. "We can both walk away right now and forget the other exists."

Apollo shook his head again, more firmly this time. "That won't work. The curse is still in place. I have a plan, though. All you have to do is . . ." He reached out and grabbed her arm. "Say you love me out loud then we can both be—"

Once again, her half-baked plan had failed. His one-track mind was still as straight-and-narrow as ever.

Her resolve sparked into a shower of panic when his grip on her arm finally registered. "Stop it! Let go of me. I don't love you. I never have."

Daphne tried to free herself, but his hand felt like an iron shackle. The rumble of a diesel truck engine—Sam's white chariot—in the distance flooded her eyes with tears.

"You don't mean that," said Apollo, sounding like he was trying to convince himself as much as her. He'd let go, but he still stared, dumbfounded that she'd actually refused to say she loved him.

Zeus came tearing out of the truck, snarling and heading

straight for Apollo. He flicked a hand, a brushing motion that sent the big dog yelping and tumbling backward.

"Zeus!" Daphne ran toward him, consoling the whimpering dog. "What's wrong with you?" she spat at Apollo.

"Zeus? This *dog* is named after my *father*?" He laughed. "Oh, that's hilarious. And totally fitting."

Sam walked up to the scene, hand on his firearm. Still holstered, thankfully, but the strap was unbuttoned. He whistled sharply and delivered a command to his partner. "Zeus, come." Zeus obeyed without hesitation, and when Sam reached Daphne's side, he gave another. "Guard."

Zeus did as asked, adding in a low, threatening growl.

"What's going on here?" asked Sam. "Are you all right, miss?"

Daphne's chest swelled with pride. He was taller and stronger than most mortal men, and she was positive Sam could definitely give Apollo a run for his money. However, seeing as the latter was a god, taller and stronger than most wasn't going to make a difference in the end.

Something else swelled in Daphne; bile crept up from the depths of her churning stomach. Sam had that look in his eyes. Serve. Protect. Defend.

Fight to the death.

When the only thing Daphne could do was stand there, Sam turned to Apollo for answers. "What seems to be the problem here, sir?"

Sam's voice was full of challenge, and Daphne cringed. Her belly clenched along with every other muscle. Sam had no way of knowing, but the tone of his voice would surely trigger Apollo. When he was in victor mode, he didn't accept merely being the winner, he became obsessed with being the absolute champion. And he didn't stop until he crushed the competition.

Daphne noticed they had an audience. Most onlookers

kept their distance, probably sensing the situation was a powder keg, one open flame away from exploding to high-heaven, but Sadie had rushed to her side, phone still in hand. Ready to call paramedics next, Daphne supposed.

Another woman, with long red hair tied into a messy ponytail at the nape of her neck, hung back. She looked positively beside herself, and Daphne thought she knew her from somewhere, but couldn't place it. Until her yellow aura surged. She was a muse. Daphne had never seen one before, but this one was even more beautiful than she'd imagined.

"I assure you, there is no problem," said Apollo calmly.

Daphne was pretty sure she knew the rest of what Apollo wanted to inform Sam. *I can crush you with my eyes closed and both arms tied behind my back.*

"Okay. Then how about you go back to whatever it is you came from and leave this woman alone."

It wasn't Deputy Carson speaking, it was Sam. His feelings for her had joined forces with his oath to serve and protect, making him take the current situation very, *very* personal.

Daphne placed a hand on Sam's chest. "Sam—Deputy Carson—it's okay. I've got everything under control." She hoped to Hades' Realm his emotions didn't make him do anything rash.

Apollo's gaze darted between her and Sam. When the obvious nature of their relationship clicked, his eyes narrowed before they landed on her. "You can't be serious, Daphne. Even in your . . . new condition. He can never offer you what I can. I can offer you freedom. If you'll just listen, I promise you'll have all that your heart desires."

Sam looked at her with questions in his eyes. "New condition?"

Daphne ignored him. She had to because she was seething at Apollo, and she needed all her focus in order to direct her rage toward the right person. She turned toward the object of her hatred and glared at him. "I'd have everything except love. Don't you get it by now? You don't really love me, you just want to win. That's all you've ever wanted. It has never been about me. It's always been about you."

The muscle over Apollo's jaw bunched as he ground his teeth, his aura revving up, his fists snapping shut like traps. Three centuries worth of anger and resentment bubbled to the surface with astonishing speed at the sight. Powerless in its intensity, Daphne let every emotion that followed burst forth.

"How would it look if the high-and-mighty golden child didn't get the girl?"

Pop.

"They'd all see you for who you really are, wouldn't they?"

Pop, pop.

"They'd know that every victory, every shining, glory-filled win was—is—a desperate cry for attention."

Pop, pop, pop.

Apollo's death stare shredded her bravado to ribbons, and suddenly, it didn't seem like such a good time for an impulse control fail. But she barely had time to backpedal when his eyebrows dipped, as though he was in pain, and he reached for her again.

"Please, Daphne. Just come with me. I can explain everything."

Sam stepped in front of her, ready to fight. "She's not going anywhere with you."

The look on Apollo's face, a mix of resolve and desperation, morphed into anger. She had to end this. Right now, and not by making herself seem less than she was, and certainly not by hurling centuries worth of frustration at a god who could take away everything—every person—she'd fallen in love with since running away to the middle of nowhere.

She would save them all by getting it over with and giving in to Apollo's demands.

She'd caused too much suffering already, and if she didn't go now, the pain for Sam—for them both—would be a thousand times worse. Not to mention he could quite possibly end up a thousand times dead.

Daphne placed her hands on Sam's shoulders, her regret so heavy she could barely look him in the eyes. She wasn't sorry she had fallen in love with him. No, the only thing she regretted was ever thinking she could outrun the curse.

"I'm sorry, Sam." She kissed his cheek softly, willing herself to remember the feel of the stubble beneath her lips. He tugged desperately at her elbows, silently pleading for her not to go, but she untangled herself from his embrace.

"This is crazy, Dee. Why are you doing this? You obviously don't want to go. He's going to end up hurting you."

"I wish I could tell you why, but I can't stay."

"Is it because you're carrying his child? Is that your new condition?"

Her soul withered. A baby. Sam thought she was leaving him because she was carrying another man's child. It had to hurt worse than being left for a doctor.

Oh gods, but it was the most horribly perfect excuse.

"Yes," she whispered, not sure she'd ever be able to forgive herself for breaking Sam's heart like this.

"I'll take care of you both. I don't care if it's not mine. Don't go with him. Stay with me," pleaded Sam.

"Sam . . . Don't. I can't."

He swallowed hard, a look of hurt flashing across his face. She'd seen it before, the night she tried to say goodbye, and it killed her. It was even worse when he nodded, finally letting her go.

Daphne turned to face Apollo, her voice steady and sure. "You got what you wanted, but know this . . . I will *never* love you." She stared into Apollo's eyes as she said it, sending all the truth and intent she could to get her message across. "Every moment you force me to spend with you will be fallow. Because I love Sam, not you."

CHAPTER TWENTY-FIVE

pollo's pulse raced. He needed to get Daphne alone, so he could explain that he wanted to be free as much as she did. That he'd finally learned his lesson. "I understand," he replied. "But we really should go now."

Her mortal turned on him suddenly. "Didn't you hear what she said, buddy? She doesn't love you. Jesus Christ, what is wrong with you?" He turned to plead with Daphne again. "Don't downplay yourself for this asshole, Dee. You deserve so much more. It doesn't have to be me, but please, *please*, don't let him trick you into thinking you're nothing without him."

"It's for the best . . . Sam, is it?" said Apollo, feeling his panic rise as he reach for Daphne again. He contemplated magicking them to Olympus as soon as he made contact. Callie would know to call her mother, Mnemosyne, down to erase everyone's memory. At least, he hoped she would. And then after the curse was broken, he'd straighten things out with her, and finally reveal his true feelings. He loved her, not Daphne. Always had.

But before he could even touch Daphne, Sam charged,

throwing his arm out hard and fast. It connected with Apollo's face, and a loud *crunch* filled the air. Apollo stepped back to maintain his balance, shocked by the fact a mortal man had very possibly just broken his nose. It throbbed painfully, and Apollo raised a hand to assess the damage. His fingers came away wet with blood.

His temper rose to the surface with the heat and force of a volcanic eruption. Why was trying to do the right thing *so fucking hard*. His face burned hot, and his eyes blazed as his victor overtook him, power surging through his body as he reached a hand toward Sam.

The man's eyes went wide, his mouth gasping for breath as Apollo curled his fingers and slowly closed them into a fist. Twisting his wrist ever so slowly, he brought the mortal before him to his knees.

Apollo was so close to breaking the curse, he couldn't stop now. Wouldn't.

"Stop it, you'll kill him!" screamed Daphne.

"We can break the curse." Apollo was vaguely aware someone was pounding on his back, but he was too focused to care. "I have a plan. I'll explain everything. Just come back with me."

The pounding continued. "I'm sorry," murmured Apollo through the building chaos. There were so many voices, too much noise. "I can't let anything get in the way."

"Stop! *Please*," cried Daphne. She was clutching her mortal protectively now, and Apollo's gaze landed on her when she said, "I'll go back with you. I promise. I'll profess love from any mountaintop you want, I swear it."

Although her promise was enough for him, it was not enough for his victor. His victor still saw the man in front of him as an obstacle to his freedom. Apollo squeezed his fist all the way closed. Then, amidst the darkness creeping along his tunneled vision, he heard Callie speak.

"Save your breath, Daphne. He won't listen. He can't," she said, her voice raw and rasping with anger. "Because he's a fucking monster."

And that was all it took for him to stop.

Apollo stood motionless as the EMTs strapped the mortal man he'd almost destroyed onto the gurney. He was deathly pale, evidence of how close he'd come to taking his last breath, and Apollo had to look away. It was a reminder of how weak he truly was.

As if testament to that truth, the sun had disappeared, casting the market in shadow. The crowd that had gathered was now dissipating, and he tried to ignore the whispers as they began to give way to confused murmurs. *Who is this guy? Does anyone know where he's from? Did you see the way Deputy Carson just dropped like that?*

Apollo was used to crowds, but this one felt different. It felt wrong. All the other times, they had been rooting for him, not against him. Now they glared at him as the walked away, arms folded instead of hands clapping.

The lights of the ambulance flashed even though the sirens had been turned off. Red reflected off Daphne's tears, making it look as though she were weeping blood. He commanded the lump in his throat to go away. Guilt had never served him well before. It would do him no good now. Priority one was getting Daphne back to Mount Olympus. What else was there left to do?

Apollo cleared his throat softly. "How much time do you need to gather your things?"

"What things?" Daphne asked bitterly, wiping the tears from her cheeks. "I don't have any *things.*"

"Okay, then we should go now."

Panic chased terror across Daphne's face, her tone softening, becoming more compliant.

"Wait, I'm sorry."

Normally, a surge of delight would zap its way from his toes straight up to his gloating ego. Instead, the guilt he pushed away earlier made the swelling in his throat come back. He swallowed, hoping it would go away again.

"Can I at least make sure he's all right?"

She was pleading with him, and a wave of heat consumed him, drowning him in the most unpleasant feeling that made answering difficult. He wished he could give her what she wanted, what he wanted too—freedom from the curse—with the snap of his fingers. Of all the power he did have, that was the one thing he had to rely on Eros for, and he still needed her participation. "He'll be fine."

He'd caused some temporary damage to the man's heart, but it was a pittance compared to the destruction he could have done.

Her voice hardened again. "You almost killed him, and I'm supposed to believe you when you tell me he'll be fine?"

"He'll be okay, I promise." He said the words, but fully expected her to push back. She was right, why should she believe anything he said? In fact, how had he gotten away with anyone believing what he'd said for this long?

"No, I want to make sure he'll be okay with my own eyes. You owe me more, but at least give me that much."

A heaviness pressed down on Apollo. He was tired of pretending, and so he relented with a nod, giving up this particular fight willingly. As much as he wanted to say no, he couldn't. He did owe Daphne. He'd waited this long for them to be free of this wretched curse, another forty-eight mortal hours wasn't going to make a difference. It might even make her more open to listening if he gave her time to say goodbye to her mortal.

Besides, it was a small sacrifice to make compared to what he knew in his heart was coming. He didn't even want to think about what was going through Callie's mind at the moment. Surely, it wasn't anything good.

"How about you call out to me in a couple of days? I'll come down and get you." He could use the time to sort through things. Figure out exactly what it was he was going to say. He had a feeling Eros was going to be a stickler about this. If not, Psyche certainly would. Daphne would undoubtedly profess her love for him now that she truly had no other option, but it wouldn't be of her own volition. She'd say the words, but they wouldn't be true because he'd trapped her. Forced her into it, yet again.

Hopefully the god of love would let that part slide.

A blonde-haired woman with ruby lips clutched a cell phone as she hugged Daphne tight. "You don't have to do anything he says, sugar. You can stay with us, for as long as you need. You hear me?"

"I wish I could," whispered Daphne.

The woman fixed a hard glare on Apollo. "You're a real sorry son-of-a-bitch, you know that? Sam's not going to take this lying down, I can guarantee you that. You hurt one hair on Dee's head, and you're gonna feel the wrath of this whole goddamned town. You hear me?"

Apollo's insides twisted. He wasn't bothered by the woman's threat; it was the conviction in her words that tightened the screws. The woman believed it was possible for an entire town to win against a god. The fact that a "whole goddamned town" would rally together to protect someone they loved, showing how much they cared with *action*, made the resentment he'd been carrying around forever seize his heart, slice in deep with its sharp claws, and squeeze.

Unconditional love like that was all he'd ever wanted.

"Come on, Zeus." The woman called over her shoulder as

she led Daphne to her beat-up vehicle and helped her into the passenger seat. She opened the back door and the dog jumped in, immediately resting his head on Daphne's shoulder. The woman slammed the car door and began to make her way around the back of the car. "The whole goddamned town, mister," she repeated, pointing at Apollo before she swung open the door and slid into the driver's seat. The vehicle's tires spun, throwing up gravel as she backed out. With that, the rusted contraption sped off through a cloud of dust toward the main road.

Apollo scrubbed a hand over his face, his skin suddenly slick with sweat as he turned to find Callie. Sure enough, there she stood, arms folded, head tilted, hip cocked. And he knew exactly why.

How quickly—how *easily*—he'd reverted into the role of the ruthless victor.

"What was that?" With just three words, her disapproval was a palpable thing writhing between them. "I mean, really? What. The fuck. Was *that*? We went over this. We practiced, and you were doing so good. I thought you'd . . ."

Anger and frustration—disappointment in himself—rushed to the surface, crashing through and overpowering him in an instant. "Learned one of your lessons?" His sardonic laugh shot out in a short, hard burst. "Sorry to disappoint you, Calliope, but this had to be done my way. The right way."

He slipped his trusty suit of armor over his wounded pride effortlessly.

"No." She shook her head. "I thought you'd finally changed." Her arms dropped like anchors to her sides, defeated.

He pushed out his chest, steeling himself. What came next was going to be painful, he just knew it.

"But I was wrong. You're never going to change. No, it's

worse than that. You're not the god I thought you were. You never have been."

And it did hurt. It hurt worse than anything he'd ever felt, even being constantly cast aside by his father. It tore him open wider than any rabid beast's teeth or claws ever had. It cut deeper than the sharpest blade during any battle he'd ever fought.

Normally, he couldn't stand being seen in a negative light. He strong-armed his way back into good graces, even if there *had* been just cause for a not-so-glowing review of him. But in this case, he had no argument, and he didn't have the will to make one up.

So he did the only thing that wouldn't make the cut deeper. He walked away, putting the distance between Callie and himself needed to spare her any more disappointment. He'd fucked up again, royally. Worse than he ever had before, and there was no excuse he could use to justify his actions. So he let his feet carry him to the sports car, a thing of beauty in stark contrast to the ugly surroundings he'd created.

He was no victor. He was a loser. In every conceivable way. The worst part had been seeing it in Callie's eyes. Hearing it in her voice. He was tarnished gold. Precious, but easily nicked and gouged. It's why he'd tried to outshine everyone else. Blind them with his greatness so they wouldn't see all his imperfections.

But she saw. Beautiful and kind and unassuming Callie. His muse had seen through his facade. Always had, and she'd stood in the shadows while he'd taken all the glory. Accepted all the credit. Hoarded every last bit of the fame she helped him win. Gave him the unconditional love he'd been too blind to see. And because of it, instead of reveling in the thrill of victory, he was drowning in the agony of defeat.

CHAPTER TWENTY-SIX

Callie wanted to slap him. Punching him in his flawless, perfect face would be satisfying as well. She could forgive a lot, and she'd excused plenty of his bad behavior over the centuries, but seeing him nearly destroy an innocent mortal to get what he wanted was more than she could bear.

He could be pretentious and conceited, caring way too much about what other people thought, but in all her years working for him, she'd never seen him act so ruthless. She knew everyone had a dark side, but these weren't powerful gods or monsters, they were innocent people. Apollo was not the god she thought she knew, and Clio had been right all along. He was an asshole.

And now, after showing his true colors, he thought he was just going to get to walk away?

She stomped after him, her anger boiling over. It bubbled in her stomach and stung her eyes, making them both burn mercilessly. She thought she didn't want an explanation, because it was so obvious he'd been acting the whole time, but now she wanted to hear it from his mouth. Not an apology, gods, it was too late for that, but why. Why he couldn't just swallow his pride and ask Eros for help. Why he always felt the need to hide behind his ego. Why he would throw everything away, including her, just so he could keep pretending he was the god of every damn thing.

"I can't do this anymore," she yelled at the back of his head.

He stopped and turned around. "Can't do what?" His pale eyes had gone dim, burdened with fear and regret. The sky darkened as he took a step toward her, reaching out a hand to her.

She stepped back, distancing herself from his advance. He dropped his arm, his expression crumbling at her retreat. She didn't care, let his light go out. It was too late for sorry.

She gulped down the sympathy trying its best to convince her to comfort him. She'd already given him too much. Once, all she'd dreamed about was being the only one he wanted. Now all she wanted was to run away.

Just like Daphne.

"Callie? Can't do what?" His voice was hesitant, testing the waters and trying to do what he always did. He might be a stickler for telling the truth, but he was a pro at ignoring it.

"I'm done," she said simply. There wasn't really anything more to say, honestly.

"With?" He peered down at her with a furrowed brow.

Hera fucking Zeus, was he really doing this? Her anger reignited, quick as lightning. "*You.* I'm done with you and your bullshit, Apollo. I've done nothing but help you win victory after victory after victory. I've stood by and watched you soak up all the glory and give nothing back for far too long."

"Callie, please stop," he said, sliding his hands into his pockets. "You'll say something you'll regret."

He looked so innocent standing there, but she knew

better. She'd fallen for it time and time again, but not today. It was the end of the line for Apollo and his selfish nature. And she was going to tell him so. Right now.

She stabbed a finger at his chest. Might as well fly high like Icarus and go out with a bang, maybe this time she'd finally break through the thick concrete that was his skull.

"Stop? So I don't say something I'll regret or so you don't have to hear the truth? Because that's the problem, isn't it? You don't want to hear the truth. You want to keep living in your own little world, expecting everyone to revolve around you. And we do. Oh, we do, and so willingly, too. Because you're beautiful and you're brilliant . . . and . . ." She shook her head, thoroughly exasperated. "Do you even know how brightly you shine? Gods, it's a sight. You're so warm when you want to be—when you *choose* to be—but you think so highly of yourself that we all get burned."

Apollo stared at her, dumfounded. The light in his eyes had gone almost completely out. Yet there was no emotion creasing his face, rendering it unreadable.

She sighed, exhausted. What had she expected? "Forget it. It doesn't matter what I think anyway."

"It does matter . . ." he began, but hesitated.

Now was not the time for hesitation. It was the moment of truth, and if he couldn't recognize that, then there was nothing else she could do. True to form, she gave him one last opportunity to come clean. "Does it?"

He took a half step towards her. "Of course it does."

And then he stood there. No clarification. No explanation. Not even an apology. Nothing.

"I'm going back to Olympus," she said, brushing past him. She was tired of waiting for him to do and say the right thing. Finally done with playing the fool.

"That's a good idea. Let's just take a few days off . . . We can . . .We should, ah, clear our heads before we figure out what to do next," he stammered as he trailed behind her.

How hysterical. No, how *fitting*. He was usually the one doing the leading, and now that he was following he was floundering so badly it was almost funny. She suddenly had the urge to unleash a maniacal laugh, but held it back. He might get the wrong impression about the depth of her hurt and anger. Besides, there was only room right now to make one thing very clear. Only one place she had just enough energy left to go.

She whipped around to discover his mouth was open, like he was going to say more, but she gave him a look that confirmed arguing would be futile. And if he was thinking he'd get the last word, he was wrong about that, too.

"No, Apollo." She shook her head. "There is no *our* heads anymore. You'll have to figure out the rest of this mess by yourself. I quit."

She turned on her heels and, for the first time ever, left him hanging. For a second, she thought her legs were going her disobey her command to *walk away*, but then her feet began to move. She folded her arms, hugging her middle in an attempt to keep herself from falling apart after only a few steps. All she wanted to do, all she was praying for at that moment, was having enough strength left to get to the nearest restroom so she could magic herself home before she burst into tears.

*A*pollo peered out of his expansive office window and down at the city streets below. He lifted his hand, a finger and thumb on the verge of a flick, but dropped it. The mortals traversing the sidewalks below continued about their business, unaware—and safe—from his divine melancholy. Knocking them down and seeing them stumble no longer calmed him. It only reminded him that Callie was right. He was a monster.

A fucking monster, to be exact.

He sighed, raking his fingers through his hair as he turned away. The air on Earth had stifled him, and he'd come back to Olympus directly after his ultimate screw up so he could think straight—breathe. He needed to focus on coming up with a plan, one that would take away the guilt and remorse insisting on plaguing him. He shook his head at the irony. He usually did the plaguing.

His gaze flicked toward the indent on the couch cushion where Callie sat so often. *Had* sat, as in, would probably never sit again because he'd been such an arrogant ass.

The nectar he'd poured beckoned to him, but he knew the

sweet, heady liquid would only make him feel better, more alive, and so he ignored it. He should punish himself, regale his body, mind and spirit with pain and suffering. It was only right.

He sank into his expensive office chair, rested his elbows on his nothing-but-the-best desk and rested his forehead on his fingers. The sun outside cast a weak light, making his office as dim as his mood. He didn't have the will to shine. Not today.

Would she notice?

Of course she would. She noticed everything. The real question was would she care.

Two sharp raps on the door sent his heart racing, and his pulse jumped when he bolted out of his chair and hurried around his desk to open it. His pulse slowed considerably, and so did his feet, with the third knock, which bore the news it wasn't Callie. Sure enough, Hermes stood on the other side of the threshold with an envelope in his hand.

"Special delivery, sunshine." Hermes handed over the envelope. "Leto asked me to give this to you."

"Hello, brother." Apollo stepped to the side. Hermes narrowed his eyes, as though considering his options, but breezed past a moment later.

Apollo let out a breath, relieved Hermes had decided something was up. And that he'd also accepted his invitation to find out what.

"You didn't point out that I was only your half sibling," said Hermes. "What's wrong?"

Apollo swallowed. "Nothing. Can't a man catch up with his little brother every now and then?"

"Okay, but we're not men, we're *gods*. Pro tip, most of us aren't known for harboring a fondness for our brethren. You think we would since we're all pretty much relate—"

Apollo shook his head, raising a hand to indicate he knew

the sordid history well and didn't need a refresher. The heavily branched family tree that started with their father—Ground Zeus—was nothing short of mind boggling. The king of gods had spun a rather large, and mostly adulterous, web from the beginning. They were deities, of course, not bound by human taboo, so it didn't necessarily matter, but still.

No wonder the inhabitants of Olympus had so many issues.

Apollo handed the nectar sitting on his desk to Hermes. "How's your collection coming along? Been anywhere good lately? How's Hades?"

Oh gods, he was beginning to sound like his mother.

Hermes accepted the offering and took a sip. "Good. Super busy, and I'm thinking of taking some time off soon. Quick little getaway to Elysium, maybe."

Traveler, messenger, conductor of souls to the Underworld, and that wasn't even the half of it. Hermes was a free spirit; he wasn't weighed down with the need for adoration like Apollo. Hermes lived in the moment, and his eternally positive outlook made Apollo a little jealous. Okay, a lot jealous. Everyone loved Hermes, even the Fates. Sometimes, Apollo wondered why his younger brother wasn't the god of sun and light instead of him.

"What about you, Mr. Brightside? Any personal victories lately?"

Apollo bristled at the casual manner with which Hermes referred to him, but rolled his shoulders and forced himself to lighten up. Maybe he could manage to not take himself so seriously and see what happened. It had worked before, with Callie. Until he'd slipped back into beast mode.

"Funny you should ask. I'm sure you've heard?"

Hermes pressed his lips together. "Well, yeah, I did just come from seeing the goddess of gossip." He took another sip of nectar.

Apollo, now sitting at his desk, opened the folder. Listed on the lonely sheet of paper was a single name, a maenad by the name of Bromie, one of Dionysus's devoted female followers. Apollo had expected at least two pages worth of names, but no one, save for a crazy, in the most literal sense, maenad had applied to be his new assistant. He closed the folder, forcing himself to ask the question on his mind before he lost his nerve.

"How do you do it, Hermes?"

"Do what?"

"Make people love you so much?"

"Easy. I'm a giver."

"A giver?"

"I give, Apollo. You take. You're a taker. People don't like takers."

Apollo nodded, a montage of memories chased each other through his mind. Callie standing on the sidelines smiling proudly through the cheering and screaming in every one.

"But they all cheer for me."

"It's complicated. People love winners because it gives them something to strive for, but by the same token, they don't suffer pompous assholes. People love me because they *like* me. You know what I'm saying?"

The concept nibbled hungrily at the crumbs of Apollo's understanding when someone knocked on the door. It was more of a pounding, actually, and he knew immediately who'd come calling. Their mother must have sent her.

Hermes swallowed the last of the nectar before getting up and walking over to Apollo's desk. "Life is not a contest, man. Just be yourself."

"What if this *is* myself?"

"It's not." Hermes set the glass down, and when he turned to go he nearly crashed into Artemis, who'd stalked into the office and was in the process of pulling a chair over to the front of Apollo's desk. "Hey, Arti. Love the Adidas get up."

Artemis stopped to clasp forearms with Hermes. "Thanks. What's up, player?"

"Protecting travelers, sticking up for thieves, ushering the dead . . . the usual." Hermes tossed a wave as he headed out the door. "See you guys later."

Artemis dropped into the chair. Knees bent, she planted her feet on the edge of Apollo's desk. "So what the fuck's your problem now? You've got mom all in a tizzy."

Apollo's twin was tall like him, lean and muscled from a continuous rotation of outdoor sports, but where he was the embodiment of the golden sun, she was the silvery moon. Striking cool eyes, dark hair, pale skin . . . and a razor-sharp tongue. Artemis said exactly what was on her mind.

"Hello to you, too, sister." He forced himself not to mention how unsanitary it was for her to have her filthy shoes on his desk.

"Don't even start with your snarky bullshit. Tell me what's going on."

Apollo leaned back in his chair and sighed, his gaze wandering toward the window. "Don't you ever get lonely?"

"Oh good gods, I came all the way up here so you could get existential on me?"

His head snapped toward her, his annoyance surging. "I'm serious, Artemis. I'm at a real crossroads here."

They were alike in many ways—strong, confident, opinionated—yet so very different. Artemis didn't care for crowds, preferring solitude among the woods with her maids. He, on the other hand, craved attention. Demanded the spotlight. Longed for adoration. All of which made him angry when he thought he wasn't being taken seriously. Artemis didn't give a satyr's ass what anyone thought.

Apollo pried his clenched jaw loose when the obvious

clicked into place. His incessant need to prove how great he was just might be the problem.

Not might be. It *was* the problem.

"Sometimes." Her gaze dipped to the toes of her cross trainers. "But then I remember I'm not truly alone. I have the trees, I have my maids, the hunt . . . and you clowns up here on Olympus to fill my days."

"Do you think you'll ever find the one?"

Her feet slid off the edge of the desk, and she purposely made a loud *thud* as they landed on the floor. Leaning further back in her chair, she calmly folded her arms across her chest and answered coolly, "I'm not looking for 'the one' and you know it."

"Daphne hates me."

"And?"

"And what? How am I supposed to win her over if she refuses to give me a chance? I wanted this curse to be broken so I could . . ." Apollo's brows crumpled. So he could what? He'd been sure for thousands of years, but once he'd resumed his pursuit of Daphne, everything had changed. "So *we* could both have the chance to feel something real."

"We? You're actually thinking about Daphne in all of this?"

Apollo pursed his lips at her. She knew the deal.

Maybe that was his other problem. The truth had been revealed—and he finally had been forced to admit it—he wasn't perfect. He wasn't even likable.

And then there was the *other* truth. The one that involved Callie.

"Sorry," continued Artemis. "It's just weird hearing you say *we*. Look, you're beating a dead pegasus. So Daphne doesn't love you, big deal. We both know why. It doesn't matter anyway."

"That no one loves me?"

"No, you jackass. I love you, Mom loves you—"

"But does dad love me?"

Artemis rolled her eyes and snorted. "Dude, you've got to get over this need to prove yourself to him. And, no, because you should be with someone else."

"How do you know?" snapped Apollo. Sweet Persephone, feeling so exposed really had a way of grating on his nerves.

"Are you serious right now, bro? I literally live under a rock and even I saw this coming."

He knew she was referring to Callie, who hated him now. His chest tightened at the thought. He missed her. The way she smiled, the way she smelled—like lemons and sunshine —the way she laughed. He even missed the way she chewed her fingernails. There was no use denying it, especially to his twin.

"What do I do?"

"Have you talked to Eros?"

"Yes."

"*Without* the ego?"

Apollo pinched the bridge of his nose. "No. I'm afraid I was rather demanding."

"What do you have against him anyway? He's nice, so's his wife. They're partners now, aren't they? Anyway, he obviously has the biggest heart on Mount Olympus. Maybe if you show him you've got one too, he'll cut you some slack."

"Arti?"

"Yeah?"

"Do you think I'm a monster?"

"You can be a real jerk sometimes," she replied, her head tilting when his shoulders slumped. "Look, you're not a monster, but you do need to stop acting like you're so much better than everyone else."

Artemis pushed herself upright and stood. The chair slid back to its original arrangement among the office furniture with a flick of her foot. "Nice talk, but I gotta run. You good?"

No, he wasn't good. Not yet, but he was beginning to see what he had to do to get there. "Thanks for being honest with me, Arti."

"Did you expect anything less?" said his twin before swinging open the door. She paused, turning in the doorway to face him. "You got this. Just make sure you face down the demons that count, okay?"

The door clicked shut behind her.

Apollo dragged in a deep breath before waving his hand over the empty glass on his desk. Rosy-gold nectar bubbled into existence until it almost reached the rim. Callie, his mother *and* father, Orea, and now Artemis. That brought the total to five.

He finished the nectar in three gulps, still swallowing the last one as he gently set the glass down. He pushed up from his chair, adjusting the cuffs of his sleeve as he strode out of his office.

He hoped to Hades' Realm the god of love was in a forgiving mood that afternoon.

CHAPTER TWENTY-EIGHT

*E*ach step dragged heavier than the last, but Apollo willed his feet to keep moving. He'd known all along this must be done. Deep down he knew it would come to this, and so he pried his reluctant fists loose, shaking his hands out like a boxer on his way into the ring.

How fitting. He truly was about to engage in the fight of his life.

Not with Eros, but with his own pride.

He barely heard his feet pound the cobbled stone, or the rumbling it produced. He did see several heads peek out of their offices, though. Demeter, Athena, sweet-natured and nurturing Hestia . . . But he ignored them, just like he paid no mind to the canaries scattering from their perches in his wake. He was on a mission.

Still, even though he knew the probability of things coming down to this very moment, when he'd have to admit defeat and beg for the mercy of love, every fiber of his being fought to remain selfish. He'd been fighting all this time, struggling to let all the hurt and anger go because he hated feeling exposed. It had been his only goal for so long; protect the vulnerable part of him that desperately longed to be loved for who he was, not who he pretended to be.

Unfortunately, that bit of new-found self discovery didn't make what he was about to do any easier.

He blew out a long breath as he walked past the large storefront window. When he halted outside the office door of Life Industries Co-Coordinators of Hearts, the door swung open before he could even knock.

They'd been waiting for the moment he'd been dreading.

His muscles tensed, and his fists automatically balled up again, preparing for a one-two punch. He inhaled another deep breath, commanding them to relax. Blessedly, they obeyed, loosening enough for the blood to flow back into his fingers. There would be no fighting this time. Couldn't be. Only begging. Hopefully it wouldn't come to that, but he was prepared to give it a try.

"Hey, Apollo," Eros tilted his head, his gaze searching for something—someone—beyond Apollo's shoulder. "How's it going?"

He could almost hear the gods-awful rending of his pride being torn down, strip by painful, demoralizing strip. "She's not with me, matchmaker. You'll be delighted to know I've failed." Even as the words left his mouth, he knew they were laced with too much condescension, and he cringed.

Old habits die hard.

"I see." Eros set down his pen and clasped his hands together, resting them on a stack of paperwork. "So then what brings you here?"

Apollo swallowed, that small but powerful voice—the victor—screaming at him in stereo along with his raw and bleeding pride from somewhere in the back of his mind. Here it was, the time of reckoning, and the part of him that needed to win didn't like what he was about to do. *Had* to do.

"Two reasons. The first is I owe you an apology. I was—

am—insecure about . . . a lot of things. I obviously put down others to make myself feel better." Apollo pressed his lips together once the words were out, waiting for the smug satisfaction to show up on Eros's face.

Eros nodded, but with no smug satisfaction, only thoughtful consideration. The voices inside Apollo's head went silent, taken aback. Way aback.

But, by gods, did his chest feel lighter?

Yes, it did . . . but not light enough.

"Second, I need you to shoot Daphne with one of your golden arrows."

Psyche sprang up from her chair and headed straight for him. She was on a mission now, too, and he felt small inside her very intent gaze. When she stopped directly in front of him and folded her arms, she said, "Wow, for a minute there I thought you'd changed."

Apollo ran a hand through his hair, realizing how his request had sounded. Not good. Condescending and demanding. "It's not for the reason you think."

"Oh? Enlighten us," she replied.

She wasn't buying it. Probably because he was having a hard time selling it. Being humble wasn't exactly his strong suit.

Eros was up from his desk now, too, standing next to Psyche. Two against one.

"You can take them both," whispered Apollo's victor.

As tempting as the thought was, he ignored it. This was his opportunity to show he was trying to make things right. Prove that he *did* have a heart, even if he didn't know how to use it.

"I want Daphne to be free, to love whomever she chooses, even if that someone isn't me. She'll never say she loves me out loud because she's not in love with me. She's in love with someone else. So, I want—" Apollo could see why Callie chewed her fingernails to Hades' Realm. Choosing words carefully was nerve-racking. "I am *asking* you to shoot her with your golden arrow. And then bind her heart to a mortal by the name of Samuel Carson."

Psyche's face went slack, her shock evident. After a second thought, it snapped into its previously pinched and hardened state. "What about you in all of this?"

Fair question, and he couldn't blame her for asking. He supposed he'd be suspicious, too, if a notoriously egotistical jerk suddenly started thinking of others.

Not only was her question fair, it was good, and the vulnerable, innocent little blue-eyed godling born on the island of Delos rushed to answer before the victor opened his mouth. "I suppose I'll take some more time to deal with my daddy issues."

He scrubbed a hand over his face. Good gods, that might take an eternity.

Eros studied him carefully, his aura pulsing a faint magenta as he evaluated Apollo's response.

"Honestly," continued Apollo with all sincerity, "the only thing I care about right now is seeing to Daphne's happiness."

Not one hundred percent accurate. He cared about Callie, and making amends. But he could only take one step at a time.

Psyche's arms dropped to her sides, the bangles on her wrist jangling, before gliding over to him. He stood perfectly still, knowing full well what she intended to do. She found his gaze and held it. When a tingling sensation crackled along his temples, he let her in without a fight.

"Hmm," she said, biting the inside of her cheek, her gaze intensifying. "Mmm hmm." She rubbed the top of her thumbnail for a few silent seconds. Satisfied, she nodded.

"Miracle of all miracles, the god of sun and light *is* thinking about someone else for a change."

Warmth filled Apollo's chest as the aura around Eros flared from magenta to deep red. "I know, I can feel it in his heart."

Apollo exhaled, the warmth in his chest spreading as the thought of Callie in her yellow sundress, her wide, sunny smile, filled his heart. "Yes, I'm telling the truth."

But not the whole truth. He desperately wanted to ask for one more thing. If Eros could spare a second golden arrow . . .

Eros and Psyche stared at him, nodding and shaking their heads. Apollo knew there was an entire conversation going on between them inside their divine melons. So did the pit of his stomach, which was starting to feel similar to a nausea-inducing boat ride.

Finally, both co-coordinators nodded. "Okay, consider it done," said Eros. "We'll go down this evening. Where is she?"

"Oklahoma," said Apollo with an exhale. Remembering what had transpired, he slid his hands into the pockets of his dress pants. "Anadarko hospital," he said quietly, and then held his breath again.

Psyche gasped. "You didn't."

The air gushed from his lungs. Apollo dropped his head, his shoulders following suit. "I did. But I stopped. He'll be okay."

Apollo glanced up to witness more intense internal discussion going on between Eros and Psyche. One eyebrow raised, Eros bit the inside of his lip. Psyche's lips were so thin they were almost invisible. They went on this way—shrugging shoulders and shaking heads while they negotiated telepathically—until they both had the same look on their faces, which was now resigned.

Eros stiffened, folding his arms and fanning out his wings. The sick feeling crept up from Apollo's stomach and into his throat. All the times he'd known better, but had self-ishly taken the glory anyway, culminated in a dizzying feeling he was about to be denied. He was going to lose big time, and he had no idea how his victor would react.

"We need to learn from our mistakes," said Eros, Psyche nodding in agreement at his side. "How else can we change, right?"

Okay. The matchmaker needed to get on with it. Just say it.

"It seems that you, Apollo, have not . . ."

Apollo dropped his head, which felt heavier than a thou-sand suns at the moment.

"Had any trouble seeing the error of your ways in this case." Eros clapped him on the shoulder before turning back toward his desk. "Well, I mean, you've had *trouble*, but it looks like you came out the victor on this one, buddy. I'll lift the curse and add the binding you've requested to my list. I'll even fast-track it for you, how does that sound?"

How did it sound? After three centuries of being cursed, it sounded pretty gods-damn amazing.

Apollo's lips twitched into a smile, floored at what simply asking for something could accomplish. It seemed a far better approach than his previous guerrilla tactics. "I appreciate this, matchmaker."

One of Eros's cheeks pushed up into an uneven grin as he sat on the edge of his desk. "Anything else we can do for you?"

The corners of Apollo's mouth fell, but he pulled them up before Eros and Psyche could see him frown. There was something else Eros could do, all right, but having him shoot Callie with a golden arrow would not be winning, it would be cheating. He had to ask for her forgiveness on his own. "No, that's it."

"Okay, well, I'm glad we could help. You've really proven yourself, Apollo. I think you're well on your way to redemption."

"Me too," said Psyche, nodding.

The corners of Apollo's lips found the strength to lift again, the genuine praise making his aura brighten. If he wasn't careful with this asking for what you want business, he might start doing it more. "Thank you."

He was surprised at how easily the words slipped out. His limbs buzzed with satisfaction as he turned toward the door. In fact, it had produced a rather potent thrill, rivaling the strongest adrenaline rush that flooded his system whenever he defeated a foe. Better, actually, and he wondered if there was a way to make the feeling last. To make someone else feel it, too.

There was only one way to find out.

The sun's rays burst through the clouds as he magicked himself down to the Caddo County Vintage and Craft Market.

CHAPTER TWENTY-NINE

*D*aphne woke to the sound of high-pitched squeaking. She'd gotten use to the whirring of medical machinery, the persistent beeping of monitors, but this new noise was not comforting. She peered into the dim room until she found the source of the alarming noise.

"Good morning. I'm Aubrey," whispered a woman in scrubs. The marker gave one last tiny shriek as the nurse finished the smiley face she'd put after her name on the white board. The cheerful drawing seemed fitting. Her sleek brown hair was swept into a perfectly positioned ponytail. In addition to not a single hair being out of place so early in the morning, she was bright-eyed and bushy-tailed. "How's our patient this morning?"

Calmer, Daphne unfolded herself from the chair she'd used as a bed and stretched. "I was hoping you could tell me," she said through a yawn.

"Okay. Let's see what we got here." The nurse tapped quietly on the computer's keyboard to pull up Sam's electronic medical chart. "Myocardial infarction?" she murmured, glancing at his sleeping form. "He's so young. He must have been under a lot of stress."

The lump in Daphne's throat dropped into the pit of her stomach like an anvil. Stress was an understatement, and the resulting heart attack had been her fault. Pretty much all her fault, and she wished it was possible for her to leave before he woke up. So she couldn't do anymore damage. "Is he going to be okay?"

"His ECG came back normal. Doctor Morrison has him on a round of sedatives so he can get some rest. We'll run a few more tests when he wakes up, and if there are no problems, it's likely he could be discharged by this evening."

Daphne exhaled. The nurse couldn't take the liberty of saying whether or not Sam would be okay, but she had given as much information as she was allowed. The corresponding smile on Aubrey's face told Daphne the prognosis was positive. "Thank you, Aubrey."

"My pleasure. Is there anything I can get you? Water? Juice?"

Daphne shook her head. "I'm good. I have everything I need. Thanks, though."

"Okay, well, if you change your mind, the nurse's station is down the hall to your left. Just come get me, okay?"

Aubrey gave Daphne a warm smile before leaving the room. She pulled a chair to the side of Sam's bed, as quietly as possible, and took his hand in hers. He was going to be okay, which meant it was time to say goodbye.

She brushed a lock of hair off of his forehead. It felt as though she'd performed the loving gesture a thousand times before. The feeling was so powerful and overwhelming it made her breath hitch. She wished she really had done it a thousand times already.

"I should have known better, huh?" she whispered. "But no, I had to go and start the chase all over again. For what it's worth, you're everything I could have asked for in a man. You really opened my eyes to how love can be, Sam Carson, and I'll never forget you."

Hot tears welled, making her eyes burn. She'd be the second woman in Sam's life to leave him. He would be devastated, but what else could she do? She bit back a sob as she leaned in to give him one last kiss.

She pressed her lips to his, leaving them there so she could remember how they felt. How perfectly they fit together. She kissed his cheek, pressing her nose into his skin and inhaling. So she wouldn't forget the way he smelled.

Daphne suppressed a sniffle that tried its best to become another hitch. It didn't really work, so she gave up and relieved the pressure building in her neck and throat by letting go of a small sob. While she wiped away her tears on her sleeve, a shuffling came from behind her, and the unmistakable scent of roses filled the air.

She waited for the nurse to say something, and when she didn't, Daphne turned. "Thanks, Aubrey, you can set them —Eros?"

"Hi Daphne." Eros made his way into the room carrying an enormous flower arrangement. He set the vase down on a ledge near the window as she continued to stare at him in amazement.

She finally regained her senses and bowed her head to the god of love.

"Has my father sent you to come get me?"

"No, not your father."

"Then who?"

Eros didn't answer, only smiled at her politely.

Daphne sighed, the urge to roll her eyes overwhelming. Sometimes even the most mild-mannered gods were infuriating. "All right. I'm ready. Let's go before he wakes up." She stood, the stinging at the back of her eyes sharpening. A thought hit her as she kissed Sam's stubbled cheek for the very last time, and when she straightened, she asked, "Do you think you can get Mnemosyne to erase his memories of loving me before we go?"

"I can," replied Eros. "Is that what you really want, though?"

What she really wanted was to stay. But that wasn't an option. The least she could do was see to it that he forgot that he ever felt anything for her. "No, but if it's between breaking his heart or him not remembering what happened between us . . ." She made that funny half sobbing, half swallowing noise again. "I don't want him to think I left because he wasn't good enough."

Eros fixed a blue-eyed gaze on her. "Do you love this mortal, Daphne?"

She didn't hesitate to answer. "With all my heart."

One of his cheeks slid up, a dimple accentuating his lopsided grin. "Ah, yes, four words I never get tired of hearing."

With that, the god of love's wings arched high above his shoulders. She shouldn't have been surprised when his golden bow materialized, but she couldn't help but gasp.

"It wasn't your father that sent me, it was Apollo. I told him if he could get you to say that you loved him out loud I would lift the curse. As you know, Apollo pissed me off years ago. Surprise, surprise, right? He said love was a joke and that my bow was a toy and . . . Well, you get the picture. I shot you with a leaden arrow and him with a golden arrow and the rest is history. I'm sorry, Daphne. My anger was so sudden, and it was back when I had trouble controlling my temper. You couldn't have known what hit you."

"Wait. So I don't actually hate Apollo?"

"Oh, no, you definitely hate Apollo. His compulsion to

chase you over the years—" Eros cleared his throat, "centuries only made your initial aversion to his advances worse."

Daphne twisted the hem of her shirt in her fingers, as though she could wring out the confusion drenching her mind. "I don't understand why you wouldn't just break the curse."

"I know, I'm complicated." Eros winked. "See, I knew it would take a lot for Apollo to learn his lesson. What better way for him to learn a thing or two about accountability than with a contest he couldn't win unless he admitted wrongdoing? You know Apollo, he can never say no to a challenge. Well, it wasn't him you ended up professing your love aloud for, it was Sam. Apollo obviously didn't take it well at first, but then the most delightful thing happened. After some reflection, and seeing you so worried about Sam, he came to us to make a deal. Lift the curse, but bind you two instead." Eros motioned between her and Sam. "Turns out Zeus's golden child does have a heart. He's just a complete novice at using it."

"Eros, please tell me what this means." She had her theories, but she needed to hear it straight from the god of love's mouth.

"I'm shooting you with a golden arrow this time."

Her chest tightened, making the rapid beating of her heart a little painful. "Will it hurt?"

"No, not if it's true love, which, don't worry, it is . . . I double checked with the Fates."

The good news should have made her happy, and it did, but it also made the tears clinging to the corners of her eyes make good on their threat. It also brought on more sobbing and a few hiccups. "But I'm not mortal. We'll barely have any time together before he's gone. So what's the point?" Her cheeks were drenched, snot clinging to the inside of her nostrils, ready to make an unsightly appearance.

Eros smacked a hand to his forehead. "Sweet Persephone, I didn't tell you? I put in a Mortality Request for you."

Daphne's heart went from an uncomfortable pitter patter to a slightly painful *boom, boom, boom*. She thought of the Sacred Forest, of her father and her family. How she'd never need money or food or even shelter if she went back. And then she thought of Sam. Sweet, caring, innocent Sam and how he made her feel. Cherished and protected. Loved.

Not controlled, and certainly not chased.

She nodded, giving Eros the go ahead to nock his arrow.

He flashed his lopsided grin once more. "Ready, Freddy?"

She was still nodding when, before she could even close her eyes, he let his arrow fly. She saw the shimmering puff of dust and heard the high-pitched whistle as it zipped through the air straight for her heart. It sounded like the sweetest of whispers and the softest of sighs, and she bit her lip to prepare for impact. When the tip sunk deep into her chest, it didn't hurt at all.

The sparkling arrow dissolved, tiny particles glittering before blinking out, and when the bubbly popping and fizzing sensation stopped, she no longer felt the urge to run.

A small moan came from Sam, his eyelids fluttering, dangerously close to opening.

"Quick, lay across his chest." Eros drew another golden arrow from his quiver. This one left a trail of sparkly love dust, too, as his wings flapped soundlessly, propelling him up toward the ceiling.

Daphne did as instructed and threw herself over Sam's chest, taking care to align her heart with his. When the arrow struck, she gasped. She couldn't help it. A true love bond felt like nothing she'd ever known. There was no use in even trying to describe it, but it was as if all the stars were twinkling inside of her at once.

Sam gasped, too, but his eyes stayed shut. A smile played

along the corners of his mouth in his sleep, and Daphne laid her head on his chest to listen to his beating heart. She almost giggled when she thought of how the opportunity to grow old with Sam in exchange for her immortality was going to be so worth it.

She glanced up at the ceiling where Eros hovered. When she lifted her head to whisper her thanks, he gave her a thumbs up and a lopsided grin before fading away.

CHAPTER THIRTY

Rough bark bit into Callie's back, but sitting in the soft grass under the swaying branches of a giant weeping willow was somehow more comforting than sitting on one of the cold, stone benches lining the path. She'd wandered into an overgrown part of the gardens to be alone with her thoughts and write. Except, a certain someone was ruining the plan by occupying her mind.

Tiny finches flitted from branch to branch in a nearby thicket of young ash trees. The breeze lifted the ends of her hair as the birds twittered and chirped. Out of habit, her eyes wandered toward the sky . . . where the sun was covered by clouds.

So he felt gloomy, did he? Fine by her. She didn't care if he ever shined again, because the happiness of the god of sun and light was no longer her problem. And he most certainly had a problem because, as she'd so thoroughly discovered, it took more than she had in her to keep him happy. So, yeah, she'd be perfectly content living out the rest of her immortal life with the world in an overcast haze.

She turned her attention back toward the last blank page

in her journal and looked down at her resignation letter with renewed focus and determination. She hadn't so much as stepped a foot inside Life Industries in weeks, but she had heard Demeter might be looking for an assistant, which would be perfect since the position was part-time. She could work for Demi half the year, during the winter months, and when Persephone came up from the Underworld to help her mother usher in spring, Callie could spend more time re-developing her inspiration skills. Get back to the basics of being a muse. Clio would love that.

Speaking of assistants, she'd heard a rumor that a maenad by the name of Bromie might be taking her place soon, which was all well and good. Once she slipped this resignation letter under his office door, Callie would officially be free of him.

And what a good riddance it would be.

Her pencil scratched *"Dear Apollo"* across the top of the page for the tenth time, and she promptly erased it again. Too nice. She was being too nice. He wasn't dear, not anymore.

Or maybe that was just a lie she was telling herself to help her get over the break-up hump.

Callie tucked her pencil behind her ear and sighed. She was usually good with words. *The best.* Apollo's voice echoed in her brain. She snorted at the hypocrisy and closed her journal. There should be no break-up hump, because there hadn't been anything to break up.

Startled, her head thumped against the tree's massive trunk when she noticed Clio sitting on a bench a few yards away. Clio patted the empty space next to her, beckoning Callie to join her. She didn't feel like talking, but knowing Clio, that was out of the question. She'd sit there patting that gods-damned bench for an eternity. Callie dragged her still emotionally drained bones up and headed over to sit next to her sister.

The seconds stretched into minutes, but Clio didn't speak. Callie kicked at a small pebble that had found its way onto the cobblestone. It went rolling over to Clio, who gently kicked it back her way without a word. When the silence grew awkward, Callie finally broke it.

"Well, aren't you going to tell me 'I told you so'?"

Clio shook her head. "No."

Callie chewed on a fingernail for half a second before replying. "I really thought he could . . ."

"I know." Clio gently pushed on Callie's wrist, guiding her hand down to her lap.

"I was rooting for him . . . And I thought if . . ."

Clio fixed her jade eyes full of sympathy on Callie. "I know."

"I was stupid." Callie wrapped her arms around her waist, shoulders hunching under the weight of her sorrow. Funny how it always seemed to show up at the most inopportune times, like now, in front of her sister.

Clio rubbed soothing circles on Callie's back. "You weren't stupid, honey. We all want to see the best in the people we love."

Callie nodded, sniffling instead of sobbing, thank the gods. Crying would only prove how strong and vast her love for Apollo had been, and how much she was drowning in its depths at the moment, still. She'd given everything to him, and he'd given her nothing in return except a broken heart.

But she'd known that going in. She'd known that since the first time he'd broken her heart, and she'd gone back for more. So whose fault was it, really?

"I know how much you love him, Callie, but—"

"*Loved* him, and I know, I've got to move on." The lump in her throat ached, her voice thick with emotion. "I'm trying, Clio, but it's going to take some time."

"I know it will, which is why I'm not going to tell you I

told you so." She tugged the end of Callie's messy pony tail. "You know I'm here for you, right? All of your sisters are here for you. Hey, what do you say we do a girls night out soon? Drink some wine, play some trivia, write some poetry. We'll make it like old times and see if any of the goddesses want to join."

Callie mumbled the most upbeat response she could muster, which wasn't very enthusiastic at all. "Sure. Just let me finish this resignation letter."

Apollo knew she'd said she couldn't work with him anymore, but hearing the words "resignation letter" straight from her mouth felt like a punch to the gut. It made things all too real.

She really wasn't coming back.

The moment he cleared his throat, both their heads snapped around. Callie's gaze turned forward once she realized it was him, but Clio's gaze, icier than the summit of Mount Olympus, stayed trained on him. If he hadn't known she was a muse, he would have sworn she was a demon whose head had rotated and come to rest at an impossible angle on her back. She continued to glare at him as she rose from the bench—again, demon-like—only breaking eye contact with him to speak to her sister.

"We'll figure out a girls night soon, okay?" Clio laid a hand on Callie's shoulder. "Do you want me to send him away?"

Callie shook her head.

Abiding by her sister's wishes, Clio made her way around the bench, taking her time with slow, deliberate steps until she stood in front of Apollo. "I swear to your fellow gods and goddesses, you hurt her any more and we're going straight to Zeus. All of us." She pinned him with a look that left no doubt her message should be received. He hadn't seen a pair of dagger eyes that sharp since the mortal woman who'd essentially said she'd sic all of Caddo County on him.

The urge to reprimand her for addressing him in such an insubordinate manner flared, making him flush. He was their patron god, after all. But he held his tongue. She was right. It was him that had been out of line. "I understand. I just want to apologize for my behavior."

"Good. You do that." Clio gave him a curt nod before taking a step backward, fading into nothing more than an apparition before dissolving completely.

Apollo sat on the cold stone bench next to Callie, his heart pounding in his chest as he clasped his hands in his lap and inspected the cuticles of his thumbs. "Can we talk?"

Callie didn't say anything. But she didn't leave either. He couldn't tell if that was a good sign or not.

"My pride got the best of me, and I know how I handled it was inexcusable. I realize it may not make a difference at this point, but I need to say two things. First, I'm so, *so* sorry, Callie. I've taken advantage of your kindness for far too long."

The seconds dragged by, and he sat quietly with his guilt and shame. Because he deserved it.

"And the second?" Her voice sounded thin. Tired.

Regret clawed at his insides. It was good to hear her voice, but it didn't sound the same. It was devoid of its soothing tone and patient pitch. Worse, the muse of his heart was drained of her sunny outlook, her infectious optimism, and he hated that he was the reason.

Another thing he'd selfishly taken.

"Thank you," he said, his voice almost breaking.

She finally looked at him, brows furrowed over lovely eyes, blue as a cloudless sky.

"I wouldn't be half the god I am if it wasn't for you. More

than half. I wouldn't be much of anything at all. I know that now. You've always been there for me."

She huffed hard and fast, shaking her head as she shrugged. "You tell me this now? What am I supposed to say to that?"

"Callie, I—"

"I don't think you realize what I was willing to give up to help you. I'm the muse of epic poetry, and I haven't written anything epic in ages. You take so much energy, Apollo. And I . . . I just don't have any more to give. I appreciate your apology, but do you blame me for not believing anything you say?"

He buried his face in his hands. The god of sun and light actually wanted to wail like an infant. His muse was leaving him, for good, and he wanted to take her in his arms, press his lips to hers, whisper in her ear how much he needed her. Of all the things he was the best at, he wished it was knowing how to return the warm smile to her beautiful face. The memory of it made him press his lips thinner. He had to keep the tortured sigh from escaping somehow. Even sad, she shined brighter than the stars on a warm summer night.

And he didn't deserve any of her light.

He leaned over, rested his forearms on his thighs and stared down at his expensive dress shoes. The gravel pathway had covered them in dust, and for once, he didn't care. "I was chasing after something that was never meant to be. I was never going to win that battle. I was a fool, Callie."

Callie went back to punishing him with the silent treatment.

He straightened. "I should go." The yellow journal she had been eyeing their first day down on Earth materialized in his hand, and he held it out to her. "I saw that you only had a few pages left. I thought you might like a new one."

CHAPTER THIRTY-ONE

Callie reached out with trembling fingers, refusing to look at him. She couldn't meet his gaze, for various reasons, but the predominant one being confusion. She did need a new journal, that was a fact, and she had admired this one, another fact, but the whole giving her a gift thing? Right now? That was bullshit.

Once a muse always a muse, and despite the facts, grace won out over pride. She looked up at him, uttering the word "thank" out loud, but when she only caught the faint outline of his form before it vanished, the "you" withered in her throat.

It was just as well. If he would have stayed, the precariously plugged dam would have sprung a leak, leaving room for a torrent of forgiveness to come gushing forth, completely out of her control.

She wasn't ready to forgive him yet. In all honesty, she might never be.

She ran her fingers over the front of the journal, trying to keep her mind blank. The advice she'd given him, *Try giving her something you know she likes, not something you think she likes,* popped into her head. Despite not wanting them to her lips tipped up at the memory of the god of every damned thing sitting on the floor partaking in a mortal activity she knew he found boring and trite.

She scowled and stuffed the journal into her bag, her emotions battling for control. Love. Hate. Sympathy. Last, but not least, anger. He hadn't even noticed, even after all she'd done to prove it, how much he meant to her.

Another fact she needed to come to terms with.

But despite *that,* he'd just given her a heartfelt gift, one he *knew* she'd like. He'd known her favorite color without having to ask. And the look in his eyes that night under the stars, how conflicted it was as they sat in the parking lot on the hood of a car and talked until dawn.

So add another feeling into the mix. Confusion. Sweet Persephone, this emotional rollercoaster was giving her whiplash.

She reached into her bag and dragged the damned thing back out, a deep loneliness breaking her will with next to no effort. So what if she wallowed in her pathetic longing for what could have been for a few minutes? It wasn't like anyone was there to witness it. When she opened the journal to inspect the blank pages, something written on one of them caught her eye. She gasped, zeroing in on the words, mortified when she recognized them as her own.

HARK OH UNIVERSE I SEEK TO FIND
THE ANSWER TO A QUESTION THINE
UNDER GOLD RAYS OF SUN DIVINE
WHY DO I SEEM TO THUS SO SHINE?

Her cheeks caught fire. He would have had to memorize the passage to copy it down, and if he'd committed it to memory, then he knew the words she'd poured onto paper were about him. It was the beginning of a poem she'd scribbled into the margin of her last journal, and now here it was in ancient Greek, written in Apollo's perfect handwriting.

Callie's heart beat furiously, and she almost threw the journal into a thicket of bushes. What kind of game was he playing? How could he add such insult to injury? Tears of frustration burned her eyes, but, per usual, she couldn't look away. Her heart pounded as she read Apollo's response.

FOR EVERY HEART THERE IS A SOUL
FOR EVERY LIE A TRUTH BE TOLD
I TELL YOU FREE MY DEAREST ONE
WITHOUT YOUR SMILE THERE IS NO SUN

He'd answered her musing with words so pure and tender and true they could only mean one thing. But it was impossible. The curse compelled him to think of no one but Daphne, the water nymph who had surely been struck by Eros's golden arrow by now, ensuring that her heart and Apollo's were forever bound.

What if it wasn't, though? What if . . .

Callie bolted up from the bench and ran out of the gardens until the soft grass gave way to hard stone. Her sandaled feet pounded over the cobbled walkway, and she didn't slow when she entered the atrium, she sped up, dashing around the enormous fountain and up the stairs of Life Industries. Journal pressed tightly to her chest with one arm, she pulled open one of the gilded doors with the other.

"Hello, darling." Leto greeted her with a smile.

Callie did not slow down, only shouted breathlessly as she flew past the reception desk. "Hi, Leto. Going to the Hall of Olympians."

The Spartan guards didn't ask to see her work badge, they simply stepped out of her way. "Thanks, guys."

She finally slowed her pace to a brisk walk once she got to the promenade. Her mind whirled with all sorts of crazy ideas, running in the background while she worked on convincing her chest to stop heaving. When she stumbled to a stop outside her destination, she knocked frantically.

"Door's open," called out a woman's melodious voice before continuing in a low murmur, "you know, we really should just leave it open."

Callie burst into the office, her attempt at a calm entrance failing. "The curse . . . *pant, pant* . . . what's going on . . . *pant* . . . with the curse?"

Eros and Psyche exchanged bewildered looks.

"It's been lifted," said Eros. "I shot Daphne with the golden arrow a while ago."

The wheezing in her chest had begun to ease, but now it was ramping up again. "Oh." In fact, her lungs couldn't seem to find a single molecule of oxygen.

"You seem upset, Callie. What's wrong?" Psyche vanished from behind her desk and reappeared by Callie's side in an instant.

"Nothing. I just came to make sure everything went okay with Apollo and Daphne. Sounds like the binding went off without a hitch. I'm . . . I'm happy it finally worked out."

"Did Apollo not tell you?" said Eros, right before he prepared to take a bite out of a powdered donut.

"Tell me what?" asked Callie, her eyes darting from Eros and the donut.

He set it down and stood. "He asked that Daphne's heart be bound to Sam's."

"When?" Callie found it hard to breathe again.

"Ah, when was it?" Eros looked at Psyche, tilting his head. "Last Tuesday night?"

"Monday," she corrected.

The floor wobbled—or maybe it had been her legs—and Callie dropped onto a nearby loveseat so that she wouldn't crumple. So it was true. Apollo had been no longer compelled to love Daphne for over a week now. That meant he had to have been curse-free when he wrote in the journal.

"The funny thing is, I was sure he was going to ask me to shoot you, too."

"Why would he do that?" asked Callie, breathing hard.

"To ensure there'd be someone who loved him no matter what."

"But he didn't?" Callie's words came out a whisper.

"Nope," said Eros. "I don't think he wanted to take that choice away from you. He realized it wouldn't be right. He's finally learning, Callie. He wants to win hearts the right way, not the easy way."

Psyche must have sensed her struggle between believing there might be a chance or there was no way in Hades' Realm it was possible. She sat down next to Callie and, putting her arms around her shoulders, spoke in a soft, soothing voice. "Hearts can change in a beat, but minds take time. Change is hard, even for gods. Sadly, most give up unless they've got something to lose, something precious and true. Then they make the effort." Psyche winked at Eros, who gave her a lopsided grin.

"To tell you the truth, I'm glad he didn't ask me to shoot you." Eros was sitting on the other side of her now, completing the love sandwich he and his partner were so good at providing to aching hearts. "Things could have gotten pretty awkward."

Callie, still clutching onto the journal as if her life depended on it, looked at him. "Why do you say that?"

"Because I don't really need to use a golden arrow on your heart, do I?"

She hugged the journal tighter—the words Apollo meant, but hadn't yet found the courage to say—to her chest, holding it as close to her heart as she could get it. "No. You don't."

He was trying to change. Apollo had done the right thing by not asking Eros to shoot her with the golden arrow. It didn't excuse the things he'd done, but it did give her hope that he would try not to resort to inscrutable means to get the love and adoration he craved so much. Yes, Apollo was trying. He just needed time to get his mind in sync with his heart.

CHAPTER THIRTY-TWO

*D*aphne took a sip of the horrible hospital cafeteria coffee and winced. Gods, why did humans punish themselves like this? She stared at the mug half full of the burnt and bitter-tasting liquid that had just assailed her taste buds. Sadie sat across from her, gleefully stabbing a fork into a pile of runny scrambled eggs doused in ketchup. It took all the strength Daphne had not to wretch.

"I don't mean to bring it up for the umpteenth time, Dee, but your ex is a real son-of-a-bitch."

Daphne held in a laugh. "His mother is quite nice, actually. She might be the goddess of gossip, but doesn't have a mean bone in her body. Or so I've heard."

"Well then, he must take after his father." Sadie set her fork on the edge of the plate.

Now Daphne held in a few choice swear words. "Pretty much. I've never met him either, but he's got a reputation for being a real . . ."

"Asshole? Enough said, sugar. Like father, like son." Sadie wiped the corners of her mouth with a crumpled paper napkin. "Speaking of, you're not going back, right? No matter what that bastard says you've got to do."

Daphne was bound to Sam. So, no, she was going nowhere. Not for a long—

Her stomach suddenly turned, causing her to lurch forward and clamp a hand over her mouth just in case. She'd have to watch Sam grow old and die before she'd even get a wrinkle. Speaking of wrinkles, how was she going to explain why she never seemed to age?

"You okay, sugar?"

Daphne sucked in a lungful of greasy cafeteria air, hoping to prevent another round of nausea. She needed to make sure the Mortality Request Eros had submitted got approved, and sooner rather than later. If Zeus didn't even know who she was, if he didn't know the circumstances surrounding the request, there was a good chance it would get denied. More than a good chance. She was a nymph, it'd be a miracle if he even looked at it.

"I don't feel so good. I need to go to the ladies' room. Can you come get me if he gets discharged?"

"Of course," said Sadie, throwing her paper napkin on top of her plate and reaching for her own cup of horrible coffee. "You go on. I'll stay right here."

Daphne dashed out of the cafeteria and hurried around the corner toward the restroom. After checking to make sure no one else was in there with her, she ducked into the last stall and slid the bolt into place.

She closed her eyes and concentrated, calling out to her father through space and time. "Father. It's me, Daphne. I need to talk to you."

Nothing.

She tried getting his attention by being a little louder. "Father, can you hear me? I need to talk to you."

Still nothing.

"Father!" She was at full volume now.

There was a faint gurgling from somewhere around the vicinity of her knees, then another. The gurgling grew louder, until it sounded like a massive bubble traveling up from the bottom of a vast ocean.

"Daphne? Is that you?"

Daphne's gaze darted around the stall, trying to locate the source of her father's voice. As if he could see her confusion, he began to laugh. It sounded like he was under water.

"Down here."

She rolled her eyes when she realized he was communicating with her through the water in the toilet bowl. His voice wasn't being carried in a bubble from a vast ocean, but an extensive sewer system. She crouched down and leaned over the seat, gathering her hair to the base of her neck to keep it out of the way. It wasn't uncommon for people to be ill in a hospital. If anyone came in, at least they'd think she'd been overcome with grief . . . or a bad case of the flu.

"Father, hi. Listen, I need you to send me to Mount Olympus as soon as possible. And by as soon as possible, I mean right now."

The face reflected in the toilet bowl water frowned at her. "You know nymphs aren't normally allowed on Mount Olympus without being invited, right?"

"Right, yes, I know. But it's urgent. I would never ask you for anything if it wasn't important. This is important. I need to talk to Zeus immediately, and you're my only way to get to Olympus."

"Zeus? Why, Daphne, that's impossible. I can't just . . . Well, I can, but . . . What do you wish to discuss with Zeus that you can't discuss with dear old dad, huh?"

"Mortality."

Peneus's eyes went wide, his mouth dropping open. "Oh, yes, he'd be the one you'd need to talk to." He tilted his head. "Mortality, huh? That's a serious discussion, indeed. May I ask why you want to become mortal?"

Daphne blew out a breath in an attempt to calm her nerves. She didn't have a whole lot of time to explain. "Because things have happened. It's a long story, but I've fallen in love with a man, and our hearts are now bound. I can't bear living while he dies a little more each moment that passes. I'd rather grow old and suffer a mortal death than be without him a single day. Please, send me to Olympus, father. *Please.*"

"Oh, my dear, that's quite a reason. If what you say is true, who am I to deny a beloved daughter her happiness? You always did have a tender heart, Daphne. If you're sure?"

"I've never been more positive of anything in my life."

"Very well. We shall miss you."

The water began to ripple, and giant bubbles rushed to the surface soon after. Daphne floated above the bowl, head swimming and with barely enough time to thank her father, or even whisper goodbye, before the world went black.

One second she'd been hovering over a hospital toilet, the next she was standing in the atrium of Olympus. It was more brilliant than she ever could have imagined, ten times more enchanting and beautiful than the Sacred Forest.

A gleaming white Pegasus grazed on tender shoots of grass at the entrance of a massive maze of gardens. Vibrant, proud peacocks strutted over the flag stones, and three waterfalls, at least two-stories high, spilled from an enormous fountain, their spray catching the sunlight and casting multicolored prisms every which way.

She thought nothing of the three nymphs featured in the

fountain, but as soon as she spied the marble statue depicting her transformation from nymph to tree, she pursed her lips. Leave it to the gods to make her pain and suffering into art.

Ignoring the irritation tightening her shoulders, she made her way over to the wide stone stairs. When she came to the massive doors, she had to use both arms, her back, and all of her leg muscles to open just one of them. She nearly tumbled down the steps when the door she'd latched herself to suddenly swung open and an impossibly tall and muscled being, smelling of smoke and iron, limped past her in a soot-stained chiton.

He stomped over the porch in his uneven gait and began to descend the stairs. Only when he stopped, his singed cloak billowing as he turned toward her, and uttered a puzzled, "huh?" did Daphne realize she'd said, "Hephaestus," out loud. She murmured a meek thank you his way and slipped inside Life Industries before the door closed again.

After walking to the reception desk, Daphne hiked herself up on tip-toe. "Excuse me. I'm sorry to bother you, but I'd like a meeting with Zeus, please."

The receptionist held the phone receiver to her chest. "Daphne? Is that you, darling? Oh it is!" She brought the phone to her ear once more. "I've got to let you go, Asteria. *Someone* is here to see Apollo."

"I'm not here to see—"

"I heard you were on vacation, darling. How was it? Were did you go? Who'd you see?"

Daphne had never met Apollo's mother, but she'd heard enough to know she wasn't subtle at collecting information. And now she also knew where he got some of his tenacity from.

Daphne took a step back and squared her shoulders. "I'm not here to see Apollo. I'm here to see Zeus."

Although it didn't disappear completely, the smile faded from Leto's face a bit. "Oh, I see. Well, he doesn't usually meet with nymphs, but he might make a concession for you since you're the apple of our Apollo's eye."

So Leto didn't know yet. Well, Daphne wasn't going to be the one to tell her. She'd leave that up to Apollo.

The clicking of Leto's mouse seemed to take forever. In reality, it only amounted to less than thirty seconds. Just when Daphne thought she might burst, Leto finally spoke again.

"Hmm. He's in a meeting right now. It doesn't say with whom, but it's ending in a few minutes. Tell you what, why don't you head on down to his office. I'll give him a ring and ask him to stick around for a few minutes before he takes off for lunch.

"Thanks." The word came out as a cross between a whisper and a croak.

"It's just down that corridor, darling." Leto gestured toward a stone archway with two massive statues of Zeus on either side, holding torches shaped like lightning bolts.

Daphne swallowed her fear as she approached the entrance and the rather life-like statues. The popping and snapping protests of restrained raw power grew louder, heat and pressure squeezed her insides as she passed between them. Those weren't torches. They were real lightning bolts.

She gasped, relieved to have made it through alive. The dimly lit passageway seemed to go on for miles, but she continued past the portraits of the Olympians until she came to a more brightly lit vestibule. She took a deep breath before knocking on the massive glass door.

"Enter." Zeus's voice boomed, even from beyond the glass, and she jumped.

She went to open the door, but it was too heavy. She grunted, pulling on the gigantic chrome handle with both hands. Her struggling succeeded in reminding her just how strong the gods and goddesses of Mount Olympus were. Vaguely aware someone got up to push the door open for her, she continued to grunt with every millimeter she managed to move it, until Apollo was holding it open and she had landed on her backside.

Daphne hopped to her feet, uneasy at his presence. The curse had been lifted, but it seemed she was still having trouble believing it. Apollo gestured for her to enter, which annoyed her, but she stalked past him with a huff and into Zeus's office where she stood and waited to be addressed.

"You must be Daphne." Zeus leaned back in his chair, arms folded, looking her up and down with a smirk.

"Yes, this is her," replied Apollo.

She held her muscles in check, so tight they began to shake. If she relaxed them she'd collapse, so she focused on her breathing instead. Slow and steady, concentrating on giving her brain oxygen so she didn't pass out. Perhaps this had been a mistake. Now that she thought about it, maybe she should have begged her father to speak to the king of the gods on her behalf.

Zeus picked up a piece of paper from the top of a stack on his desk. He squinted, trying to read what was written on it before giving up with a sigh. "Sweet Persephone. My eyes aren't what they used to be," he mumbled, slipping on a pair of glasses.

Daphne looked at Apollo, who lifted a brow at her in return. What had he said to Zeus? Eros said he lifted the curse, and she hadn't felt the need to run, so what in Hades' Realm was going on?

"A tree for over three centuries, is that right?"

"Yes, sir." She shot Apollo a sideways glance. "And whatever Apollo has told you, it's not true."

"So you *don't* deserve to be happy?," replied Zeus. "Because Apollo, here, told me you do."

"No, I do . . . I just . . . I thought that . . ." she floundered. Here she'd thought Apollo had been trying to convince his father not to grant her mortality, to refuse her happiness out of spite even though she *knew* he'd sent Eros to free her.

"That a son of mine wasn't capable of such selflessness?" asked Zeus.

The tips of her ears seared hot, and the weight of rushing to judgment—and her feeble attempt at forgiveness—pushed down on her. Apollo had come to plead her case, to make sure his father even knew there was a request.

She looked up at Apollo, knowing she should say more, but not quite able. "Thank you."

"You're welcome," he said softly. "I wish nothing but happiness for you."

Zeus studied them both intently, but when his gaze fell on Apollo, the corners of his mouth lifted. "You've done a good thing, son."

Daphne swallowed around the lump in her throat, her heart aching when she saw Apollo's face. His eyes were closed, and his head was tilted upward, as if basking in the warmth of the sun. His chin trembled with emotion before he let out a long exhale. As he did so, it hit her. Apollo had never heard words of acceptance from Zeus.

Apollo's aura surged when he bowed his head, and she watched his shoulders relax as he released some of his anger and resentment with quiet grace.

Her heart pounded in her ears. She understood now. The curse had never been about catching her. It had always been about him letting go. And judging by the small but promising exchange between father and son she'd just witnessed, he was finally beginning to learn how.

A loud crackling filling the air forced her gaze back to

Zeus, and she inhaled sharply at the sight of electricity snapping and popping off the ends of his fingers like sparklers. Just like the statues.

He nodded at Apollo before turning his attention on her and wiggling his fingers. "As for you, Daphne, your request has been approved. Brace yourself. Mortality tends to hurt a bit."

CHAPTER THIRTY-THREE

"Sugar? Sugar, come on now. Wake up."

The tapping on Daphne's cheek became more insistent. So did the pounding in her head, which was decidedly more painful. She peeled her eyes open, immediately discovering they were as scratchy as a harpy's claws. Shock threaded through her. Nothing was as crisp as it had been with her immortal eyes. Her bones ached. Her muscles were sore, and her lungs burned, more fragile now than before, and when she coughed, she thought they might explode from the force.

"Good Lord, Dee. You scared the shit outta me." Sadie stared down at her, face etched with worry and relief at the same time. "I knew you were going to the ladies' room, but when you didn't come out for a full forty-five minutes, I thought, well, that can't be good. So I came in to see what was taking you so dang long and found you sprawled out over the toilet bowl."

Daphne probed a sore temple. "I must have fainted."

"Well, no shit, Sherlock. When's the last time you ate?"

Sadie slid her purse from her shoulder. It landed on the tiled floor with a heavy *thud*.

Daphne winced, the sound rating a solid 3.5 on the Richter scale. "I don't remember." She moved on to rubbing her forehead. It had been at least twenty-four hours. And why was Sadie calling her Sherlock?

"Hold on, let me see what I got." Sadie dug around in her knock-off designer purse. Like a magician pulling a rabbit out of a hat, she held out a packet of saltine crackers. "Here. Eat these. I'll go get you some water. Don't try and get up, now. Just stay put until I get back, okay?"

Daphne slumped against the wall, still a touch light-headed. She was a mortal now. Being dizzy, she had a feeling, was going to be the least of the physical weaknesses she was going to have to get used to. A tiny smile curled her lips as she abandoned her forehead to place a hand over her heart.

After a few more packets of crackers and half a bottle of water, the rolling waves of nausea subsided to a more manageable rippling. When Sadie helped her to her feet, a burst of emotion hit Daphne from out of nowhere, causing her to throw her arms around the woman.

Sudden mood swings must also be a mortal thing.

"Thank you," she whispered, squeezing Sadie tight.

"Sure thing, sugar." Sadie patted her on the back. "You all right?"

Daphne finally released her. "I'm perfect."

"You're good now that you got something in your stomach?"

Daphne nodded.

"How about we go see how Sammy's doing, then?"

They gathered their things, which were mostly saltine wrappers and spent tissues, and left the ladies' room. On the way out, they passed a woman in scrubs, her hair teased and sprayed into a similar fashion as Sadie's.

"Sadie Carson?"

"Trudie Diaz?" screeched Sadie. "Well, my stars. What's it been? Fifteen years?" She hugged the woman, rocking both of them from side-to-side.

When both women broke apart, they began a synchronized series of claps and stomps while shouting the words *"go!"* and *"warriors!"* and *"defense!"* After their routine was over, they loosened their rigid limbs and slumped into each other in fit of giggles. It was not unlike a pair of nymphs dancing in the moonlight.

Daphne waited politely as the two women engaged in a thorough rundown on the whereabouts of the Anadarko High class of 1990. After several minutes of Sadie waltzing down memory lane, she couldn't keep the line of impatience from thinning her lips.

Trudie cleared her throat. "You know, I was actually just looking for you, Sades. Sammy's awake and asking for someone named Daphne?"

The weariness left Daphne's bones, the urge to collapse into an exhausted heap replaced by the need to *move* as fast as her newly mortal feet could carry her. Sam was awake and asking for her.

"Oh my gawd. I didn't even introduce y'all, did I? Trudie, this is Daphne Brooks, Sammy's girlfriend," said Sadie with an air of pride. "I'll take her up."

Trudie nodded. "Nice to meet you, Daphne. And It was nice seeing you, Sades. We need to do lunch sometime and catch up."

"Sounds like a plan, girl." Sadie hooked one arm around Daphne's elbow and waved with the other as she led her toward the elevator. "Toodles."

Daphne punched the button for the fifth floor, and when the elevator stopped at the third floor to let more people on, she thought her head might burst.

She'd done it. Immortal life was over as she knew it and she couldn't be more ecstatic about it, but all she wanted to do now was to see Sam. When one of them pressed the button for the fourth floor, she thought her head might explode.

By the time the elevator doors closed and they were moving once more, Sadie was all but laughing out loud. "Anxious much, Dee?"

"Well, yeah. He's asking for me."

Sadie let a chuckle slip. "Yep."

"What?"

"I knew it the minute Sammy walked into the salon that day you two were gonna end up together." Sadie inspected her hot pink fake nails before looking up. "Something just came over me, you know? I said to myself, 'Sadie, these two need to be together' and now look at you. I know it's only been a couple of months, but if I didn't know better, I'd say y'all are in L-O-V-E." She started ticking off couples on her fingers. "Tommy and Belinda. Frankie and Carla. June and Tanner . . . Shit, they oughtta just start calling me cupid."

Daphne couldn't deny a single word coming out of Sadie's mouth. In fact, all she could do was shake her head and grin like a satyr about to get it on.

The elevator doors had barely opened before she was off like a bat out of Hades' Realm towards Sam's room. The tiny butterfly wings in her belly urged her to break out in a run. What an odd turn of events. She was running toward a man, not away from one.

Sam's face lit up when he saw her, and it made her insides melt. They damn near turned to lava when he lifted an arm toward her, beckoning her to come closer.

And she did, without hesitation. She went to his bedside and wrapped her arms around him, practically climbing over the rail to be next to him. On top of him.

Her immortal senses were diluted, but she could still smell the outdoors on his skin, even through the antiseptic of the hospital. And it was no wonder she could, her nose was buried deep enough into the stubble under his jaw.

"Hey, nature girl." He stroked her hair.

"Hey," she said, reluctantly coming up for air. Pesky moral lungs. "I'm sorry."

"For what?" He held her face in his hands, brushing away a tear that had managed to escape.

"Starting up the chase again," whispered Daphne.

He pulled her toward him, hugging her to his chest in a full bear hug. "Dee, that's on him. None of this was your fault."

Not entirely true, but that was water under the bridge now. Nothing else mattered but this moment. Daphne stayed in Sam's embrace, taking a few moments to relish the sheer bliss she felt inside his arms before gathered herself and sitting up.

"How long was I out?" asked Sam. "More important, how's the baby? Is everything okay?"

"Baby?" whisper-yelled Sadie. "What baby?"

Daphne chewed her lip. She knew this would come back to haunt her. She shook her head as she bent the truth one last time. "There is no baby. It was a false alarm."

"Is that why your ex lost interest?" asked Sam. "No pawn to control you with?"

So not her ex, but that was beside the point.

"Let's just say he won't be bothering us anymore and leave it at that," replied Daphne.

One of Sam's eyebrows arched when he shot Sadie a look. "Sadie? What'd you do?"

Sadie rolled her eyes. "Other than imparting a few choice words? Nothing. I'm a lover not a fighter, Sammy. Although,

I am prepared to scratch his damn eyes outta his fool head if he ever comes after Dee again."

Sam's expression went dark. "So where is he now?"

Sadie assumed her trademark pose—chomping on her gum with her arms crossed. "Gone back to his ivory tower, I suppose."

"Yeah," added Daphne. "He's had a change of heart."

Sam didn't look convinced. "Guys like that rarely have a change of heart. I'd like you to move into the house." Sam's cheeks ruddied slightly when his eyes met hers. "If you don't mind."

"I don't mind." Daphne placed her hand in his and squeezed. "Not at all."

Sam sighed, nodding his head. "Good." His head dropped onto the pillow, sinking in as he turned to look at her. "You know, I had the strangest dream."

"Yeah?" Without thinking, she swept a lock of hair off his forehead. She smiled. Nine hundred and ninety-eight more times left, and it probably still wouldn't be enough.

"Yeah, I dreamt a man was floating up there." Sam pointed at the ceiling, just in front of the foot of the bed. Exactly where Eros had been. "I know it sounds crazy, but it seemed so real. He had a bow and these big old set of wings." He jammed his tongue into the corner of his mouth, remembering. His brows furrowed, and he looked at her with sorrow in his eyes, as if he'd been the one who'd caused her pain. "And you were there, too. Crying. You were so sad, Dee, and it was breaking my heart. But then all of the sudden—"

Daphne jumped up and kissed him. "Shhhh," she whispered before giving him another kiss. "Save your energy so we can blow this vegetable stand, huh?"

"But—"

She placed a finger to his lips. "It was probably the sedatives." She laughed, hoping she was convincing enough.

"Or, you know . . ." said Sadie, inspecting her nails before looking up and winking. "It could have been Cupid doing some fine-ass matchmaking."

CHAPTER THIRTY-FOUR

The maenad looked as though she'd just rolled out of the Sacred Forest. Her hair was wild, with bits of leaves and twigs poking through here and there, and her baggy shirt was crumpled and falling off one shoulder. Apollo could smell her high blood alcohol level from where he sat, which was a good ten feet away.

"Here's your coffee, boss. Lots of cream and sugar, right?" She sat the cup, half empty and with a ring of lipstick around the rim, on his desk.

"I take my coffee black, Bromie. No cream. No sugar." He'd told her that several times already. "Why don't you just finish that one. And, please, there's no need to call me that, okay?"

Hearing someone else call him "boss" not only felt altogether wrong, it was a painful reminder of the one thing that had been right in his life.

"Oh, yeah. Duh. My bad." She picked up the coffee and took a huge gulp before sitting on the arm of one of the chairs. She inspected her black combat boots for a few seconds, tapping her foot on the floor a couple of times before staring at him with vacant look on her face. It was obvious working in a professional setting as an assistant was new to her.

"Um, I think you got some mail and stuff? But I'm not sure where I put it?"

Apollo shifted in his chair, his teeth clenching. Why was the majority of what came out of her mouth a question? Questions still made him nervous. "It's fine, Bromie. I'm sure it will turn up."

"Ohhhh, I remember now." She got up, took her sweet time meandering over to his desk, setting her coffee down on the edge. It almost tipped over, but he caught it in the nick of time while she liberated the backpack from her shoulders. She swung it to the ground and unzipped it, and empty wine bottles clanked together as she dug through the bag. "Here it is." She pulled out a handful of wrinkled and wine-splattered mail and unceremoniously tossed it over to him.

Apollo pinched the bridge of his nose, fully expecting to taste blood in his mouth from biting his lip so hard. He didn't need a ceremony, but she could have at least weeded out the junk mail. "Thank you, Bromie."

She hoisted the backpack onto her shoulders again. "So, like, I've got some Dion-related stuff I need to do today? I guess call me if you need me?" She batted her thickly mascaraed, and badly smudged, eyelashes at him.

He was trying to turn over a new leaf, but quite frankly, he'd rather have no assistant than this assistant. Scratch that, he did want an assistant, he just wanted it to be Callie. Scratch *that*. He'd rather have Callie at his side, as an equal. She was a revered muse, and he would treat her as such. No, better than that. He'd treat her like gold. No, even better than gold. Platinum.

A precious diamond.

Bromie swiped her coffee off his desk and slinked toward

the door. He might have flinched when she suddenly turned around when she reached it. Maenads were unpredictable. And crazy. Did he mention crazy?

"I heard what you did for that nymph. Like, stopped chasing her and everything, so she was free to give her heart to that mortal dude she loved or whatever? That must have been, like, really hard for you. I can't imagine ever not worshiping Dion."

Just when he thought the heaviness in his heart couldn't weigh any more, or the stone in his gut couldn't drop any farther, both took the express route all the way down to rock-bottom.

First of all, a literal madwoman who didn't have the best track record when it came to bad behavior—namely ripping innocent men apart just to impress the god of drunken frat boys—reminding him of his very recent, very painful past felt a lot like reopening a healing wound with a seam ripper. It was definitely the pot calling the kettle black.

But maybe she was doing some soul searching, and perhaps the sacrifices he'd made, the steps he'd taken to get to higher ground, could help her figure some things out. "It was at first. But when you finally see the light, some things just . . . change."

"Well, it was a totally cool thing to do." She took another swig of coffee. "You're all right, sun dude."

Did she just call him sun dude? And did she say he was all right?

The boulder in his stomach shrunk to medium-sized rock status. "Thank you for saying so, Bromie."

"Sure thing. And, hey, if you ever want to party with us, let me know."

He raised his hand to wave goodbye. "I'll let you know."

There was no way in Hades' Realm he was going to party with Dionysus or his groupies—they were stark raving mad and he was too old for that—but it sure did feel good to be invited. It meant people were starting to like him, and as he was finding out, being liked was better than being worshipped.

"Hey, Bromie?"

"Yeah?" answered the maenad, huffing slightly.

"If you ever need a friend, someone to talk to, about anything, my door is always open."

A half-smile lifted her cheek, and with a quick nod she slipped out the door.

Alone once again, Apollo turned his attention to the stack of crinkled mail. One piece of mail in particular, smaller than the rest, caught his attention—a square envelope.

A yellow square envelope.

He slid a letter opener through the top, the satisfying sound it made as it left cleanly ripped edges in its wake brightening his mood a bit. When he unfolded the note inside, a shot of adrenaline buzzed through his limbs, and his heart nearly exploded.

> I know you're trying & that counts
> I needed time to figure things out
> 7 long weeks to think it through
> My conclusion? Turn me over . . .

Apollo's hands trembled as he did as instructed and flipped the note over. In fact, his whole body quaked. The message on the other side could be good, what he'd been hoping for, or it could be bad. What he'd been simultaneously dreading.

I'd be lying if I said I didn't miss you
How about a real date this time?
Look out your window . . .

The chair spun in a circle, empty, as Apollo vanished and reappeared at the window. Parked on the city street down below, Callie sat in a convertible yellow Corvette, in that yellow sundress he loved. When their eyes met, she lifted a hand in a tentative wave. It pained him how unsure it was, and that her smile was hesitant. She actually thought he wouldn't be happy to see her?

He appeared in the seat next to her, controlling the urge to take her in his arms. He was determined not to take anything else from her. "Hello."

"Oh, hi."

"Nice car." He ran a hand over the dashboard.

"The best."

He chuckled at her quick wit, realizing it might have been one of the things he'd missed the most. Who was he kidding? He'd missed everything about her. "You do know that some gods aren't motivated by material things, right?" His lips lifted into a playful smirk as he tossed her a sideways glance.

Her smile widened. "You sure about that, boss?"

Sweet Persephone, he didn't just want to hold her, he wanted to kiss her.

His eyes remained locked on hers. "Positive."

She didn't look away, which was promising. "Where do you want to go?"

He shook his head and shrugged his shoulders. "Anywhere."

The sun, the moon, the stars . . . He'd go anywhere, as long as she was by his side. And if she wanted, he'd give her any of those things, too.

She arched an eyebrow. "Anywhere? Because I know a certain someone who'd *love* to see you."

He knew what she was angling at, and he admitted it wasn't a bad idea. "Are you milking my newfound likability for all it's worth, Calliope?"

"Maaaybe," she said with a grin.

The sunset cast a golden glow over everything. Its light reflected off of the city full of mirrored skyscrapers, but it was her beauty—inside and out—that blinded him. She'd been right there, the whole time, and he'd taken her adoration for granted. Mistaken her love for worship. He'd been a fool, too bent on winning to see that he'd really been losing.

Not anymore.

Apollo slipped on a pair of sunglasses that had magically appeared in his hand. "Okay then, you've inspired me, my muse. Let's go pay a visit to that old crow, Corvus."

CHAPTER THIRTY-FIVE

The stars were much closer from the top of Mount Olympus. Callie watched breathlessly as Apollo grew in size, reached up, and plucked a handful of them out of the night sky.

He shrank just as breathtakingly, and when he opened his hand a crow sat perched in his palm.

"Hello, my friend." Apollo's greeting held a hint of cautious optimism.

"Friend?" croaked the bird, flapping its glossy black wings. "Am I free, then?"

"I'm afraid I set your fate in stone long ago, Corvus," Apollo answered. "It's your fate to shine in the night sky for all of eternity."

The great crow, almost as large as a raven, hopped onto Apollo's forearm. "Then why have you summoned me, Phoebus Apollo?

"To make amends."

Corvus squawked, his feathers ruffling so thoroughly he nearly fell from Apollo's arm.

Callie swallowed hard as Apollo silently regarded the

bird. With the smallest of sighs, he began his apology. "I admit that perhaps I overreacted a bit by cursing you."

Corvus stilled—stunned, no doubt—his only movement the jerky tilting motion of his head. After a few moments of pondering Apollo's words, he lifted his wings in a human expression of exasperation. "Then you see that figs are hard to resist!"

"I do," Apollo said with the faintest of smiles. "But do you see that lying to a god that holds truth above all else might have been a mistake?"

Corvus bobbed his head. "I do, I do."

Apollo sighed, deeper than before. "I wish I could take it back, my friend, so that you could fly free once more, but I can't. You've become a fixture in the universe. I'm sorry."

The crow considered his words, walking up and down Apollo's arm as he did so. "Ah, the past cannot be changed. It is best to look toward what is yet to come, is it not?"

Apollo smiled, clearly relieved his apology had been accepted. "It seems you've grown wiser with your tenure in the sky."

"I have had ample time to think the matter over." Corvus's staccato cawing resembled laughter.

Callie couldn't help but giggle at the bird's quip, and before long, Apollo chuckled along with her. Corvus continued to squawk-laugh as he took flight, heading back to his place among the constellations willingly, satisfied that the god of sun and light had considered him important enough to apologize.

Callie could see Apollo still struggled to lay his regret to rest.

"I think he really appreciated your visit," she said, looking into his eyes.

A new-found humility shined hopeful in his. "You think so?"

The pull was strong. Stronger than it had ever been before, and Callie stepped toward him, falling into arms that enveloped her without hesitation. "I know so."

She didn't know, or care, quite frankly, how long they stayed embracing. It might have been minutes or it might have been years. Perhaps even decades. All she knew was his warmth felt good.

"Callie?"

The silky comfort of his voice wrapped itself around her, and it took a second for her to answer. "Yes?"

"Do you really think I'm a monster?"

She could feel his anxiety, rigid and unsure, coiled just below the surface as he held her, and her contentment turned to sadness. She had ample experience with feelings of uncertainty, but now that she knew what being one hundred percent positive felt like, too, his question proved that what she thought really did matter.

"No, but you did have me pretty scared for a couple centuries."

He pulled her closer, squeezing tighter. "Gods, I missed you. So much."

She returned the favor by melting into him. "Oh, you just missed me bringing you coffee."

He released her, gently guiding her back so he could look into her eyes. "No, Callie. I have never missed anyone as much as I missed you. I may be slow on the uptake with certain things, but telling the truth isn't one of them."

Apollo had longed for others, that was no secret—Cassandra, Hyacinthus, and for the longest time, Daphne—but it was also true that he never lied. He may have said and done hurtful things out of anger, but he'd never resorted to lying. Not once in his whole existence. True, he sometimes had trouble finding the right words, but when he said something, he meant it.

Aura firing up a brilliant gold, Apollo tilted his head. "My muse," he whispered. With complete adoration, he held her face in his hands as he looked into her eyes, and when he leaned in to kiss her, all the anger and resentment she'd once carried slipped away. The moment his lips met hers, she finally let her love for him catch fire. The certainty it would burn forever engulfed her. She was standing in the middle of a supernova, after all.

Apollo broke the kiss. Not because he wanted to, because he *had* to. There was one thing left he needed to prove. "Come with me. Now."

One of Callie's eyebrows slid up. "I thought you weren't going to be so bossy anymore, boss?"

There was no time to explain how he needed to make this all come around, full circle. "Do you trust me?"

"Of course."

"Do you love me?"

"Gee, I don't know," she teased, the rising sun glinting off her hair, creating a halo around her face.

Zeus Almighty she's beautiful. And I want no other for the rest of my days.

"Are you willing to say it out loud?" he asked her.

"Only every day for the rest of my life," she answered.

"Then take my hand." He held it out, and she took it.

He snapped his fingers, and when they appeared just outside the Hall of Olympians, he all but pulled her under the enormous frieze and dragged her down the promenade. He wanted no more time wasted.

He knocked once before walking through a very particular office door with his beloved muse in tow. Two sets of divine eyes, one the bluest of blues, one gold, and two sets of divine wings, one feathered, one as delicate as a butterfly's greeted him.

"Good morning, Eros. Psyche." Apollo's heart pounded in his chest. "I have another request. I mean, that is if I may be so honored."

"Oh, really? And what might this request be? Wait, let me guess." said Eros, a lopsided grin inching up his face. "You want me to shoot you."

"And her. Callie, too. Both golden arrows this time."

"I thought you'd never ask." Eros glanced at Psyche, who'd stopped signing paperwork. "What do you think, butterfly? Should I shoot him?"

Psyche turned her head, locking her golden eyes on Callie's. Psyche's eyebrows lifted in question, and a smile widened Callie's lips.

"Oh, yes. I love him, as sure as the sun shines." She tilted her head back and closed her eyes, clasping her hands over her heart and saying very loudly and very clearly, "I love Apollo, the god of sun and light."

He pulled her into his arms, unabashed. "And I love you, my one and only muse."

"Whelp, I think that does it," said Eros, walking over to the credenza and pulling a drawer open. "You said two golden arrows, right?"

"Very funny, matchmaker." Apollo threw him a nervous look.

Eros pulled two golden arrows out of his quiver, and handed one over to Psyche, who was now holding a bow of her own. "Alrighty, let's do this. You want to get that side, and I'll get this one?'

"Sounds like a plan, my love," said Psyche, positioning herself behind Callie at the same time Eros went to stand behind Apollo.

Eros and Psyche stood there, bows and arrows raised. Apollo held Callie in his arms, ready for impact, but when neither co-coordinator let their arrows fly, his brows crumpled.

"What is it? What are you waiting for?"

"Kiss," said Eros, one eye closed. "You've gotta kiss, sunshine."

"Oh, yes. Yes, of course." Apollo looked into Callie's eyes, and without further instruction, leaned down to kiss her smiling lips.

It didn't take long for Apollo to forget where he was, and when his kiss turned passionate, he was vaguely aware of someone commenting, "Yeah, get in there, buddy."

What he was acutely aware of, however, was the moment the arrow sank. He was temporarily blinded by a swirling kaleidoscope of pinks and reds and magentas exploding across the inside of his lids. Until he opened his eyes and all he saw was blue.

Two breathtaking, not-a-cloud-in-the-sky blue eyes staring back at him.

"Boom," said Eros, giving Psyche a high-five. "Direct hit."

"I must say, that is the greatest thing I've ever experienced," said Apollo, still trying to catch his breath. "Even better than the thrill of victory, which I would know."

Eros shook his head, but grinned in delight just the same. "I told you, my friend. Love ain't no joke."

CHAPTER THIRTY-SIX

The sun filtered down through the trees, dappling the ground with shadows and golden light. A gentle breeze blew, lifting the ends of Daphne's hair and making her smile.

"I'm so glad you could make it, Zephyrs," she whispered. The god of the west wind circled around her in response, enveloping her in a warm hug before swirling away.

When she looked up, she saw hundreds of tiny gossamer wings fluttering around in the treetops. She knew the original love birds, Eros and Psyche, were there, and her smile widened.

The face of a beautiful dark-haired woman emerged from a nearby tree. Daphne blinked, unsure if what her mortal eyes had just seen was real. The nymph was still there, and Daphne caught the movement of her lips, but couldn't make out the words her mouth was forming. No longer a magical being, Daphne had lost her ability to speak the language of the forest, and instead, the only thing she heard was the rustling of leaves.

Despite this, Daphne understood what her cousin had

been trying to say. In her heart of mortal hearts, she knew the words Orea had said were, "Congratulations, dear cousin."

Daphne nodded and, unable to hold back her emotion any longer, a tear skimmed her cheek as it fell. After centuries of discord between them, Orea had finally let her jealousy go, coming to wish Daphne well and say farewell before blending in with the bark once more.

Daphne scanned the trees, wondering how many more of her relatives had come to attend her wedding.

All of them, she hoped. It made her sad she would never see them again, but she knew that every time she walked barefoot through the woods, dove under the cool waves, danced under the moonlight . . . they would be there.

"Shoot, Dee. Stop crying, would you? You're gonna ruin your makeup."

Daphne whirled around at the sudden appearance of her maid of honor, wondering for a fraction of a second if Sadie possessed a bit of the magic she'd given up. Was it possible the woman was part nymph? Because where Sadie and the tissue she was thrusting toward her had suddenly come from, Daphne hadn't a clue.

She accepted the tissue and dabbed at the corners of her eyes. "I know, I know. But I just can't help it. A year ago, I thought I'd never be able to stop running."

"You sure did come from outta nowhere, didn't you? But then you found love and now look at you. Oh, come here, sugar." Sadie folded her into a hug, almost knocking the garland of delicate flowers nestled atop Daphne's loose waves. "You and Sam were meant to be, I truly believe that. You two are gonna grow so old together."

Grow old. Together. Earning each wrinkle by laughing and loving and living every beat her fragile mortal heart had left to the fullest. She couldn't imagine anything more divine.

Sadie sniffed when she finally released Daphne. "I'll take that." She held out her palm, indicating Daphne should place the used tissue in it. "And you take this."

Daphne made the switch, taking the bouquet of wild flowers in exchange for the crumpled up tissue, which Sadie stuffed inside her bra.

Ah, no magic. Just stealth and ingenuity.

A warm, velvet muzzle nudged her shoulder and Daphne turned around and reached up to run her hand along Delilah's forehead. "That's right, girl. I'm never leaving. Promise."

Zeus whined, wanting his turn. She giggled at the bowtie he wore on his collar. He was such a good boy—the best boy. She bent down to scratch between his ears as he patiently waited to walk her down the aisle, which wasn't even an aisle, but the narrow trail that led to the river behind the farmhouse.

Several of Judy's wind chimes hung from the surrounding trees, tinkling as she peered down the trail at Sam. She locked eyes with him as he stood under the gorgeous trellis he'd built for their special day. The flowers floating lazily in the river beyond had been her idea. The small watercolor landscapes and feathers, a nod to Sam's heritage, that adorned the spot on which they would say their vows, his.

She smiled at the man who was also patiently waiting for his turn. He smiled back, pressing his lips together as his chest swelled. She couldn't see the tears in his eyes, but she knew they were there.

Sadie started down the path to take her place, Jimmy already standing next to Sam. Everyone was there. Judy and Jud, Edna, sans her ever-present baseball cap, ready to officiate the intimate ceremony. Sampson was in search of tender morsels, wandering absently off to the side, Delilah joining him in his quest. Barney, looking at Sadie with pure adoration. Daphne had a feeling the god of love would be visiting Oklahoma again very soon. Maybe he'd even strike while he was already here. Otherwise, she might have to do a little matchmaking of her own back at the Bullpen when the dancing started later in the evening.

"Thank you," she said, lifting her eyes and whispering toward the heavens, to the gods and goddesses of Mount Olympus who had chosen to listen to their hearts.

One god, in particular.

The sun kissed Daphne's cheeks as she peered up into the cloudless blue sky, and Apollo sent her his blessing as he dried her tears of happiness. She hoped she was worthy of the simple but elegant white dress she'd borrowed. Adorned with the most brilliant turquoise beads, it barely brushed the soft earth. As she walked barefoot toward the man with whom she couldn't wait to spend the rest of her days, she thought . . .

There could not be a better place to set my roots than here.

ABOUT THE AUTHOR

Kerri lives in Michigan with her husband, son, and cat they lovingly but aptly refer to as The Maleficence. When she's not writing, she's probably raking leaves, shoveling snow, or looking into where science is on that human cloning thing. For news and updates, visit kerrikeberly.com to subscribe to her mailing list.